PORTAL

AN URBAN FANTASY TRILOGY WITH TWISTS AND TURNS

E. G. BATEMAN

CORNERDOWN PUBLISHING

For the people who inspire me, teach me and believe in me.

PROLOGUE

Previously, in *FADE*.

My awakening—my introduction to the world of trackers and faders—happened about three years ago in the courtyard of a Glastonbury bookshop. But my experience was different to most. I was at the center of an electromagnetic pulse and energy wave which destroyed digital devices near me, toppled furniture, and set off car and house alarms in the distance. I had gained the Sight *and* seen my first fader, Connor.

A day later, while I was spending the day with a friend, my home exploded, and my father was presumed dead. I was taken to the military academy where my dad had previously worked, and there I learned that I had the ability to be a tracker. What would I track? Faders!

At the academy, I was taught that faders were monsters. They looked like humans but could make themselves invisible. I was also told that faders were responsible for murdering my father, so I was happy to learn how to hunt them. Because my awakening had been unusual, and I could now affect electrical objects around me, the agency wanted to investigate my potential abilities.

At the academy, I began to rebuild my life. I learned how to blink-in. That's, what they called the ability to see the faders. I trained and made new friends: Marcus, Orla, Zoe, and Nathan. I became particularly close to Marcus.

I learned that the fader who had killed my dad was still after me and, in an attempt to get to me, had murdered two of the other students at the academy, including Zoe's boyfriend and Marcus's best friend, Nathan. I was moved for my own safety to another academy in Colorado. My friends, Marcus, Orla, and Zoe, came to Colorado with me. We made a new friend, Hannah, who became Zoe's girlfriend, and life carried on...

Until I learned that my dad hadn't died in the explosion at all; he had been saved by the fader, Connor. I also discovered the reason we had the special ability to see faders was because we *were* faders. The agency was giving us a drug which stopped us from developing fully and had been doing this to trackers for at least seventy years. It's amazing what you can get away with when you control the narrative—the victor had well and truly rewritten history.

The agency scientists inserted a special inhibitor into my head which allowed them to study my abilities, but I wouldn't be able to access those abilities myself. However, we still managed to escape from the Base—Orla, Marcus, Zoe, Hannah, and me. Then I met another person I'd presumed dead: my grandmother, Vanessa. She had also been a tracker but had been able to develop into a fader.

We were hiding in a safe house in Arizona when I found

Zoe and Hannah seemingly dead with Connor crouching over them. Marcus, telling me he believed something was off about Connor, escaped with me into the Arizona night. That night, Marcus also told me he had always known we were faders, but he didn't care. He was happy to hunt them down. He was addicted to a special kind of energy that faders produce, but he was so sensitive to it, he could sense it in trackers and regular humans, too.

I also learned that it had been Marcus who had murdered his best friend Nathan and tried to drain the energy from Zoe and Hannah. In the dark, I got away from Marcus but broke my ankle in the process. Marcus found me, but so did Connor. To stop Marcus from killing Connor, I slashed at the back of my neck and removed the inhibitor, using my ability to kill Marcus and save Connor.

We spent a couple of weeks at a farm where my ankle was treated. Finally, we traveled on to a vineyard in a remote area of California. There were many faders hiding out there, and we were invited to join a resistance group called the Network. They were planning to fight back against the agency.

I was tired and in physical and emotional pain. But as I looked at the faders around me, men, women and children living in perpetual fear, I became angry.

THEN, in *THE NETWORK*

WE DISCOVERED THAT 'THE NETWORK' referred to lines of energy which crisscross the earth, known as ley lines. I learned that my ability to affect electrical signals increased greatly when I was close to them. This was the same for all of us with extra abilities.

I was recovering from by broken ankle, plagued with thoughts and dreams about Marcus and trying to ignore Connor's attempts to get closer to me.

The plan was simple. We knew we weren't strong enough to actually fight the agency. They were everywhere. They were in governments, and the military all around the world. Our best hope was to alert the faders who didn't know about them yet. Give them somewhere safe to hide. The problem was, David, the fader we needed to carry out this mission, had been captured by the agency whilst in the vicinity of the Colorado base. Getting him out meant breaking back into the facility we'd just broken out of. We engaged the reluctant help of a fader called Vince, who could fade without emitting.

We were able to get David out, and Jodi, a fader who I'd taken part in capturing. I learned that David had been a student at the Washington State academy where my grand-father had died. He had been so traumatized by events there, that he wouldn't even attempt to fade. On our way to deliver David's carefully scripted message to all faders, everywhere, we were betrayed to the agents by Vince. They had set up a barrier which stopped us from fading through it. But we were at the ley line, and David's ability to commu-nicate telepathically was so strong, he realized he was able to hear the mind of the tracker. David changed his message to 'trackers are faders.'

David had another ability that no one knew about and that he only suspected. Connor faded us all, and as David delivered his message, he, too, faded as he ran to us, but his fader mist wasn't yellow, it was red. It encompassed us all, and we collapsed to the ground. When we came to, the agents, their leader, Major Tomowski, and Vince were all gone. We had traveled to another earth.

We were initially arrested but discovered that Zoe's problem of constantly emitting meant she had great standing in this world. Unlike our world, most of its inhabitants were faders. They called it Full-Earth and were aware of our earth but were unable to travel to it; they called our earth Half-Earth. We also learned there was another earth which they called Broken-Earth. Most of its inhabitants had died in radiation storms.

When we were able to travel back to our earth, we found our friends under siege from the agency. Vanessa, my grandmother, had been shot and was dying. As a last act of defiance, she sacrificed herself to hide the cube technology we used to escape.

We began to rescue faders and trackers from our world. During an operation to rescue Orla's parents, we found ourselves trapped on our earth, unable to return to the new earth. I had a cube filled with David's red fader energy. I took up all the energy and used nanites to incorporate the mist into my body. It worked, I was able to get us home safely, but I was still to learn the action came at a cost...

1

———

I*f I'd known the consequences, would I have done anything differently?*

I WOKE with a start in my bedroom at the Brightling L.A., Residence on what the locals called Full-Earth.

"What?" I asked into the darkness.

Turning on the light, I sat up and looked around. The room appeared empty. I blinked in, sweeping the room with my Sight. There was no yellow mist indicating that a fader had walked through the room.

Was that you? I asked silently into my mind. There was no response from David.

I must have been dreaming, I thought.

My arm was itching again. I pulled up the sleeve of my pajama top. It had been a month since I'd used the red cube, and the itching in my arm was just getting worse. I'd already cut my nails short to limit the damage I could do. At this rate I'd be sleeping in mittens. I reached over to the jar of cream the doctor had given me and smoothed it over the skin. Lying back, I thought about what I'd done; taking the nanite pen and the cube filled with an eerie red light from David and dragging it up and down my arm until it the cube and pen were empty in the hope that I'd be able to create a portal. It had worked, we'd escaped, but shortly after that happened, I stopped being able to conjure energy balls or make the lights flicker. I couldn't make a portal. I couldn't even fade anymore.

I wondered, if I'd known the potential consequences, would I have thought twice about it? We were in a bad situation rescuing Orla's parents. Even if I'd known the risks, I'd have done it anyway. I couldn't let any harm come to Orla's family or her boyfriend, Jason. We might have been able to escape another way, but the agents had placed booby-trapped inhibitors into her parents, telling them it would reactivate their tracker glands. Believing the faders had taken their children, of course they were willing to have the procedure. The problem was, the agents had remotes that would activate the inhibitors and kill Orla's parents if they reappeared. Getting them off our earth was the only option for them. I stroked my itchy arm. It felt lumpy. Great, I thought. Now I'm allergic to the cream. Just what I need the night before the first day at my new job.

I flicked off the light and lay in the darkness listening to the quiet of the residence. It was nice to finally experience peace in the house. Zoe and Hannah had moved into the Citadel with Hannah's parents. I was sad to see them go but happy they were safe. They had visited a couple of times over the last month, and we were planning to visit them soon in their new place before the binding ceremony when Zoe would be forever connected to this earth and replenish its ribbon. I didn't really understand what that meant, but it hadn't done the previous Brightling any harm, and it meant that Zoe would be safe and treated well for the rest of her life. Orla and Jason were down the hall. Dad, Connor, David, and Sofia were all still here, and we had visitors every day. We'd rescued over forty trackers and faders from our earth. James, the Mayor of L.A., had worked wonders finding places for them to stay, setting them up with work and school. Jodi was living in an apartment in the city, and the girls had started attending a school nearby, but they visited almost daily as Sofia watched the girls after school until Jodi finished work. I closed my eyes and returned to sleep because I was about to start my own first day at work.

As I dressed, sounds of activity in the house filtered through to me. I opened my door and the smells of breakfast hit my nose and stomach immediately. I walked down the hallway just as the doorbell buzzed. The panel showed that James and Heidi were at the door. I waved my tag at the panel and said, "Open."

"Not recognized," said the panel.

I did it again.

"Not recognized. Initiating security protocols," said the panel.

"Wait, what security protocols?" I looked around.

"Anyone?" I called.

The door buzzed again and Sofia appeared beside me.

"There's something wrong with the panel. It won't open the door," I said.

"Open," Sofia said, waving her tag at the door. The door opened to reveal Heidi and James. Sofia shrugged and said, "Good morning, I'm making breakfast," and headed back to the kitchen.

"Hi, Jenna," Heidi said, hugging me.

"Good Morning," James said,

"What have you got there?" I asked, pointing at the bags they carried.

"Two hundred nanite pens and cubes, for our friends on BE. We're meeting Kim here to transport them before we go to work," James said.

"Can't we just get Kim and her friends off that planet?" I asked.

"Hopefully. I'm having meetings with anyone who will listen. But how about you? Are you looking forward to your first day at work?" James asked.

"Raring to go," I said

"Good to hear it," James said as he followed Sofia towards the kitchen.

Heidi's communicator beeped. "Oh. You have an intruder inside the front entrance," she said glancing around with her brows furrowed.

"It didn't recognize me. The house is initiating security protocols. Whatever that means," I said, shaking my head.

Heidi waved her hand at it. "Cancel security protocols."

"Why didn't you come through the ribbon in the garden?" I asked.

"The mayor insisted we come in that monstrous SVU," she said.

"SUV. He can drive it?" I asked, closing the door.

"Hell no," Sean said from the other side of the door I was closing in his face.

I jumped back and let him in.

"I'm the mayor's driver now. I'll have to get myself a hat," he said.

"You drove it back from Canada?" I asked.

"He had it brought back in a hopper. Then he had the audacity to take all the best parts out of it. It runs on those bloody cubes now. I just drove it from the outskirts of L.A.

Anyway, I'd love to chat but I smell bacon." He carried on in.

I closed the door. With Heidi there, I tried the panel again, and it still refused to recognize me. It threatened me with security protocols again.

"What are the security protocols? I'm half expecting little machine guns to pop up out of the floor."

"It alerts me. I would have sent the officers in," she said, scrolling through menus.

"What are you doing?" I asked from over her shoulder.

"I've never experienced this problem before. I'm just creating you a new profile and deleting your old one. You'll have to present your tag again, like the first time."

We went through the process again, and it recognized me.

"Thank the Gods!" I said and exhaled loudly.

"Strange. But it's okay now," Heidi said, taking her bags into the living room.

I stood, staring at the door, and muttered, "Technology!"

I heard a muttered comment and turned to see who had spoken.

"Hmm?" There was no one there. Perhaps I heard them speaking in the living room. I rubbed at my arm and walked through the house.

I had toast for breakfast and headed out with Sean, James, Heidi, and Orla.

"The roads are shocking here. Someone should complain to the mayor," Orla said.

"They don't get used very much, although that might change. I seem to have started a trend. The engineer who updated the power supply wants to build his own,"

"Don't the incs use them?" I asked.

"Incs tend to live closer to hopper routes for convenience. The roads get better in the towns because bicycles are popular, but they're not very wide"

"You'll be popular, hogging the road with this monster," Orla said.

"People don't mind. It's unusual, they wave," Sean said.

We were in the car for nearly two hours.

"Are we there yet?" Orla asked for the third time. Each time she sounded more and more like a petulant child.

Heidi was in fits of giggles.

"If you ask that again, Orla McGinness, you'll be walking," Sean said.

"Pah! You can't get the staff," Orla stuck her tongue out at Sean through the rearview mirror.

"Aren't you his staff, too?" Heidi grinned.

"Well, there's no need to be rude," Orla said with an exaggerated bristle.

"Isn't this taking a large slice out of your working day?" I asked James.

"Well, yes. It is a little indulgent. I think we'll need to revert to standard travel methods for the rest of the week," James said.

"But what about my job?" Sean asked.

"I've received a lot of requests to see the vehicle. Speak to Yolanda, she'll sort out a schedule of journeys for you," James said.

"Your man will have to bring you in tomorrow," Orla said, like I needed to be reminded that I couldn't fade.

Sean dropped us at a ribbon gate and hopper station. James entered the gate, and Orla, Heidi, and I took a hopper the rest of the way.

Twenty minutes later, we arrived at the office building. We entered through the lobby doors and followed a long hallway to the back of the building where a small area was filled with people waiting for an elevator. The elevator doors opened. It was tiny. Three people stepped in, and the doors closed.

"We'll be here forever," Orla said.

I counted the people ahead of me. It would have to make five more trips before I could go up. I wished I'd gone to the bathroom but I wasn't giving up my place in the queue now.

"This is ridiculous. Why don't they have more elevators? Or one that holds at least ten people," I said.

"It could be made of gold, too," said someone farther down in the line.

A few people chuckled. Orla laughed.

"Why are you waiting?" I asked Heidi.

"I have to get you safely to your office," she said.

"Well, I'm safely in the building. Won't that do?" I asked.

"Hell, to the no," Heidi said.

A few people in the queue glanced at her with quizzical expressions.

I raised my eyebrows at Orla, but she kept her face down.

"Could you not just flash your badge and say it's police business?" Orla whispered to Heidi.

"That would be a lie," Heidi said.

"Sure, only a bit of one," Orla said.

The young woman standing behind us in the line had tilted her head out slightly, to discreetly look at our tags. I held mine out for her to see. She blushed and averted her eyes.

"You can see if you like, I don't mind," I said.

"I'm sorry. I noticed your gold tag and wondered why you would choose to travel in this thing," said the young woman, indicating the elevator.

I looked at her. Her skirt suit didn't appear to be something worn by catering or cleaning staff, which was what most of the incs here were.

"Her fade is temporarily banjaxed," Orla said.

"Banjaxed?" the woman asked.

"Up the swanny, on the fritz, busted, broken," Orla clarified.

"I understand," said the young woman.

"I'm Orla, this is Jenna, and this is Heidi."

"Hello, I'm Maggie. I assume this is your first day," she said nervously to Heidi

"I'm just ensuring these two get to work safely. They get into a lot of trouble. I mean, a lot," Heidi said.

Orla guffawed, and Maggie smiled uncertainly.

"Look at that. You found your first work friend," Orla said.

I knew instantly what was coming.

"So, Jenna, sweetie. You know I love you to the moon and back," Orla said.

"You can go. It's fine." I sighed.

"I don't want to be a bad friend," Orla said.

"Just go. I get it." I rolled my eyes.

"I'll have a nice cup of coffee waiting for you on the top floor, but I just cannot do that tiny, squeaky death box," Orla said, heading back out of the door.

Heidi looked at me and watched Orla's retreat, indecision on her face.

"You can go, too, if you like," I said.

"No, I'll stay with you," Heidi said, glancing nervously at the elevator as we shuffled closer to it.

"She'll be flying out of the front door, shopping for shoes," I said.

"You think?" Heidi squeaked. She bolted.

"You really think your friend would go to shops instead of to work?" Maggie asked.

"No, not really, but Heidi looked like she was going to faint before getting into the elevator," I said.

"It's usually psychological," Maggie said.

"No, I think the elevator just looks woefully inadequate," I said.

"I mean the fading. Losing the ability to fade. It comes back. The trick is not to worry about it. Or so I hear. I'm sorry, you probably already know that," Maggie said.

"I didn't. Thanks. You're likely right," I said.

"Where are you going to be working?" Maggie asked.

"In the mayor's campaign office. Stuffing envelopes, I suppose. Where do you work?" I asked.

"I'm in the mayor's mailroom. I'll probably be mailing out your envelopes." Maggie laughed.

We chatted until we were at the front of the line. We stepped in. Maggie pressed the M button for me, the floor below it for herself, and floor seventeen for a man who got in with us and just went into a world of his own. The doors squealed so loudly as they closed, I winced. The elevator juddered and jerked its way slowly upward.

"You can actually hear the rust," I said.

The man flicked an annoyed look at me, then breathed in and appeared not to breathe out again.

"I try not to think about it," Maggie said.

The man stood there. He seemed to be focused on a single point while sweat patches appeared on his shirt at every shudder.

I took my cue from the man and held my breath pretty much all the way up. He got out on the seventeenth floor, and the elevator continued its erratic journey.

"It must be well-made. I mean, it's working, isn't it? They wouldn't use it if it were actually dangerous," I said

"One of these broke down in another building a few weeks ago. A lady had a heart attack in it. By the time they got to her it was too late,"

"That's shocking. Couldn't someone have just faded in through the wall with a nanite pen?"

"Emergency calls get diverted from incs all the time. It must be very different where you're from." Maggie shrugged.

"That's the truth. Where I'm from there are only a few faders. Most people are incs,"

"Did you live in the Citadel?" Maggie asked as the doors opened for her stop.

"No. I'm from what you call Half-Earth," I said as the doors closed on her slack-jawed face.

The doors opened on the mayor's floor, and I stepped out on shaky legs, glad to be alive. True to her word, Orla was standing there with a mug of coffee for me, and Heidi stood next to her with Yolanda, the mayor's assistant.

"I am never getting into that thing again," I said.

"Don't worry. It's not so bad going down. When the mayor's floor calls the lift, it comes straight here. You won't have to wait forever." Yolanda said.

"It turns out, the wait was the best part," I said.

We walked down the hallway to the main office and waved to Yolanda as she took a call at her desk. She smiled and waved back. Orla showed me to our desks. She'd already laid claim to the one by the window. I looked at the paraphernalia on the desks. Sure enough, we were stuffing envelopes.

"What are you going to do today?" I asked as Heidi took a seat in the corner.

"I've got a bunch of reports to do. Believe it or not, being your liaison comes with a lot of paperwork." She smiled.

We got started. Heidi didn't get much of her paperwork done as we chatted away. Before I knew it, lunchtime had come around.

"We're heading out to a cafe down the street," said Yolanda, appearing at the door to our office.

My first thought was that I was hungry. My second thought was of the elevator.

"You go ahead. I brought a book," I said.

"So did I. I'll stay here with you," Heidi said, pretending she wasn't staying because it was her job to keep an eye on me.

"Don't worry, I won't let her out of my sight," Yolanda said as she and Orla left.

"That means they'll both be shopping for shoes," I said.

"I'm not falling for that one again,"

I laughed.

"It's the elevator, isn't it," Heidi said.

"I've already called Connor. He's coming to pick me up after work," I said.

"Great," Heidi said, barely containing her relief at this news.

"There's food in the break room," Heidi said.

We went down the hall and entered the break room which had a couple of sofas and a few tables and chairs scattered about. One wall had a vertical conveyor about a foot wide, rising from the floor and disappearing into the ceiling. A couple of feet along the wall, it came out of the ceiling and slid downwards. Glimpses of bright ribbon light shone through the edges of the boxes as they moved along. A display showed different foods. Heidi selected a sandwich and a drink and flashed her tag. The boxes continued smoothly up until her sandwich appeared and was pushed to an open box at the side. Her drink followed.

My eyes widened at the sleek, modern contraption. I didn't feel like food anymore. I felt angry and could only think of one place to direct it.

"Are you okay?" Heidi said, clearly alarmed at the sudden shift in my emotions.

I pivoted, left the break room, and marched to James's office. He was at his door with his jacket and satchel.

"Are you heading out?" I asked. The sharpness in my own voice almost made me jump.

"Yes...er...I've got a meeting in San Francisco in a half hour. Can I help?" He sounded wary.

"You're on your way out? Perfect. Come with me," I said.

I led him to the door that was used only by the incs and held it open for him.

"Oh, I've never been through here before," he said.

We walked to the doors, and I called the elevator.

"Is there a problem?" James asked. He pulled at his collar.

Just as Orla had said, the elevator arrived quickly, with its doors squealing rustily open.

"You're heading downstairs. Let's go," I said.

James stepped in with me. He was a tall, broad-shouldered man, and the tiny space became instantly claustrophobic. I pressed the button for the ground floor, and the elevator squealed, juddered, and jerked its way, painfully slowly, to the ground floor. The doors opened, and several incs jumped back to see the mayor exiting their elevator covered in sweat.

"Well, that was an experience," James said.

"That's not the best part," I said.

We entered the hallway to the front of the building, but

partway down I opened the door to the ground floor break room.

"Do you see how smoothly this system runs through the whole building from top to bottom? It's carrying snacks. That thing at the back of the building is supposedly built to carry humans."

"Jenna, you make a compelling case. I can assure you, we are on the same page," James said, patting his forehead with his handkerchief.

Having made my point, I sighed loudly, the frustration leaving me. "I have to go back up in that bloody thing again. Have a good meeting, James." I smiled.

I made my way back to the elevator and waited. There were only three of us, so I was back in the break room in a few minutes.

"Better?" Heidi asked.

"Can I get a sandwich now?" I asked.

"You feel like you need one," she said.

I laughed.

I selected a sandwich and drink, then waved my tag.

"Not recognized." I slumped.

"I'll get it. It can take a while for the updated information to get around the whole system," Heidi said.

We ate and chatted. I wondered if James would be able to do anything about the elevator. There didn't seem to be enough space to fit a bigger elevator in the back of the building, but there were three vertical ribbons at the front which seemed excessive.

James returned from his meeting at four p.m. and glanced in at me as he hurried past our office. I managed an embarrassed smile before he disappeared into his office and closed the door. I wondered if this would be my last day of working here.

James announced at the end of that day that two vertical ribbons were enough and the third was going to be turned into an elevator, powered by ribbon energy, big enough to hold twelve people. Work would commence soon.

"He really is a good guy," Heidi said.

"I hope he'll still be my friend. I know this isn't my world and things work differently here, but sometimes, however I look at something, I can't help but see it as wrong," I said.

"Jenna, that elevator is definitely wrong. I think that's what James likes about you Half-Earthers. Seeing things through your eyes gives him a wider view," Heidi said.

"Are you causing trouble again?" Connor asked from the doorway.

"Do you even have to ask?" Orla asked.

He laughed.

"That's my girl. Are you ready to go?" he asked.

"I just want to say goodnight to a new friend."

We headed down one flight of stairs to the mayor's mailroom.

"Hi, how's your day been?" I Maggie asked.

"Very well, thank you," she replied.

She seemed a little cool. I wasn't sure what to make of it.

"Okay, have a nice evening."

We turned to leave.

"Erm...I heard what you did," she said. "And I heard the mayor looked like he was going to faint when he left the elevator."

"That's an exaggeration," I said. But not by much, I thought.

"Thank you anyway," she said.

Connor and I headed back up to the office to pick up my things.

"So, is she your friend or not? She seemed conflicted," Connor said.

"Hmm. I noticed that, too." I shrugged.

Connor faded me down to the ground floor and back to the residence. After that, he took me to work and picked me up every day.

2

———

"How's it going with your friend/not friend in the mailroom?" Orla asked as we set the table for dinner.

"Who's this?" Dad asked.

"Jenna's forcing an inc at work to be her friend. She doesn't seem very happy about it, but Jenna doesn't care. She's decided they're friends and that's that," Orla said.

"Do you two not spend lunch together?" Dad asked, surprised.

"Orla doesn't like to be cooped up. She spends lunch breaks outside with Yolanda while Heidi and I head down the stairs to the mayor's mailroom and meet Maggie for a sandwich."

To Orla, I said, "Maggie's fine. We're friends, but I think she's had some preconceptions about faders. She doesn't talk to any other faders, and she pretends we're not friends around her inc colleagues. Luckily, they all go downstairs to have lunch with other people, so we pretty much have the break room to ourselves,"

At the end of the week, Connor arrived, as usual, to go home, but I had an idea.

We walked down the stairs to the mailroom. Maggie and her colleagues were getting ready to leave. At the sight of us, a young man picked up his bag and barged past us. Connor watched him walk down the hallway.

"Please excuse Kevan, he's moody."

"Have you ever wondered what it's like to fade?" I Maggie asked.

"Every day of my life," she said.

"Would you like to try?"

"Erm..." She waved her silver tag at me.

"This is Connor. He can fade other people," I said.

Heads lifted with curiosity in the office.

"I've never heard of that. Is that real?" she asked.

"It often makes people dizzy or sick the first time," Connor said.

"Right, yes, I know that." She lifted a trash can and put it on the desk next to her.

"May I touch your arm?" Connor asked.

Maggie nodded, and Connor reached out to both of us. The three of us faded. I could see her raising her arm to look at it in fascination. We reappeared, and Maggie swooned, then sat immediately on the floor with her head between her knees, taking in large gulps of air.

"Can I try?" a young man asked, stumbling to get around the desk.

"Sure," Connor said.

I stepped away from him and over to Maggie who had tears in her eyes.

"I never thought I would experience that," she said.

Connor and the young man remained faded for a few

minutes, and I was just about to blink in when the trash can rattled with the splash of vomit.

"Yuk!" I said.

"At least I didn't do that," Maggie said.

Maggie's remaining colleagues were all incs. They allowed Connor to fade them, and each had an equally emotional response. Two had thrown up into the trashcan. They left gabbling excitedly.

One of the young men ran back and picked up the can. "I'll clean this out in the bathroom." He walked away holding it at arm's length.

"I need to get home. I'll see you tomorrow?" Maggie said.

"Would you like to take the ribbon down with us?" I asked.

"If I'm not going to throw up in the lobby, that would be wonderful," Maggie said.

We walked to the ribbon, faded, and stepped in.

I woke up later than usual on the Saturday morning to the sound of people talking in the living room. I climbed out of bed feeling stiff, with my arm still itching. On two feet I felt a little dizzy and sat back down on the bed. Having decided I had gotten up too quickly, I raised myself slowly and headed to the bathroom. My dizzy spell forgotten, I dressed and headed out to see what was happening.

Connor, Orla, and Jason were standing around the table at the other end of the room. It looked like they were planning another rescue operation. Connor glanced up and winked at me. My heart skipped a beat. I smiled, and he returned to his discussion.

I passed David who was sitting at a side table tucking in to a pile of toast.

"Morning, David," I said walking past him.

He looked back at me and narrowed his eyes as he stared.

"Come on, let's give her some air," Dad said.

I opened my eyes. I lay on the couch staring up at Connor.

"What happened?" I asked.

"You fainted," Connor said.

"I did?" I had no recollection of feeling like I was going to faint.

"One second, you were gazing lovingly across the room at your man, and the next, you were heading for the floor. If David hadn't been there to catch you, you'd have cracked your skull," added Orla.

"You were looking at me strangely," I said to David, who was hovering over me.

"You said good morning, and I answered in your head, because I was eating. But it was like you weren't in there. Then I watched your face drain of color and I realized you were going to topple," he said.

"Well, good catch. Thanks," I said.

Dad passed a glass of water to me, and I took a sip and tried to ignore everyone gawking at me. I felt embarrassed.

"Okay, nothing to see here, move along," I said.

Connor leaned in and kissed me.

"Are you feeling okay?" he asked.

"Erm..." I managed.

"I think she's..." David said.

I stared down at Dad picking up broken glass from the floor, then glanced at my empty hand.

"What happened?" I asked.

"You hadn't finished fainting," Orla said.

I scratched my arm. It was red and lumpy.

"I've called the doctor," Sofia said. "She'll just be a couple of minutes."

A moment later, I stared into an unfamiliar face while a light was flashed into my eyes.

"I'm Dr. Hade. I hear you keep fainting."

"I heard that, too. Do you know why?" I asked.

"From what I understand, you've been experimenting on yourself with red mist," she said with one eyebrow raised and a glance at my arm.

"Oh! You think it's that. I didn't understand the implications. I still don't," I admitted.

"I don't think anyone does. How's your arm?" she asked as she scrolled through a pad.

"I think I might be having an allergic reaction to the cream," I said.

She examined my red and lumpy arm.

"I'll try you with a different ointment. Can you confirm your identity with the pad please?"

I waved my hand across her panel.

"Not recognized," it said.

"Not this again," I sighed.

"Is there more than one Jennifer Banks here?" the doctor asked.

"No. This happened a week ago. My login had to be reset," I said.

"Interesting. I'll scan it myself," she said, waving her tag over the panel. "The ointment should be delivered within the hour. Otherwise, you need to spend some time resting."

Sofia walked the doctor to the door.

"Right. Bed for you," Connor said. He took me up easily in his arms.

"But it's Saturday. Why couldn't I have been ill on a work day?"

"Put her downstairs in Zoe's room. It's quieter down there," Orla said as we left the room.

"Hmm." Connor stood at the top of the narrow staircase with me in his arms.

"It's okay, I can walk from here," I said.

"No. I said I'd carry you, and carry you I shall, my lady." He hoisted me over his shoulder into a fireman's lift and started down the stairs.

I pulled up the back of his t-shirt and tickled his back.

"Do you want me to drop you down the stairs? Two can play at that game."

He tickled my waist, and I squealed.

"Do I have to come down there?" called my dad.

We stopped immediately.

Connor tucked me into bed. "I'm not surprised by this. You need to rest. You haven't stopped." He leaned in to kiss me but pulled back. "You know, you fainted when I kissed you. I can't figure out if this means I'm a good kisser or a bad kisser."

I grabbed his collar and pulled him to me. "Mmm... Good," I said after delivering a kiss.

"Get some rest, beautiful," he said as he closed the door and I closed my eyes, convinced that I wouldn't be able to sleep.

I KNEW I HAD FADED, but I couldn't understand where I was. I tried to materialize but I felt like the weight of the world was crushing me. I couldn't breathe; It was like I was drowning.

The door burst open, and David ran in. I was standing,

shivering and taking in huge gasps of air in the middle of Zoe's bedroom. I couldn't quite breathe in as much air as I wanted. David pulled the throw from the bed and covered me. I realized I'd been naked.

Connor came running through the open door. "What's happened? What's wrong?"

"I heard her screaming," David said.

"I was right there in the den. I didn't hear a thing," Connor said.

"I heard in here." David tapped his head.

"Jenna, what happened?" Connor asked.

"I think I had a nightmare. I was drowning. Why am I naked? I thought we were done with all that," I said, pulling the cover more securely around myself. I looked at the bed and, sure enough, the clothes I'd been wearing were lying there like I'd faded right out of them.

"Come on, get back into bed," Connor said.

"I think she should sleep back upstairs. Not underground like this," David said pointedly.

"Do you think she might have faded and sleepwalked?" Connor asked David, looking with a shudder at the walls to the basement room we were in.

"Could be." David shrugged. He seemed perturbed and left the room without another word.

"How are you?" Connor asked.

"I feel a bit freaked. I'm annoyed at all this fainting and drama, and my arm's really itchy again," I said, scratching. "I'll go up to my own bed." I closed the door, glad to be alone. I wiped sweat from my face and shakily pulled on Hannah's robe. After what Connor had said about sleepwalking, I couldn't get back onto ground level fast enough. I snatched my clothes out of the bed and left.

I walked straight along the hallway to my room and

changed into my pajamas, climbed into my bed, and went back to sleep. The doctor had been right. I really was tired. I slept through the rest of the day and the whole night.

I woke and checked that I was still in my pajamas. All was present and correct. I washed and dressed. That feeling of suffocating wouldn't leave me, and neither would the itchy arm.

"What's happening?" I Connor asked, entering the living room to find more people than usual.

"The people from Broken-Earth have been and gone back with more food and blankets. Orla had a call from her parents who seem to be enjoying Full-Earth Ireland. I think they're going to stay so they can visit their kids in minutes from where they are. They're talking about opening a bingo hall, and being from our earth, the locals are treating them like celebrities. Sean's friends are visiting Los Angeles, and as far as I can tell, Scruffy and Felix seem to have taken to each other quite well."

I looked at my cat and Jason's dog. They were at opposite ends of the room staring suspiciously at each other like they had been for the past month.

"If you say so," I said. "I'm going to assume those two guys are from the Brotherhood." I nodded towards two men in brown robes.

One of them was talking with my dad, and the other was mingling, if you could call wandering around sniffing people, mingling. It looked weird enough, but little Milly was walking behind him, copying him. Occasionally, he stopped and turned quickly, and Milly froze. The man chuckled and continued.

"The Brothers have come to check out anyone planning to visit Zoe and Hannah in the Citadel. David's a definite no because of his abilities. They've explained the rules to us.

We can fade in and out through the gate, but once there, fading is not permitted. It's a perfect city for incs to live in. I think life's a little slower. Oh, and last night, Orla had Heidi calling incs 'muggles'. She thinks it's hilarious," Connor said, shaking his head and rolling his eyes.

I smiled. I thought it was hilarious, too.

I wondered if David had taken a peek into the minds of the Brothers, which Dad had told me was considered an offence.

"Every time I even consider it, the sniffy guy gives me a funny look. He seems to be able to tell when I'm directing my thoughts towards them," David sent.

"Why am I not surprised you're in here?" I sent, tapping the side of my head.

"I'll tell you the truth. Since you pulled that trick with my red energy, it's a struggle to stay out of your head. I think we might have some kind of link. I don't understand it yet, but it's something we need to talk about."

"No offence, but yuk!"

"How are you feeling, sweetheart?" Dad asked.

"Much better thanks." I hugged my dad.

"This is Brother Damon," Dad introduced the man he'd been speaking to.

We shook hands, and he smiled at me. "It's a pleasure to meet you. I hear you're quite the anomaly. Are you planning on coming to the Citadel?" he asked.

"Yes, I'd like to come." I was suddenly aware of a sniffing sound beside me.

The second monk was staring at me with a confused expression.

"This is Brother Justin," Damon said.

"You're right," Milly said, sniffing at my jumper. "She does smell funny."

I stroked Milly's hair. "Where's your mom?" I asked.

"She's at work. Auntie Sofia's making sure we don't get into trouble," Milly said.

"I think Justin's got a fan." Damon chuckled.

Damon looked at Justin and raised his eyebrows. Justin gave an almost imperceptible nod. Apparently, I was good to go.

I found Orla in the garden with Heidi.

"Hey, our daisy's up and about. You're not going to faint again, are you?" Orla said.

"I don't think so," I said.

I felt a tap on my neck and turned to find Sofia with a nanite pen.

"The doctor sent it for your allergies," she said and wandered off.

"How are you?" Orla asked.

"Good. Tired but good," I said.

"We were just talking about the differences between our worlds. What has surprised you the most about our world?" Heidi asked.

"I'm more surprised by the similarities than the differences. Like the escalators at the convention center," I said.

"The what?" Heidi asked.

"Yes, the moving staircase, and how it swept around like a grand staircase," Orla said.

"What makes people on two worlds invent escalators?" I asked.

"They'd already been invented when the worlds diverged," Dad said, walking towards us.

"How do you even know that?" I asked.

"The same thought struck me, so I looked it up."

"When are we going to the Citadel?" I asked.

"Tomorrow," Dad said.

"I miss Zoe and Hannah. I'm glad they're somewhere safe, though," I said.

"Yep! And with Hannah's parents, that's four less to worry about. I worry about the rest of us. There's a lot we still don't understand about this place, like who attacked Zoe at the convention hall, and why," Orla said.

"I guess no world's perfect, but we seem to fit into this one better," I said.

"Well, you'd say that. They treat you and Zoe like fecking rock stars," Orla said. "The rest of us can't live here for free forever."

"We're working now. We're fully paid-up members of society," I said

"Sean's also got a plan to solve that problem," David sent.

"What's that?" I asked, sensing his amusement.

"He hasn't shared it with anyone yet. I'd hate to spoil the surprise," he sent.

3

Later that day after the visitors had gone, I found some alone time in the garden. I sat on the bench by the pond and quieted my mind. I lifted my right hand and focused. I tried imagining a small ball of white energy appearing in my palm, slowly undulating, then slightly faster with my pulse, but there was nothing. I held out my left hand and visualized a red ball of energy appearing. I was even disappointed to see there was no red. I had hoped some kind of ability would have come back by now. I felt useless. I could no longer protect the people I loved and the people who still had to be saved. I wondered if I just needed a jump start. I thought, if I could get a hint of white and red energy in my hands, I could smash my hands together.

"I wouldn't do that," came David's voice from the kitchen.

"*What would happen?*" I asked him through our mind link.

"*I have no clue, but does it feel like a good idea to you?*"

"*Maybe not,*" I said.

"Just because you can do something, doesn't mean you should," he added.

"But I can't do it, that's the problem,"

"Perhaps, instead of forcing it, you need to be asking yourself why it won't work," David said, now at my shoulder.

"Maybe I'm just broken. Perhaps I should go live on Broken-Earth now," I said.

"Just try to get your strength up first. We need you back on the team."

"I'm off the team?" I was offended. I pretty much thought of it as *my* team.

"Do you want to risk everyone's safety by fainting in the middle of a rescue?"

"Well, no." I was stuck and I knew it.

"Just get better and no dawdling." He smiled.

"Why, what are you thinking?" I asked.

"When you get back from the Citadel, we need to continue rescuing faders and trackers from our earth," he said.

I nodded, then smiled, seeing Connor walking towards us.

"How many do you think we'll be able to bring over before the locals start to have a problem with it?" Connor asked, handing me a mug of coffee.

"Who could have a problem with us saving lives?" I asked.

"James is already meeting with a lot of resistance to his plans to help the survivors on Broken-Earth," Connor said.

"But those people are desperate and dying." I was shocked.

"The people of this earth are afraid of what diseases they might bring over with them again. We're trying to save people from two other earths. Some people see this as a mathematical problem," he said.

"Three into one doesn't go," I said, realizing his point.

He nodded.

"I don't want to keep bringing refugees here," David said.

"You don't?" I asked, confused now.

"I want to build an army," he said and walked away.

"*Hey, no walking away with that. An army for what?*" I sent, but I already knew.

"*I'm taking Craig down, once and for all,*" he sent back.

"Well, this just got complicated," I said to Connor who was still staring after David with his mouth hanging open.

"*David, they're not going to let us amass an army here,*" I sent.

"*I'm not staying here,*" he said.

I filled Connor in on the rest of our conversation. We followed David into the house to find him talking with my dad.

"We've still got safe houses on our earth. The winery wasn't compromised as we'd thought, and there are others. We still need this earth. I can't fade like you, I can only portal, so I'll portal them here, then back to a safe house," he said.

"I don't know if I can fade like I used to. I'm still too scared to try," I admitted.

"I think that's something else you need to find out," David said.

"I don't see how we can fight them head-on. The Agency is global. Craig Tomowski is just one nasty face. For every face we know, there are hundreds we don't know. They are in every government and every military on our earth," Dad said.

"You're right, of course. We need to fight them in other

ways. I want to disrupt their communications and corrupt their data. I want to take away their trackers. I think we can make their entire network unsustainable," David said.

After dinner, I found David sitting on the garden seat by the ribbon and Jason standing near. I watched as David concentrated, listening across the earths for people needing help. It occurred to me how much he had changed since I'd met him. I remembered the man who'd woken up from a drug-induced coma inside Cheyenne mountain. He had been terrified of fading, knowing somehow that he didn't fade the same as the other faders. Since we had crossed to this earth, he had gained in strength and confidence. He owned what he was and was no longer afraid of it. We'd have been dead without David many times over. I hoped he would come to forgive Vince for his betrayal. Vince had remained on Broken-Earth except for when they visited us. David and Vince wouldn't talk to each other during those visits, but it was their close connection that made the crossing so fast. There was no searching like David did here to find people on our earth. The connection to wherever Vince was on Broken-Earth was almost instant. I wondered how long it would take for Vince to start showing signs of the sun sickness they all had.

"It can take years if he's careful. Kim is evidence of that. I think it helps that they weren't born into it," David sent.

I blushed, feeling I'd been caught gossiping when all I'd been doing was thinking private thoughts. Or thoughts that used to be private before I knew David.

"Anything?" Jason asked.

"Nothing on your father or the others, I'm sorry," David said.

"But you'll keep trying?"

"I try every day. I'll keep trying," David said.

Jason walked past me into the house, and I patted his arm as he passed. He nodded but didn't speak.

"Vince is coming," David said.

Three people appeared in the garden: Vince, Kim, and Kyle.

David stood from the seat, hugged Kim, and shook Kyle's hand. Vince walked to the seat and sat where David had been sitting.

"Hi, Vince. How are you?" I asked.

"I'm okay. I hear you've been unwell."

"I'm feeling a lot better, thanks. I think I just needed a rest," I said. "How are things over there? Are we making a difference?"

"There are people alive today who would have been dead if not for the help we've received from here. The storms are increasing again. We're going to have to move south. The equator is the safest place we can get to now, but it won't be like that forever. That would have been difficult before. They have little enough food and medical supplies to keep themselves alive. We're hoping we can buy safe passage across the border with some of the supplies you've given us. It will take a few weeks to organize."

"I don't understand. How many of you are there?"

"Around ninety in our group,"

"Can't you cross over and travel on this side?"

"Callan told us that Mayor James has people protesting outside his building. He's been so helpful to us. We don't want to make things difficult for him."

"But you could come straight here and ribbon out direct to Chile. No one would even need to know," I said.

"They'd know when ninety people suddenly appeared through their gate," he said. "And the panels on the gates record the trips."

"I didn't know the trips were recorded. Not that it matters, I suppose. How about asking David to do it? With strong access to the energy in the ribbon, he could just drop you straight there,"

"He could, but James has been asked to ensure this Earth does not interfere beyond providing humanitarian aid while it's still being discussed," said Vince.

"I'm sure we can think of something. Are you still in that bunker?"

"We've moved. We're right here, on the other side. It made more sense for moving the supplies,"

"So, we're kind of neighbors." I smiled.

"I'll never understand why you're so kind to me," Vince said.

"Because I can see you're a good man," I said.

"Maybe I had to lose everything to find that out." He glanced up at David.

"Maybe," I said.

I wandered over to where David and Kim were speaking. David was showing Kim the little metal spork Craig had thrown at him.

"I remember this, from the kitchen at the academy. I remember Chris putting it in his pocket," said Kim.

"He stabbed Craig in the shoulder with it, before Craig—"

"It's all right. It was a long time ago," said Kim, covering David's hand.

"It's every night for me," David said. "If only I'd taken Cindy's father's advice and kept away."

The moment looked personal so I turned away. I looked at Vince. He was staring at David, looking hopeless.

"You are welcome to stay," Sofia said, bringing out bags of food and clothes.

"No, we need to take the supplies back. Thank you, though, Sofia," said Kim.

After they had returned to Broken-Earth, I watched as David walked back to his seat by the ribbon.

"Do you think you'll ever forgive him?"

"Unlikely," came the bitter response.

I LAY AWAKE, unable to rest with everything whirling around in my head. Concerns about the future turned into memories from the past. My first kiss with Marcus, being dragged by him through the Arizona desert. Then I remembered events from my childhood, things I didn't even know were in my own memories. The face of my mother came so clearly to me, I cried. That had never happened before.

I sat up and switched on the light.

"Why won't you let me rest?" I said to my brain, as I massaged my temples.

I lifted my head to a light tap on the door.

"Hello?" It was after two a.m.

Orla popped her head around the door. "I saw your light was on. Can you not sleep either?"

"It seems to be eluding me tonight," I said.

She came in and sat on my bed.

"You know when Jodi came to pick up the girls tonight?" she asked.

I nodded.

"I was watching them hugging their mum, and she was telling them about her day at work while Milly was sitting on her knee. Out of nowhere, I just remembered how we used to call their homes 'nests' like they were insects. I was hit with such a feeling of shame." She covered her face as though to hide from the embarrassment.

"I'd forgotten about that. How did we believe it all? How are generations of families so easily fooled?" I asked.

She had no answer.

I noticed that she was wearing her jeans and a t-shirt. "Why are you dressed?"

"I have a secret. Get dressed and I'll show you," she said, jumping up.

I met her in the garden. It was beautifully lit at night, with low lighting in the flowers and trees and around the pond.

"What are you up to?" I asked.

"When did you last fade? I mean yourself, without Connor doing it for you?" she asked. "You can't see what my secret is without fading, and we're running out of time."

I took a deep breath and closed my eyes.

"It's fine," whispered Orla.

It was like just being told that was enough. I finally relaxed and faded. I opened my eyes. I was still in the garden, and Orla was at the gate. She swiped her hand past the panel and said, "L.A Central," before fading.

We stepped through.

It was almost three a.m. when we materialized on the platform in front of the ribbon. It was empty and eerie.

"It's hard to believe this is L.A. There is literally no one out," I said, turning my head in all directions. "Where is everyone?"

"People are either at home or where they need to be at this time."

We walked out onto the pathway.

"So, why are we here? What's your secret?"

"You know what I miss most from home? Well, from every-where since we've been here?" she asked, looking at her watch.

"What?"

The time ticked over to three a.m. exactly, and the heavens opened. Or to be more precise, the sprinklers opened.

I realized she was right. Every night the domed areas rained between three and four a.m. By the morning, everything was dry again.

We danced and ran around in the rain like idiots for twenty minutes, then sat soaked through under the cover of a hopper stop.

"There you go! Now you know you can still fade. See what you might have missed," Orla said.

"What, catching my death? Yeah, thanks." I smiled. "I didn't think I'd be able to do it. I closed my eyes and was just about to give in when you said, 'It's fine.' Then it just worked."

"When I said what? I didn't say a thing," Orla said.

I looked at her, but she appeared to be serious. I'd definitely heard it, and it wasn't David's voice.

I noticed James' building which was directly opposite. There were posters taped to the lampposts.

"What's that?" I asked.

We stood and walked across the street to read the posters.

NO BROKENS

BROKENS BRING DISEASE

"This is awful," I said.

"Yes, they've been here for a couple of weeks since word got out that James was trying to help the Brokens. I hate calling them that. They're just people," Orla said.

"Connor and I had been fading in through the mayor's private ribbon in the lower ground floor and I hadn't been going out of the building at lunchtime, or I'd have known this was going on. Why didn't you say anything?"

"With your sense of justice? No way. You'd have gotten yourself torn to shreds by an angry mob."

I looked up and down the street and shuddered. "Come on. Let's get home."

We walked to the station and ribboned back to the garden. Even knowing the gates recorded our movements, I didn't feel comfortable with Orla coming out alone at night.

"I don't want to spoil your fun but I'm not sure it's safe to keep doing this. Going out at night, especially there. If those hateful people were still around..."

"How would they know who I was?" Orla asked.

"How did that man know who Zoe was at the conference hall?" I countered.

"The party was thrown in her honor. But you're right all the same. Maybe I'll just play in the garden from now on. I love the rain, but it's not worth dying for," Orla said.

"I'm going to see if I can get a couple hours sleep," I said.

I got out of my wet clothes, pulled on my pajamas, and dropped off straight away.

4

———————

I woke from a nightmare, covered in sweat. I'd been dreaming about the two agents I'd accidentally sent into oblivion between the universes. The scenario was still playing in my head as I lay there, awake, recalling how I intended to throw a ball of energy but doing it with my left hand, the portal opening around them and swallowing them up. Watching them float off into the void with horror on their faces, grabbing at nothing as the portal faded. I threw my arm across my eyes as though that would wipe away the image.

Part of me was glad I couldn't make portals anymore. One doctor said he was surprised that I'd been able to use David's red energy at all. He said that since it hadn't killed me, he expected it to dissipate quickly. I'd been frightened that it would take over and, like David, I wouldn't be able to fade like other faders. I'd just be creating portals. I had never imagined I'd lose my ability to control electricity and create energy balls. I'd gotten used to that. It had come in handy, and I kind of liked it. At least now I knew I could still fade. I had hope that the other abilities would come back, too. I glanced at the clock: six a.m. I'd managed a couple of hours. There would be no more sleep for me. I got up and headed for the bathroom.

CONNOR, Orla, Milly, Ava, and I were the only ones visiting the Citadel that day. We gathered in the garden. As I was no longer nervous about fading, Connor didn't need to fade me through the ribbon. He watched me fade myself and smiled. We arrived minutes later at the center of the Citadel. This was not the Glastonbury I'd seen before. On my earth, the town had been to the west of the tor, but here, the tor was at the center of a walled town which seemed to go down into three or four distinct tiers. The top of the tor was level with a monastery at the top of the town. The ribbon station was about two thirds of the way up. An iron gate in the wall barred the entrance to the monastery. The town spilled out around it, all under a huge dome. The moment we arrived, the hairs on the back of my neck jumped up. The energy of the ribbon seemed even stronger here, than it had felt travelling through it. When we stepped out of the gate it was deactivated, and the familiar whine of fade inhibitors filled the air. I shuddered involuntarily and wondered if that sound would ever not remind me of the day the major had caught up to us on that hillside in California.

I peered through the railings leading up to the level above us. That way seemed to be populated exclusively by the Brothers and guarded. I guessed we weren't going that way. We were met by Brothers Damon and Justin.

"Hello, Milly," Justin said.

"She insisted on coming to see you," Orla said.

"I'm happy to see you again," Justin said as Milly danced around them, sniffing.

"I'm not sure how much of this is playing or if she might actually have some talent," Justin said.

"Couldn't you just, you know..." Orla gave a couple of loud sniffs.

Justin smiled. "She's too young for me to sense her abilities. We won't know for a few years yet."

"Milly, are you ready to come and see your friends?" Justin asked.

"Yes," Milly ran to the guarded gate towards the monastery.

"She's not up that way," Justin said.

"Yes, she is. She's right at the top," Milly shouted, pointing to St. Michael's tower.

Ava walked to the gate, reached out her hand, and Milly took it.

"Well, let's go this way for now," Ava said.

Milly followed her sister back towards us but kept looking over her shoulder, up at the window in the top of the tower.

We wandered down a small winding, cobble-paved path and through a gate, and the town opened up before us. It was like walking through Rome: plazas, restaurants, coffee shops. I blinked in, and sure enough, there was not a single fader.

"*You're missing a real treat,*" I sent to David, but it felt like the words went no farther than my own head. It was strange to not have him around in there. I assumed they had technology which blocked the communication.

We came to an iron gate which opened to a small courtyard in the front of a quaint house. Zoe and Hannah sat at a table in the courtyard under a palm with huge leaves. When they saw us, Zoe jumped up to the gate, moved her tag across the panel, and the door opened. We headed up the path and entered a lovely, cottage-style home. The girls showed us around. The house was furnished with old, quirky, wooden furniture, and there was a Victorian roll-top bath in the corner of the master bedroom. We entered a second bedroom.

"Is this where I'll stay when I'm visiting?" Orla asked.

Zoe and Hannah looked at each other and back at Orla.

"They try to discourage visitors. This is kind of a one-off. You saw what happened at the mayor's party. The whole point of this place is to keep Zoe safe," Hannah said.

"But we can come and stay at the residence. The gate in our bedroom there only comes here," Zoe said.

"And we have to take our security detail," Hannah said.

"What are they like? Have you met them yet?" Connor asked.

"Hi," Damon said, and Justin waved.

"Oh, that's you guys," Connor said.

"Won't you be up in your ivory tower?" I asked, pointing up towards the monastery on the top level.

"Our brotherhood is made up of many levels, much like the town. We don't quite have top-level credentials yet. We live on this level. Next door to the Brightling," Damon said.

"Oh!" I mouthed silently at Zoe.

"Living next door to monks. That'll put a dampener on things," Connor said.

Hannah flushed bright red.

"So, are you like ninja monks?" I asked, trying to change the subject as we headed back downstairs.

"I don't know what that is," Damon said, glancing at Justin who shrugged.

"Ancient Japanese warriors," Connor said.

"Oh, you mean Shinobi. No, we're nothing like that. Were they monks?" Justin asked.

"Or turtles," Orla said, drawing another confused glance from the monks.

We entered a brightly lit conservatory on the side of the house with art equipment set up and a dressmaker's dummy.

I studied Zoe's work in progress on the easel. It was a painting of Hannah standing at the dummy putting pins into a beautiful blue-and-gold brocade fabric. Blue material was hanging over a tailor's dummy, but it was plain.

"Zoe got a little creative with the material," Hannah said.

"Now she wants the material in the picture, and it doesn't exist," Zoe said.

"It is beautiful," I said, appreciating Zoe's talent.

"Where are your parents staying?" Connor Hannah asked.

"Just a few streets away," Hannah said.

"Let's go to the plaza for a coffee," Zoe said, keen to show off her new neighborhood.

We walked out of the gate, down a path, and into a plaza.

"You sure have fallen on your feet, Mrs.," Orla said at a table outside the café in the early evening, under lights.

As we sat drinking coffee, I took in our surroundings, and Connor's hand slipped into mine.

"This is kind of where we met," he said.

"Yes, Glastonbury, a world away." I smiled.

"You were wearing that horrible hat," he said

"I loved that hat."

"That street was pretty old. I wonder if that building's a café here, too," he suggested.

"A lot of the old town was destroyed in the storms, before they built the domes," Zoe said.

"It's so odd. We never even had the storms, and I wonder

why they just stopped here but went on to destroy Broken-Earth," I said.

"That was us. You don't know?" Justin said, sitting up straight and leaning forward.

"Oh dear," Damon said, smiling. "He's off."

"This is important. If they're going to be staying here, they need to know our history,"

"I'd love to hear about it," I said.

"This is where the storms were worst. A group of five brave monks came together right here and prayed. One called out to the Divine Light for forgiveness and protection. The storms subsided around them and the ribbon appeared. From that day, the five called them-selves The Brotherhood of the Divine Light. The word spread, and believers flocked to this place. The very first dome was built from wood, stone, and lead to protect the monks praying in the tower and on top of the tor. Then the monastery was built around them. It was built in less than a year. The monks were secluded away, but the Order grew. People joined from all over the world.

"You mean *men*," Orla said.

"At first. The monks had originally come from a Bene-dictine order. Of course, they were excommunicated from the Church for praying to what was considered to be a heathen deity. Since then, there have always been five leaders and they are called The Five. They no longer had to follow the rules of the Christian church, so women were allowed to join. It's called a Brotherhood to honor that first group of monks. Women can choose to be called Brother or Sister," Justin said.

"Oh, well, that's all right then," Orla said, appearing annoyed at having nothing to be annoyed about.

"Over the years, the town was built around the monastery—"

I yawned.

"Sorry," I said, embarrassed.

"You're still under the doctor's instructions to rest. We should get you back to the residence," Damon said.

We walked back up to the ribbon gate. I looked up at the tower, a very slight shimmering ribbon flowed down from the top.

"What's that?" I asked.

"That's St. Michael's Tower," Justin said.

I opened my mouth to clarify my question but just yawned again.

"We can have a few people at the ceremony. Not many, because the place will be full of kings and queens," Zoe said.

"I expect the Kardashians will be there. They're everywhere," Orla added.

"Hannah's parents are coming. I'd like you and Orla to come."

"We'd love to. Great! I need a new outfit," Orla said.

"It's a while yet, Orla. You've got time" I laughed. "Thanks, Zoe. We'll see you there," I added.

Minutes later, we were back at the residence in California and it was daylight again. I yawned as soon as I entered the garden.

"Day, night, day, night. How does this not drive them all crackers?" Orla asked.

'My body says night," I kissed Connor and headed off to get ready for bed.

Within ten minutes, I pulled the covers over my head and went straight to sleep.

I woke up cold and uncomfortable. I was outside, on the ground. It was first light, but I felt I'd only just closed my eyes. I sat up, looking around, confused. I was on a building site. A security light came on, lighting up the area. I was sitting next to a digger, and the area was fenced off with white boards surrounding me on all sides. I was blocked in. I had no idea where I was but at least I was clothed.

A loud squeak made me look up in time to see a window opening.

"Who's there? Jenna? Is that you, love?" Mrs. Cowan asked.

I realized I was in the remains of our house in Oxfordshire.

"How did you get in there? I'm coming down," she said.

A moment after she closed her window, one of the boards rattled. It was a door, and the rattling was a padlock being opened from the outside. A large-sounding dog was barking. I cast my gaze about, desperate to find somewhere to hide.

I jumped up and turned, ready to climb into the digger, but it was gone. Just like that, the world had wobbled, and I was somewhere else.

It was dark again, and I was surrounded by more evidence of destruction. Most of the room had disappeared, but I recognized small patches of unblackened wallpaper. This was where we'd placed the gate posts. Where I'd last seen my grandmother. I was at the ranch in Canada where Vanessa had died, and I wasn't alone.

Two men were standing directly in front of me, within arm's reach. If they had been facing me, I would have been in trouble. I stood silently, not even breathing as they waved a device that appeared to be a metal detector in front of them.

I stared at my hand, willing an energy ball to appear. Of course, nothing happened.

"Is this definitely where they found the cube device?"

"It was over in the corner next to the unexploded grenade, but what was left of the body was here. There's evidence of another cube and some kind of posts here, but they were destroyed beyond..."

One of the men stepped backwards, and I stepped back, too, thinking this was it. Everything blurred again. I was on the hill where we had originally crossed to Full-Earth. I wasn't sure which side I was on. This must all be a dream, I thought, but it felt so real. And again, I travelled. I was in Helen's office at Hilltop. There was a dark spray pattern on the wall behind her desk. The picture of Mum and Dad at dinner with Helen was still on the wall. I ran and grabbed it. I turned, everything blurred again. I was in the dark, inside a room. I didn't know where I was.

"It's nice to finally be alone," Zoe said.

"I'm sorry, I..." I said.

Hannah screamed.

And once more.

A room filled with people appeared around me. They jumped up at my arrival. I saw Vince and stepped towards him.

"I can't stop it," I said. By now I was crying and shaking.

He reached for me.

It happened again. I was back in my bedroom, and Vince was standing with his arms around me, looking startled.

"She's back," called Connor.

David was already in the room, and footsteps came running along the hallway.

"I don't know what's happening," I cried.

David's face was a mask of annoyance, to be suddenly face-to-face with Vince again, but he turned away to focus on me.

He grabbed a hold of me. "Look at me. Feel my hands on your shoulders. You're here with us. Be here with us. Here's Connor. Feel his hand in your hand. You're here. You're grounded."

I burst into tears and fell into Connor's arms.

Dad walked into the room, and behind him came Orla and Jason.

"Zoe's just been on saying she was... Oh, you're here," Orla said, her eyebrows raised to find Vince there. He just shrugged and shook his head.

I still had the framed photograph in my hand and held it out to my dad. As he took it, the sleeve on my arm rose to reveal that the lumps had raised farther and were now in a pattern of hexagons around my wrist. We all stared at it. I was dumbfounded. Connor lifted my sleeve. The pattern covered my arm up to my elbow. Red around the edges but the inside of each shape was gold like the nanite tags.

"What is it?" I asked, my voice squeaking out in horror.

"We'll find out, sweetheart," Dad said.

I dropped down on the bed, exhausted.

"I'll make you a cup of tea," Orla said, heading off with the others.

I sat quietly with Connor. A few minutes later, we both looked up to the sound of voices at the door.

"I'll give it to her, she wants to talk to me," David said.

"Tell her to get some rest," Orla said.

The door knocked, and David came in with my tea.

"What do you want to know?" he asked.

"What exactly happens when you fade to another place?" I asked.

"I understand it much better now. I emit the red mist, a portal forms within it, and I step into it. As you know, I can emit and make the portal without fading now but I fade to step into it."

"That's what I don't understand. I didn't feel like I was making portals. It felt more like they were just happening around me," I said.

"Vince just told me he hadn't faded before he went through. That's new," David said.

"I don't know, it all happened so fast. I went from our old house to the ranch in Canada. They're both on the same earth. I thought portals only crossed between universes, I'm confused." I closed my eyes.

David walked back to the door but turned around. "Listen, about Vince. If I promise to try to talk to him, will you not drag him across worlds and drop him in front of my face again?"

"I'll do my best." I smiled.

"You get some rest," Connor said, attempting to release my hand.

"Don't leave," I said, refusing to let go. "God knows where I might end up."

"I'm here," he said.

He sat up on my bed next to me as I lay down to sleep. He held my hand and didn't let go.

5

———

Dad and I sat in Dr. Hade's office. I expected her to want to examine me, but she just asked me to place my hands on two panels which were on top of the arms of the chair.

"Do you know what this is on my arm?" I asked.

"It's what happens when you take ill-advised actions and you're lucky enough to not die," she said.

"So, you don't know," Dad said.

The doctor sighed.

"It's nothing I've ever seen or read about. I can't tell you if it will progress. I can't tell you if your daughter will be covered from head to toe in red and gold hexagons by the end of the week."

I didn't like Dr. Hade. She was snippy.

"Where did you go when you were red-misting all over the place?" The doctor asked.

"I don't really remember everything. I recall seeing the remains of our old house, the academy, Broken Earth. That's all."

"You went to Broken Earth? You'll be lucky if you haven't

picked up some nasty disease on your travels," Dr. Hade said with a disapproving shake of her head.

"I didn't do it intentionally," I said. She was getting on my nerves.

"I need to take a blood sample, is that okay?" she asked.

"That's fine. Just leave me enough to get home." I smiled. She didn't smile back.

She tapped the screen on her panel a few times, then stood and took two wipes from a packet and walked around the desk.

"Okay, you're all done," she said

"What about the blood?"

"The nanites take it."

"Clever little buggers," Dad said as I stood, rolling down my sleeve.

A beeping sound came from her panel. She reached back over the desk, picked it up. and turned it around to read it.

"That's odd. The nanites haven't returned. Can you sit back down?"

I sat in the chair and placed my hands onto the panels again. She pressed a couple of buttons, and this time, she waited. It beeped again.

"It looks like we're going to have to do this the old-fashioned way." She went to a cupboard, took out a box and blew dust off it. She opened it to reveal a syringe, a leather strap and some vials. Returning to me, she assessed the equipment in her hands doubtfully. "I think I should get the nurse to do this."

"Have you not done this before?" My dad was incredulous.

"Not since medical school. It just doesn't come up." She left the room.

"Okay, now I'm nervous," I said.

"Roll up your sleeve. If I can find a rat's veins, I can find yours," Dad said.

He put the band around my arm.

"Erm..." said the doctor from the doorway.

We ignored her.

Dad reached over to the doctor's desk and pulled out one of her sterile cloths. "This'll do," he said and wiped my skin.

"Slight sting," Dad said before inserting the needle.

"Do you say that to the rats?" I asked.

The doctor walked over and was watching Dad loosen the band around my arm.

"Wow!" said the nurse who was sticking his head out from behind Dr. Hade.

"Is that enough?" Dad asked, who had filled three vials.

"Yes. That's good. Thank you. Although you didn't need to. I brought the nurse," said the doctor.

We watched as the nurse stared at the doctor with horror on his face.

"Oh!" Dad said, removing the needle. "That felt like it was being pushed out."

"That's the nanites getting rid of the foreign object," said the doctor as she walked around to the panel. "Well, I'm going to need some time to work over the data. I'll contact you," said Dr. Hade, and we left.

"I don't like her very much. She's snippy," Dad said.

I smiled. "That wasn't bad for a doctor's appointment. At least there were no electrodes. I have issues with doctors now. Honestly, from my experiences over the last couple of years, I'd rather let a horse doctor treat me."

"Or a rat doctor?" Dad asked.

We found the art shop I'd been searching for and

bought some gifts for Zoe. Then walked along the sidewalk and wandered into a park. We found a park bench and sat together. The temperature was lovely. It was always lovely; warm but not too warm, not too dry, not too humid. Dad seemed to be thinking the same thing. He dropped his head back, taking in the huge, transparent dome.

"It must cost a fortune to run these domes," he said.

"I don't think anyone pays for it. It all just comes from the ribbon," I said.

"A never-ending supply of free energy. Back on our Earth they'd be charging for it anyway," he said.

I traced the pattern of hexagons around my wrist.

"How are you, little duck?" Dad asked as we wandered along the path.

"I'm okay. A bit scared, I suppose, but I don't feel like I'm going to fly apart any second or leap to another earth."

"You know when it's going to happen?" he asked.

"I remember feeling, I don't know, wobbly. Just before it happened each time," I said.

"Well, that's good to know. I have to admit I do feel like I'm flying apart sometimes," Dad said.

"What do you mean?" I asked.

"I was selected by the agency at university. I signed the Official Secrets Act, and they dropped it all on me—the faders, or monsters as they referred to them. Protecting the human race from that horror was my life after that. Then I went to the academy and met your mum. We were both dedicated and worked hard in our own ways towards the same goal. We had you, and that just made us more driven, because we had to protect a world with you in it. I can't tell you the number of times I cursed the fact that I couldn't see the faders like your mum could.

"So, half of my life has been fighting for a cause that was

a lie. You'd think I would have felt empty after discovering the truth, but the fact is, my life now feels just as full as it always did. I've never been so sure of being on the right side. We've met some pretty special people in the last couple of years. Of course, I'll miss your mum till I die…"

"Oh my God! You want to marry Sofia. Dad, that's brilliant." I threw my arms around him. "Have you asked her?"

"Not yet. It's not just that, there's something else—"

"She's pregnant? I'm going to be a big sister?" I squealed and hugged him again.

"Could I please reach the end of a sentence in this conversation? It seems like red misting isn't the only thing you've picked up from David."

I froze. Could I be reading Dad's mind? That could be potentially gross, I thought.

"Think something. Think of a number," I concentrated. I strained.

"Nope. You're just really transparent," I said. "Dad, that's fantastic news."

"I'm relieved. I was worried you might not approve."

"Why wouldn't I approve?"

"She's not your mum."

"You've spent too much time alone. Besides, Mrs. Cowan could do with a bit of competition. Come on, let's get back to the house. I want to hug Sofia." I jumped up off the bench, eager to get back to the residence. I hugged dad again, then intended to march us back to the closest gate.

With my arm still around my dad, I turned towards the park's exit and wobbled.

I found myself in the kitchen at the residence. Dad was blinking.

"Oops," I said.

"I think I need to sit down," Dad said, dropping on to a stool at the breakfast bar.

A minute later, the comms panel chimed, and James's name appeared.

"Answer," I told the panel. "Hello?" I said.

"Thank the Divine Light," James said. "Your security team is going crazy. They looked up and you were gone."

"Apparently, we took a shortcut," Dad said.

"We have a security team?" I asked.

Orla walked into the room waving her communicator.

"Of course, you've got a security team. We all have. Although a fat lot of good yours is with you pinging all over the place. I've got Heidi on, she's freaking out," Orla said.

"Seriously? It's been like, ten seconds," I said.

"Well at least they're on the right earth and at the right destination," came Heidi's voice through the speaker on Orla's communicator.

"I'll call off the search party," James said before disconnecting.

"Where's Sofia?" Dad asked

"We went shopping. She's putting away her things. I needed company to buy a new outfit for the ceremony. Jason's gone off with Sean and the lads..."

"And Callan," added Heidi's disembodied voice.

I remembered that Connor had said he was going somewhere with Sean.

"They're planning something they want to do during the holidays. I don't know what," continued Orla. "Do you know what's going on, Mr. B?"

"My lips are sealed," Dad said.

"So, you know," I said.

"I'll never tell," Dad said, wandering out to the hallway.

"Sofia was buying some pretty baggy tops. I have a theory," Orla said.

"You mean that she's pregnant," I said.

"She is? I was just being gossipy. That's grand." She looked at me. "Is it grand?"

"It's fully grand," I confirmed. "He's about to ask her to marry him."

"What, now?"

"I think so."

"To make an honest woman of her?" Orla asked.

"I think he would have asked her anyway."

Dad came back into the room. "Tell her I'm in the garden." He walked straight out.

Sofia appeared at the door looking nervous. "I hear you've been speaking with your father."

I went to her and hugged her. "Congratulations, Sofia. I'm so happy for you both and I'm proud that I'm going to be a big sister."

"Thank you, Jenna. That means the world to me." She smiled.

"Oh, Dad's in the garden," I said.

"That's nice. Would you like a cup of coffee?" she asked.

"No, thanks. I think he's waiting for you," I urged.

"I'll just make a cup of coffee first." A tiny smile made its way to her lips before she could hide it.

"You know!" I accused.

"He's a whole heap of nerves," she said as we peeked out of the window to see Dad marching forward and backwards by the pond.

"Oh, for God's sake. Put the man out of his misery. He looks like he's going to have a heart attack," Orla said.

Sofia put down the coffee mug. "I'm a whole heap of nerves, too."

"So you should be. On your way, Miss." Orla pointed to the door, and Sofia headed out.

She took three steps then nervously turned back to us. We shooed her away then ran over to the kitchen window to watch.

We couldn't hear from so far away, but Dad had assumed the same posture he used when he was preparing to educate me about something I wasn't interested in, like airborne microbes and cleaning my bedroom.

"That's how he stands in class when he's about to deliver a really boring lecture on ionic bonding or some such nonsense," Orla said, whispering, even though we didn't need to.

"God, I hope he doesn't pull out a flip chart," I said.

"And a laser pointer," Orla said.

We giggled.

The front door buzzed. We glanced at each other.

"Well, I'm not getting it," I said.

Orla took out her communicator and pressed a button.

"Is that you at the door?" she asked.

"Yes," came Heidi's voice.

"Just come in," Orla said.

"I don't want to be rude," Heidi said.

"Just come in," we both said.

"He's taking a very long time about it. What if she's said no?" I said.

"I'm sure he hasn't gotten to the proposal part yet," Orla said.

"The proposal part of the proposal?" I asked.

"Exactly," she said with no irony.

"What are you doing?" said Heidi from directly behind us.

"Holy Mother of God. Do you need to sneak up on people like that?" Orla said.

"But—" Heidi said.

I pulled her up to the window.

"Dad's about to propose to Sofia," I said.

"Really?" Heidi squealed loudly.

Dad glanced towards the house. Orla and I ducked down fast then pulled Heidi down.

"Shh!" we both said.

We raised our heads. Just in time to see my dad going down onto one knee.

"Oh, he's old-school. How lovely," Orla said with a catch in her voice.

He pulled a little box from his pocket, opened it, and presented it to Sofia.

Sofia stepped back, covering her mouth with both hands.

"Pah! Like she didn't know it was coming. Well played, Sofia, well played," Orla said.

Sofia nodded 'yes', and the three of us jumped up and cheered. Heidi was crying floods of tears.

"Are you okay?" I asked through my own tears.

"I'm feeling so much joy right now. Mine, yours, theirs, and the baby's," she said, then froze, fearful that she'd given away a secret.

"Wait, you know about the baby?" I asked.

"Oh, yes, I began to feel it a couple of weeks ago. I usually sense them at about four or five months. I think it comes with the child's self-awareness," Heidi said. She wandered off to find a tissue.

"That's incredible," Orla said, wiping her face. "Ooh! A wedding. I need a new outfit."

"You just bought one."

"But that's for Zoe's ceremony. Now I need a new, new outfit."

I shook my head and laughed. "You need help."

"Thanks. We'll go after we've been to the Citadel."

I knew she had intentionally misunderstood me, but I didn't mind.

Dad burst through the door. "She said yes!"

"Well, where is she?" I asked.

"Oh. I left her in the garden," he turned around, and bolted back out.

That night, Connor stayed with me again, holding my hand to be sure I didn't disappear. I woke in the night to find he had snuggled down behind me on top of the sheets and was fast asleep. I pulled up the blanket from the bottom of the bed to cover him. I lay down feeling a kind of contentment I didn't initially recognize.

"*Safe,*" came the word, sighing from the back of my mind.

My eyes shot open. I'd heard it. I hadn't imagined it. I knew it wasn't David. I knew it wasn't anyone near me. This was a voice inside my mind.

"*Who's there?*" I asked silently.

Nothing.

I wondered if I was losing it.

Strangely, I didn't feel like I was in danger, but I did not like unanswered questions. I wasn't sure who to talk to about this. A picture of Dr. Hade flashed into my mind. Hell no. I thought of Helen back at Hilltop. I thought of the spray of blood on the wall behind her desk. I'd have talked to her about it.

I took Connor's arm and pulled it across me. He stirred, stroked my arm, and returned to sleep, as did I.

6

———

The day of the ceremony finally arrived.

"Jason," shouted Orla in the hallway outside the door, "I can't find my new shoes."

"They're in the bottom of the wardrobe," he called back.

"I just looked there."

"They're in the bottom of *my* wardrobe because there's no room in the bottom of yours, because of all the shoes."

"Oh right. Thanks. Love you," hollered Orla.

Orla thumped my door. "Are you getting up or what? We've got some kind of ceremony to get to." There was a pause. "Are you there or did you vanish again?"

"I'm here. Be out soon," I said.

"She's got a point. What kind of ceremony is this?" Connor asked who was still sneaking in to sleep next to me.

"No idea. Out you get." I kissed him then threw him out of the room.

Fifteen minutes later, I was washed, dressed, and eating toast in the kitchen.

"What's that?" Orla asked, staring suspiciously at the box in my hand.

"It's a gift for Zoe," I said.

"A gift? This is a gift thing? No one told me. I didn't get her anything." Her voice had raised several octaves.

"It's just a set of nice paintbrushes."

Orla looked mortified.

"It's from all of us." I added.

"Oh." Orla calmed down. "Oh well, that's all right then."

Orla turned to Jason. "You know what to do?"

"Yes, you've gone over it a million times. We'll start getting the place ready the second you leave. The caterers are due here in an hour with the food. Sofia and Neil are already getting the flowers. It's all good. Go."

"Okay. Come on, Jenna, we'll be late for the...thing,"

Orla and I faded through the ribbon.

We arrived at the Citadel at two-forty p.m., twenty minutes before the ceremony was due to start.

"Thank the Divine Light, we were just about to come and find you," Justin said.

The gate was deactivated as we walked out. Throngs of people were waving and cheering, and flowers decorated the streets.

Justin stopped with a puzzled face and sniffed at me. He shook his head. "You smell different every time I see you."

"Is that bad?" I asked.

"It's confusing, but I don't sense any harm, it's not a problem," he said.

"It is for Heidi. She's had to reset my identity on the system three times now," I said.

I looked up at the ancient tor which, in this world had the monastery built onto it. The strange vertical ribbon I'd seen previously was no longer there. I wondered if my eyes had been playing tricks on me. We made our way up through the guarded gates to a circular room adjacent to the tower. Zoe was already seated on a dais in the middle of the old section, ahead of us. She was beautiful, dressed in a black pant suit. Hannah had a front-row seat in a dark red dress and rows of people behind were in expensive finery.

Hannah waved us over. "I saved you seats. If you feel daggers staring into the back of your head, there are some presidents, prime ministers, and royalty back there who think they should be in this row."

I gazed around the room. It was a round brick building. Sections of the wall were ribbons of energy. Between the ribbons, flowers adorned the walls. It was mesmerizing. A pattern of rich, polished wood curved in from the edges of the high ceiling, and met the old wall of the ancient tower. Looking through the arched doorway to the dais where Zoe sat, I spied glass tendrils spiraling down to several feet above her head. The glass shone in the reflection of the ribbons around it. Behind Zoe were five empty, large wooden chairs arranged around the far wall.

I blinked in and whispered, "Are we supposed to see anything? Because all I see is yellow."

A bell sounded, and the assembled Brothers muttered prayers. I couldn't work out what they were saying. Singing began and continued for about ten minutes. Then three men and one woman in plain robes but with colored silken tabards proceeded from the entrance. As they each reached the dais, they bowed to Zoe and walked around to the left and seated themselves in four of the five large, wooden chairs situated at the far side, leaving the middle chair empty. I guessed these were the Five.

"It looks like they've forgotten someone," I whispered to Orla, nodding towards the empty chair.

One of the men turned and seemed to be staring straight

at me from the other side of the room. He was staring so intensely, I felt uncomfortable.

"They are four of the Five," whispered Brother Damon from behind me.

The hanging glass tendrils slowly turned.

"Are you seeing this?" Hannah said.

I blinked in again and was amazed to see that the yellow mist emitting from Zoe was coiling upwards into the ceiling through the glass spirals. This kept going until the yellow had almost completely gone. Sighs and gasps escaped the assembled guests behind us. Suddenly, the light changed direction and came down onto Zoe like a white waterfall. The light shot through her body and along crystal channels inset into the floor to the ribbons in the wall. The gasps were louder now. The ribbon sections brightened so much that I almost had to shield my eyes, and everyone inside and outside cheered.

I leaned to Orla to comment when the voice in my head screamed "ABOMINATION." I jumped at the sound. Orla, and Hannah's parents glanced briefly at me. Clearly, it had just been in my head. For a moment, I thought I might have screamed it myself.

"Can you hold this, please?" I whispered, passing Zoe's gift to Orla. I sat on my hands, fearful that I'd jump up and do something shocking.

I glanced up to see the same member of the Five staring at me again. It was unnerving.

"Why does that guy keep staring at me?" I asked.

"Maybe because you jumped up in the middle of the ceremony like you'd been bitten by a snake," said Mr. Deschene.

"He's not staring at you," Damon said from the seat behind.

"No. He's definitely staring at me."

"He's blind."

"Oh!" I had no comeback for that. But it still looked like he was staring at me.

"That was incredible," Hannah said.

I blinked out but the white light continued flowing down from above her, through her, and into the floor.

"What happens with the light?" I Hannah asked.

"It stays in the ribbon," Hannah said.

"But I can still see it," I said.

"Sorry about that. We should have warned you about it. Zoe says you call it an after-image. It was amazing, wasn't it," Damon said.

"She's connected to this earth now, purifying the ribbon," Hannah said.

I wasn't seeing an after-image.

"I'll never forget that as long as I live," Hannah said.

Zoe stood from the chair, stepped down from the dais, and walked down the aisle. She stopped when she got to us and whispered, "Well, that's a load off my mind."

Damon stood and stepped out in front of her, and we filed out. I stared transfixed at the ribbon of energy continuing to flow down through the center of the ceiling and followed her out. I wondered why no one else seemed able to see it. I also wondered why it made me, or this other thing inside me, incredibly angry.

We were in a procession going down to the plaza where a street party was being held. Zoe was being introduced to VIPs, but she was definitely the most VIP today.

I looked across the plaza to see five people in robes heading in a different direction into the monastery.

"Oh, the fifth member of the band has appeared," I said to Orla, but she was chatting with Hannah. As I watched, the blind man paused, turned, and looked straight at me with a strange little smile on his face before disappearing through the door. I shuddered and my creep-radar went off in my head.

After an hour at the party, Damon asked us to head inside Zoe and Hannah's house. On the way, we weaved past security people who were walking around scanning people's bags and clothes.

"Is that a metal detector?" Orla asked.

Damon shrugged. "Similar. It's for security."

I momentarily froze. Something about a metal detector was prodding at my mind. I couldn't quite grasp it.

Zoe and Hannah came in and flopped onto chairs.

"I'm exhausted," Hannah said.

"Hey, don't be flagging. We've still got the L.A Party," Orla said, realizing that she was still holding Zoe's gift. "This is for you, Zozo. Happy... Ribbon... day."

"We call it Brightling Day," Damon said.

"Ooh, a present," Zoe said, pulling it open to inspect the paintbrushes. "Nice quality. Thank you." She hugged Orla.

"Well, you know. They're from all of us," Orla said, looking at me apologetically.

I smiled, happy to look away from Zoe and the strange light.

"Come on then. Party number two," Orla said.

We gathered at the gate in Zoe's house while Damon called the ribbon.

I tried not to look at Zoe but couldn't help it. The light was pouring into her head and out through her feet.

"What?" Zoe asked, aware of the scrutiny.

"You look really great in that outfit," I said.

"Thanks," she said, grinning.

I smiled and diverted my gaze.

We arrived in Zoe and Hannah's bedroom in the basement of the residence. I glanced quickly at Zoe—yes, it was still there. Damon went ahead of her, and Justin followed.

As we rounded the corner into the living room, a cheer went up, and the party began.

After a few minutes, Heidi took me aside. "Can we talk?"

"Sure. What's up?"

We wandered into the garden.

"I was going to ask you that. You seem angry," she said.

"I'm fine," I said.

"Jenna—"

"There is something I need to talk to someone about, but can it be tomorrow? Let's make today about Zoe."

"Okay. But I'm concerned and I have my nanite pen. If I feel you're going cray-cray, I'm knocking you out."

I sighed.

We walked back into the house. Dad and Sofia had clearly told Zoe their news because Zoe was delivering ecstatic hugs. I looked away. Her wavy chimney-pot head was irritating.

Heading towards Connor, I made to walk past Orla, but stopped.

"Really? Cray-cray? Did you have to?"

"Yes! House," Orla shouted.

A few people around the room groaned, they were all from my Earth.

"Orla, please tell me you haven't all been playing Half-Earth Out-of-Date Slang Bingo with Heidi."

"This isn't an admission of guilt, but would you be mad if I said yes?"

"You know you're going to Hell, right?" I said as I moved on toward Connor.

I almost reached him first, but Milly came flying past me

and dived at Connor. He lifted her up, and she hugged him. When I stood next to them, Milly reached out and tapped my cheek.

"I love you," Milly said.

I laughed.

"Well, Jenna loves you, too, pumpkin," Connor said.

"Not Jenna, silly. But Jenna's nice, too. She saved Mamma," Milly said. She wriggled out of Connor's arms and ran off.

"That kid is weird. Cute but weird." He shook his head.

I just followed Milly with my gaze as she skipped through the house to the garden.

"What did that even mean?" I said.

"She's seven. It could mean anything," Connor said. "Well. I've heard about this ceremony from everyone except you."

"Hannah tells it way better than I do," I started to say but was interrupted by a poke in the back. I turned to find Zoe standing there with an energy waterfall crashing into her from above.

"Thanks for my brushes. They're lovely." She hugged me.

"Do you feel any different?" I asked.

"You wouldn't believe how different. I feel alive and free from the weariness that's dogged me for months and months."

"You're certainly a lot more tactile than usual." I laughed. I was focusing so hard on her face, trying not to see it.

Heidi was looking at me nervously. Did she think I was going to hurt my friend?

Hannah came up and passed Zoe a drink.

"Hannah, tell Connor about the ceremony. You tell it beautifully."

Hannah launched into her description immediately.

I excused myself and made my way to the door. I turned to make sure that Heidi was following me. I headed to my room and sat on the edge of the bed, waiting a few moments for her to appear.

"It's every time you look at Zoe. I sense a deep anger. I'm worried about you, Jenna,"

"Do you see anything different about Zoe?" I asked.

"She's stopped drowning out everything else with yellow when she shines," she said.

"During the ceremony, the yellow mist was drawn up into a spiral and disappeared through the ceiling,"

"Yes, I've read about that."

"Then, a flood of white energy that looked like the ribbon came down, went through her, and seemed to disperse into the ribbons in the wall all around,"

"Yes, that's the connection between the Brightling and the ribbon being made. That's the end of the ceremony, followed by the procession to the celebrations," she said.

"I can still see it," I said.

"Still see what?" Heidi was clearly confused.

"I still see the ribbon coming down from, I don't know, somewhere, and flowing down through her into the floor. But as far as I can tell, no one else can see it."

"Have you asked the Brothers?" Heidi asked.

"I haven't said anything to anyone. People are going to think I'm crazy."

I wanted to tell her about the voices. I needed to tell someone I could trust, but I didn't want to worry the people around me.

I walked around the party avoiding Zoe. I tried my best

to concentrate on what people were saying to me and just get through it. Hours later, the party was mercifully over. Everyone had gone. I'd closed my eyes and hugged Zoe. I felt nothing but love for her. The last person to leave was Heidi.

"I'll call you tomorrow, and we can talk some more," she said and left.

We rested for an hour. Dad put on a pot of coffee, and the conversation turned to wedding and baby plans. Dad and Sofia were talking about moving out after the wedding. I'd expected that, and it was okay. Orla hijacked the conversation every time it appeared there might be an excuse for shopping.

Jason came in from the garden.

"Anything?" Orla asked.

He shook his head.

I made my way into the garden, past David, who was still at the ribbon, down to the pond, and stood, gazing into it. Thoughts flew through my mind too fast for me grasp. It was as though someone else was flicking through my memories like a photo album. It stopped. My mind's eye was looking at the security people with metal detectors.

"*Why is this important?*" the voices asked.

I stared at the image, shocked that this other entity, which I had only suspected, had spoken directly to me. I wanted to ask it who or what the hell it was, but it was forcing this image upon me. Then it hit me. I remembered the seconds I had spent in the desolated farmhouse. The men, what they were saying. They had found a cube. How could I have forgotten that Major Tomowski had a Full-Earth energy cube?

"He what?" came David's voice.

We gathered around the dining table. Dad, Sofia, Orla,

James, David, and Scarlett, a friend of James who was an engineer in Ribbon Technology from the university.

"What are they going to be able to get from the cube and the gate posts?" Dad asked.

"It depends what condition the items are in and how good their engineers are," said Scarlett. "From what you said, it sounds like the posts and one cube were destroyed."

"The other cube may have been intact, but as I remember, they were both pretty low on energy," I said.

"That's right. Callan took the two full cubes with him," Connor said.

"But what can they do with just a cube?" Orla asked.

"We started with a cube. Well, it wasn't a cube at first, but it's still the same principal. Everything you see here began with the invention of the energy cube. It was created as a device for drawing energy from the ribbon to provide light and power," said Scarlett.

"But they don't know about the ribbon," I said.

"If they don't have access to the ribbon, all they need are a few faders to fill it," James said.

I remembered the cube exploding at the exhibition hall party. It was a tiny cube, but the explosion was devastating. I knew instantly that Tomowski would pursue this with everything he had.

"We need to get that thing back. Where are they likely to be working on it?" I Dad asked.

"There are facilities and labs all over the world. I'd have said the safest place was the mountain, but since you infiltrated it, that's probably changed."

"Then what we need is someone who knows where it is," I said.

"I asked Yolanda to call Heidi and Callan. They should really be in on this," James said.

"I'll try, Heidi," Orla said.

...

Heidi's panel buzzed. It was the residence calling and her panel was showing that she'd missed a call from Yolanda. She jumped out of bed.

"Delay," she said, knowing that an automated voice at the residence would be telling the caller that she would join them momentarily. She pulled on a shirt and smoothed her hair. She looked decent above the waist and decided that would do.

"Answer," she said and was faced with Orla.

"Hello, Orla. Is something wrong?" she asked. "Is Jenna okay?"

"What? Jenna's fine. Can you come over here? And bring Callan. James is here, too. We're having a meeting," Orla said.

Heidi flicked her eyes to the side and said, "I'm home at the moment. I'll see if I can contact Callan."

"Heidi. You and Callan are the worst kept secret on the three Earths. I know he's there," Orla said.

Heidi blushed, and Callan leaned into view with an awkward wave.

"Did David tell you?" he asked.

"No. You did when you popped your head into view. I was totally bluffing," Orla said.

Heidi's blush grew hotter and Callan chuckled.

"We'll be there in ten minutes," said Callan before disconnecting.

"We could be there in five," Heidi said.

"We could..." said Callan, leaping onto the bed.

"You're such a hottie," Heidi said, using another word she'd picked up from Orla.

Callan smiled. "You really like them, don't you?"

"They have such a strong aura of honesty and fairness. They remind me of you. It's impossible to not like them. And they're different and exciting. I love that I see things in a different way because of them." She paused.

"What?" Callan asked.

"I've been sensing something different in Jenna. It scares me a little," she said hesitantly, with her eyes lowered.

"Something like what?"

"Anger, grief, sadness, all mixed up together. It's not there all the time, but it's there."

"She's been through a lot," he said.

"Yes, but still. I didn't sense it as strong as this before."

"Can you dig for more?"

"You know how it works. I don't go in, the feelings come out. It's been there since that thing on her arm appeared, and it really spiked today. I've never seen anything like that before."

"But she's still a good person?"

"Yes. She glows beautifully when she's happy. Even more so when she's happy for others. Even for us. Come on, let's get over there."

"Okay, but you should probably get some more clothes on first," he said.

She picked up his socks and threw them at him.

...

AFTER WE UPDATED Heidi and Callan to the situation, they just sat there, silent, turning it over in their minds.

"We have to get it back," said Callan.

"It's been months. They must have gotten somewhere with it by now," Heidi said.

They were replaying a conversation that had taken place before they'd arrived.

"That's the conclusion we came to," James said.

"Do you know where it is?" Heidi asked.

"We're going to ask an old friend," I said.

"You'll need to make some arrangements," James told Callan while he pressed a button on his panel.

Callan looked at his own panel as the details arrived. "This is going to take a couple of days."

"That's fine. I'll see you ladies at the office," James said before leaving with Scarlett.

7

Orla and I arrived at the office building. Justin and Heidi had finally decided I wasn't a threat to Zoe. I was happy to be back at work. Maggie was standing in the lobby. I wasn't sure if I should speak to her, knowing that she didn't want to be alienated from her inc friends. I had decided to just walk ahead when she reached out and touched my arm.

"Hi," Maggie said. "I heard you've been unwell. I'm happy you're back. Did you enjoy the holiday?"

"Hey, Maggie, I'm feeling much better now, thanks. And I was better in time for the holiday." I did a double-take, the others I'd seen queued up at the back of the building were now waiting for an elevator at the front. "They did it already? That's fantastic."

"Life is so much better here. Some of us go out for lunch now. We never used to bother."

"I'm really pleased for you. Hey, my fade came back. It looks like we're both having good times."

"Oh. So, Connor won't be coming again?" Maggie appeared disappointed, and I realized she'd probably wanted to try fading again.

"I can ask him to pop in occasionally," I said.

Orla glanced at me. James had asked Connor to be careful with fading incs. If they started turning into faders it could severely upset the balance of the society. I thought once or twice wouldn't hurt.

"Oh, it's all right. My dad was really angry about it anyway." She looked down.

"Why would he be angry?" I asked.

"Just, he thought it might not be safe." She averted her gaze. She wasn't giving me the whole truth.

"Let's meet for lunch. We could go to the Italian place," I suggested.

"Sure, that would be great," she said.

Maggie went up in the new elevator while Orla and I stepped into the ribbon to the top floor.

"I'm happy to see you back here," James said, popping his head into the office later that morning.

"Well, I'm happy to be stuffing envelopes for you, Mr. Mayor," I said with a smile.

"James looked at me with an uncertain half smile, and I realized Orla was also staring at me strangely,"

"What have I said?" I asked.

"Sweetie, neither of us knows if you're being sarcastic," Orla said.

"What? No! I mean it. What you've done for the incs in this building is wonderful. I'm proud to be on your team."

James came into the office and sat on the edge of a low filing cabinet.

"Stuffing envelopes helps, but I want you to know that I value your perspective and your input, both of you."

"Thank you. That's a lovely thing to say," Orla said.

"Your ten-thirty is here," said Yolanda from the doorway.

We continued with our work until lunchtime when we went down a level to meet Maggie for pizza. As we walked into the office, one of her colleagues tutted. I didn't see which one it was.

"I'm sorry about earlier. Some of my workmates are resentful of faders. They just don't know you yet. You two are so friendly for faders," Maggie said as we waited for our pizza at the restaurant.

"Well, we've had an inc try to shoot our best friend in the back, so believe me when I say, you're right up there with the best of the incs that we've met," Orla said.

"Why would someone shoot your friend?"

"She's the Brightling," I said.

"You know the Brightling?"

"Yes, she came here with us from our earth."

"Oh. I didn't know that." Maggie looked awkward.

"Why are incs so against her?" I asked.

"It's not her, personally." Her eyes darted about like she wanted to bolt.

"I thought it probably wasn't. But we're new here and we don't understand it. It's great to find a friend like you who can just explain it so we understand and don't make fools of ourselves," Orla said. She had seen Maggie's discomfort, too.

"Yay! Food," I said as the waiter came to the table and handed out pizzas and drinks.

"It's hard to explain," Maggie said.

"We can just talk about something else if you prefer," I said. She was caving, but I didn't want her to think we were pushing her for information, which we were.

"This is the first new Brightling since I've been born. But I've been told that whenever there's a new one, the ribbon gets stronger and the faders find more ways to use it. They create new technology that leaves us farther and farther behind. The farther behind we are, the less we're considered true members of society and the more we're treated like cattle." Maggie drew in a breath then blew it out. She stared at her food.

"That's horrible, to feel so marginalized," I said.

"It's not a reason to try to kill your friend. I'm sorry that happened."

"I'm from a country with a sad past of people doing awful things in the name of religion and freedom, but it wound up being mostly about revenge. It takes a lot to turn away from that way of thinking," Orla said.

"Well, we can narrow that gap between us, can't we. It's a start," I said.

Maggie nodded and smiled.

"What did you do on Brightling Day?" Maggie asked.

"We went to the ceremony," I said.

"You actually saw it all? What was it like?"

"It was hands down the weirdest thing I've seen in my life, and I've seen some weird stuff. Mostly since I've been here, though," said Orla

"I heard Emperor Alexander VI of Russia was there. He is so handsome," Maggie said.

"See? It's that kind of thing that blows my mind. They have a Russian Emperor here," Orla said.

"There were some important-looking people there. Most of them seemed annoyed that we were in the front row. I tried not to gawk at them," I said.

"Anyway, more importantly, what do you do for fun around here?" Orla asked.

"I go to the picture house, or skating."

And the conversation moved on.

Later at home, I sat with Orla, Jason, and Connor in the garden.

"What did you think about what Maggie said at lunch today?" Orla asked.

"You mean the part about incs being treated like cattle?" I asked.

She nodded.

Connor sat forward.

"It sounded to me like someone else's words were coming out of her mouth," I said.

"That's exactly what I thought," she said.

"Have you seen much of the guy with the bad attitude?" Connor asked, referring to the young man in her office who had barged into us.

"The second I turn up, he goes," I said.

"I didn't get a good vibe from him. What does Heidi make of him?" Orla asked

"I don't think she's seen him," I said.

"Maybe that's something you should arrange," Jason said.

The next day at the office, I mentioned it to Heidi.

"Are you sure he intended to walk into you aggressively? If you were blocking the doorway, he might have expected that you would fade to allow him to walk through," she said.

"Possibly, but he storms out every time I show up," I said.

"Very well. I'll go down there now."

"What are you going to say?" Orla asked.

"I'll think of something," Heidi stood and left the office, heading for the stairs.

Orla and I looked at each other, then bolted from our desks to follow.

The mailroom was the first office on the right from the stairwell. We stood around the corner, unable to go any farther as the front office wall was glass. We listened as Heidi spoke.

"Hello. I'm Heidi. I work up in the mayor's suite. You may have seen me around. The mayor's just asked me to check that you're finding the new elevator serviceable. Not having any problems with it?"

Several voices, including Maggie's, responded that it was great, wonderful, and a joy.

"And you?" Heidi asked.

There was a long pause. I could tell that Orla was getting ready to poke her head around the corner and I was getting ready to yank it back if she moved an inch.

"It's great," said a flat, somber voice.

"Well, that's lovely. Thank you all for your input," Heidi said.

She walked back to us. I opened my mouth to speak, and she shook her head and walked straight through the doorway back to the stairwell. We followed. As the door closed, she turned to us.

"Hostile, hostile, hostile, so hostile," she said, shaking out her hands and bouncing on the balls of her feet.

"Bad then," Orla said.

"I've never been faced with someone so angry without backup before. I'm going to start carrying my weapons again. I don't feel like you two are safe here," Heidi said.

"Calm down. It's just one person. Maybe you can get a look through his things after he's gone home," I said.

"That's a good idea. I'm calling Callan," Heidi took out her communicator and muttered into it as we returned to the mayor's floor.

Back at home, I stepped out of the shower and looked at my lumpy arm. I tried hard not to scratch it during the day but suspected I was still scratching it in my sleep. I dried myself and pulled on my comfortable sweats, walked out of the bathroom, and found Orla leaning against the wall.

"At last. I thought you'd moved in," said Orla.

"Sorry, it's free now."

"I don't want the bathroom, you eejit, I want you. Heidi and Callan are here with news, they don't want to tell us until you're there, and we've been waiting ages. Come on."

We headed into the living room. "Sorry to keep you waiting," I said.

"We've been here less than three minutes," said Callan.

I looked at Orla.

"Well, it's seemed like ages in my mind," she said.

I shook my head.

"I don't recommend the inside of Orla's head to anyone. It's all shoes, shoes, shoes," David said, walking past with a bag of Cheetos.

I did a double-take at the snacks.

"Hey! Where did you—"

"Heidi and I searched Kevan's desk about an hour ago," said Callan. Dragging me back to the subject, he said, "The drawers are full of anti-Brightling leaflets. That's not against the law, but there was a letter from the mayor's team to a catering staff company, requesting support for the event where Zoe was targeted, along with a few other letters, stuff about the rest of you. He's been arrested and is being interviewed now."

"That's great news. I hope you can gather up the lot of them," Orla said.

"There's some bad news. Your friend Maggie was arrested, too. She's just been released," Heidi said.

"Why was she arrested?" I asked.

"Kevan is her boyfriend," Heidi said.

Orla facepalmed.

"Maybe she won't know it was us," I said.

"She may have seen me at the station," Heidi said

"But equally she may not have," Orla said.

"No, she saw me. I was trying to break it to you gently."

"What are we going to do?" I sat on the edge of the sofa.

"I'm going to ask David if he could scare up another Earth for me to go and live on," Orla said.

"I'll join you," I said.

"You've done nothing wrong. If you had known he was her boyfriend, would you have done anything differently?" Heidi asked.

"No, I guess not," I said

The next day, Orla and I stuffed envelopes in silence, occasionally glancing at the clock and each other.

"Five minutes to go. Are we going down?" Orla asked.

"Is she even here? What if she got fired?"

"I'm sure we'd have heard. Let's just go."

Lunchtime came, and we headed down the stairs, through the stairwell door, and around the corner to Maggie's office.

"Look, she's not there. Come on, we'll head back up." Orla said

We turned to find Maggie standing behind us having come out of the ladies' bathroom. Her eyes were red and puffy.

"Oh, sweetie," Orla said.

Maggie walked past us and into her office. She picked up her bag and left.

"I feel awful," I said.

"Let's just give her some time."

We returned to our floor and went back to work.

8

─────────

Dr. Anil Narayan stood at the door to Neil's old office. "Can I help you Dr. Narayan?" asked the room's new incumbent.

"No, no. Just thinking," said the old Indian scientist.

He returned to his office and sifted through the pictures and scans of the mysterious cube which had been retrieved from the faders in Canada. This information had been sent out to every agency lab in the world.

It looked like some kind of trendy adaptor or a night-light. He had been surprised not to find an Apple logo on it. A cube, with rounded corners, one side had a button on it and the other sides were made from a translucent glass.

Sitting, he hit the Play button on his laptop and viewed the videos he'd received from Major Tomowski.

It didn't take long to realize the cube was powered by fader energy. This had been what they'd been striving for all these years—a way to tap into the power harnessed by those with the ability to fade.

He watched as the first video began with a lab tech

announcing it was test number eleven. He had already watched tests one to ten.

"It is clear this cube is intended to be used by faders, but none of the faders we've captured seem to have any knowledge of its existence."

The video showed a boy of about twelve years, waking on a gurney in a room, empty, with the exception of a small trolley and the cube placed in a little cage atop it. The boy took in his surroundings and immediately faded. Moments later came the sound of an electrical discharge, and the boy reappeared unconscious in the room having tried to go beyond the forcefield created by the posts in the corners of the room.

"Observe how the subject barely glanced at the cube and certainly with no recognition," said the narrator.

The boy raised his head and staggered to his feet. "What have you done to me?" he yelled at the camera high on the wall.

"Please switch on the cube. If you can switch it on, we'll let you leave," came a woman's soft voice through a speaker into the room.

Dr. Narayan leaned closer to the screen as the boy attempted to pick up the cube and found the cage secured to the surface of the trolley.

"What is it? Why does it glow like me?"

No response.

He pressed the button, stiffened, and collapsed.

The screen changed to another face. Probably a former tracker, seated in the observation room above the experimentation labs.

"Ryan, I'd like you to describe what you saw," said a woman in a lab coat.

The boy looked like he had been beaten. He looked frightened.

"The cube has a glow, not bright, but it glows yellow like they do...like I would."

"And what did you see when the fader pushed the button?" she asked.

"The fader emitted, and it went into the little box," said Ryan.

"Did anything happen to the cube?" the woman asked.

"It went a little bit brighter for a second but went back to a dim glow."

The video switched back to the room where another fader was lying unconscious. It was an older man. Dr. Narayan waited for the man on the gurney to stir, but nothing happened. After a few minutes, a man in a white lab coat flanked by an agent entered to check the man's vitals.

He looked up at the camera. "Another dud," he called while waving his hand in front of his neck, making the 'cut' signal.

"This subject has been in a drug-induced coma for seven years. Subjects who have been unconscious for an extended length of time can't always be awakened, but they can still be of use in other experiments," said the narrator.

Dr. Narayan paused the video and returned to the scans of the object which showed a box with plastic and glass surfaces and a button with wires leading to a point on the inner wall of the cube. There didn't seem to be anything special about the cube. He glanced at the paused video, closed it, and scrolled down the files knowing that nothing different had happened in any of the first batch of experiments, except that a couple of the subjects had actually died after touching the button. That didn't make sense. And who had invented it? To his knowledge, the faders were a disorganized bunch, and half of them, when caught, didn't seem even to know what they were. The idea that some super-scientific underground fader organization existed was beyond ludicrous. And why would they use a technology that could kill them?

Dr. Narayan's expertise was in biology. He didn't like to admit it, but Neil Banks's knowledge of molecular chemistry would have been very handy.

He clicked on a different folder called Cube Two. He opened a couple of schematic files. To his eyes, they seemed identical to the original cube. He opened the first video file.

A naked girl was lying on the floor of the room. They'd clearly skipped past the part where she woke, faded, and knocked herself out on the forcefield.

The cube was on the trolley. It appeared similar but not identical. He switched screens to look at the schematic again. The style of the cube was crude, even for a prototype. When he switched back, the girl was sitting up.

"Press the button on the cube, please," said that same soft female voice.

"Bite me," she shouted back, looking around until she spied the camera. She flipped the bird.

"We'll let you go if you press the button. That's all we need. That's the only reason you're here," said the voice.

The girl cast about. She couldn't fade. There was nowhere for her to go. She sighed, stood, and walked to the trolley.

She reached down to the cube and pressed the button. Nothing seemed to happen to her. She picked up the trolley and smashed it into one of the posts in the corner. The door flew open as she faded. An agent ran in with a dart gun and shouted "Oh shi…"

The camera switched to Ryan and the woman again.

"Yes!" said Ryan, looking through the observation mirror.

The woman's hand came up and slapped him across the mouth. Ryan froze. She immediately returned to her keyboard.

"What did you see?" she asked.

"Nothing," said Ryan.

She stared at him. Her eyes were shark-like, flat and emotionless.

"She didn't emit. There was no yellow. Nothing went into the box," he said.

Dr. Narayan heard a loud sizzle and the two on the screen looked down through the mirrored glass towards the hallway outside the test room. Two loud reports came immediately after. When he returned his gaze back to her, she was staring at him, smiling.

"Clean up on aisle three," she said.

"What the hell is wrong with you? That was a young girl. Someone's daughter," he said.

"That was a little monster. The daughter of monsters. If you knew what your kind were responsible for…" She had leaned in towards him, and he shrank back.

She sat upright and looked up, presumably at the person behind the camera. "Let's have a little break, shall we?"

The movie file ended.

Dr. Narayan sat back in his chair before leaning forward again to compose an email to Major Tomowski. He began to type but stopped. Closed the app and checked the time. America would be up by now. He lifted his desk phone and called there instead.

"Tomowski."

"Good morning, Major. How are you?"

"Doctor. You got anything?

"Have any further tests been carried out on Cube One?"

"I've got some asshole here who wants to drill into it," Tomowski said.

"You have engineers on it? You need scientists," said the doctor. "We need to find out what's inside it."

"That's what the idiot with the drill keeps saying," Tomowski said. "I have scientists, too. They're dipping it in something to work out the density of the gas inside."

"I was about to suggest that. I look forward to hearing the results," said the doctor.

"How is Operation Dreamcatcher going at your end?" Tomowski asked.

"To plan. Yours?"

"The same. How many viable subjects do you have now?"

"Fourteen. I saw your report. Two hundred and twenty-seven. That's impressive."

"We should have done this years ago. This is going to save a fortune for the program going forward. Good luck, Doctor," Tomowski said.

The receiver went dead. "And goodbye to you," Dr. Narayan said.

He left his office and walked along the hallway to doors, guarded by two large, armed agents, which led to the agency section of the building. He flashed his ID at the scanner and headed through the doorway into the section which was off-limits to all but a few on the base. He paused at the door to the stairwell, but lately he'd been feeling the years in his hips and knees. He moved on to the elevator and down to basement level one.

The smell of disinfectant was strong, and the floors shone in the overhead lights. He felt comforted. The order around him did not reflect the chaos this program was going through.

Walking through a side door onto a ward, he moved past unconscious faders. He kept a few here for study. The facilities weren't great. Most were either experimented on and discarded or flown to Colorado. They had been planning to expand the facilities down here, but that was not going to be needed for a while. The program was on the verge of collapse since the telepathic fader's message had been received by virtually every fader and tracker on the planet. The agency had been stretched to capacity handling the situation. They tried to spin it, suggesting that it was a fader trick, but it seemed the veneer of their lies was thinner than they had realized. When faced with the truth, the trackers had accepted it immediately.

The sprinkler systems installed in every tracker's home on the base had long ago been fitted with a nerve agent. At the touch of a button, windows were sealed and the system activated. Most of the older trackers on the base were eliminated. The younger ones were either tranquillized or caged. The agency had been lucky; only about a hundred or so had been out in the field. The missing trackers were reported as escaped from a mental institution. Thanks to agents in policing, government, and media, very little news had made it to the outside world.

He entered the second ward and studied the charts for the comatose patients around him. All girls age fourteen and older, all artificially inseminated. The program would grow again, but they were playing a long game.

Dr. Narayan headed back up to his office to write up his

notes. He'd finish late, but it was preferable to starting early. He entered his office.

He glanced down at the tracker in the corner of his room who was, unsurprisingly, sitting in her chair. He checked the restraints. "What are you? Eighteen? I might have another job for you," he said.

Sitting at his desk, he began to type.

9

It was strange to be back at Hilltop. Not least because it was so quiet. I had expected uniformed agents everywhere, but it was deserted.

We stood at the entrance to the med center. The team consisted of Connor, Vince, David, and me. Vince was there because he was able to fade without emitting, therefore being invisible to trackers. Connor's ability to share out the abilities of other faders meant that none of us could be seen by the trackers. I didn't have any concerns relying heavily on Vince again. I felt confident in him. David had told me he had torn his way through Vince's mind and he had no intention of betraying us again, but I hadn't needed that.

We entered the center and made our way down to the labs, looking out for anti-fade posts. Dad's office door now held a different name, one that was unfamiliar to me.

Dr. Narayan, the little Indian scientist who had experimented on me so long ago, sat at his desk seemingly oblivious to our presence. We walked around the desk to see his papers and screen. I didn't understand anything on the papers, but his screen held images of an x-ray of the cube. A noise from the corner of the room drew my attention.

One of the students sat chained to a chair. I recognized her as one of Tiffany's friends but couldn't remember her name.

"When we take him, she'll be punished," I said. I half expected Vince to complain.

"We'll need to do this quickly," Vince said.

"Are there cameras in here?" Connor asked, looking into the corners of the room.

"There's nothing I could do with them even if there were. We should get the laptop, too," I said.

"Okay. As quick as we can. Remember, the paperwork is extra. What we need is in his head," David said.

Standing behind Dr. Narayan, we separated and materialized. Connor's ability sharing, no longer allowed us all to remain hidden. David emitted, creating a portal. Vince grabbed the doctor, pulling him out of his chair.

"What the...?" The doctor saw me and stopped speaking.

Connor went to the girl on the chair who was sitting staring with her mouth agape. I followed him.

"Remember me?" I asked.

She nodded.

"What kind of device is in her? Poison or explosive?" I asked, turning to Dr. Narayan.

"I don't know. They don't tell me these things."

"As I recall, Doctor, you're the one who carries out the procedure. Would you like to try that again?"

"Explosive. There's one inside me, too," he said.

I looked at David, but he shrugged; he couldn't read the doctor.

I sighed. Thinking. The doctor was sweating.

"Jenna?" Connor said.

"Get his head on the desk," I said.

"Scalpels?" I asked the girl.

"Over there in the glass-fronted cabinet," she said.

The doctor struggled in Vince's grip.

"I recommend holding still, my friend. We don't want to leave you paralyzed," Vince said.

I checked the back of his neck. He had an insertion scar.

"Are you okay doing this?" Connor asked.

Okay? No, I wasn't okay. This was gross.

"Can you confirm where it is?" I asked instead.

Connor faded a finger and poked around.

"It's an inch in, about half an inch up from the scar," he said.

"I don't suppose you could give me that in metric."

"Holy Mother! Twenty-five-point-four millimeters in, twelve-point-seven millimeters up," shouted the doctor.

"Thanks, Doc," I said as chirpily as I could manage.

Vince put his hand over the man's mouth and held his head down from the front.

I paused with the scalpel in my hand.

"Are you sure?" Connor said.

I cut.

The doctor did his best to scream through Vince's hand.

I moved to dig my finger in, but Connor put his hand over mine.

"Let me," he said.

He faded his fingers and dipped them into the bottom of the doctor's head.

"Hold still," he said to the doctor who had begun shifting.

Connor had materialized just the very edges of his fingertips to slide the capsule out. He was the only fader I had ever met who could fade parts of his body independently. It was remarkable to witness.

I turned the capsule over in my hand. "It's got liquid in it. It's poison. I placed it on the desk.

The doctor was whimpering and still slightly shifting. Too late, I realized he had reached into the pocket of his lab coat.

"No..." I cried. Just as the girl stiffened and dropped to the floor.

Connor grabbed the doctor and pushed him towards the portal, fading him at the same time he shoved him through.

Vince got busy grabbing any paperwork he could see before heading through to the Full-Earth. I stared at the girl: Laurie. I finally remembered her name. I took the laptop and stuffed it into a bag. Taking in the room one last time, I walked into the portal with David.

Callan and Heidi stood waiting on the other side. "How did it go?"

"One casualty," Connor said.

Dr. Narayan looked confused. "Where am I?"

I stared into his eyes for a long moment, then Heidi tapped him on the neck with her pen, and he slumped in Connor's arms.

"James isn't comfortable with us kidnapping people. What are you going to do with him?" Callan asked.

I hadn't even thought beyond grabbing him. I didn't have a clue.

"Could we take him to Broken-Earth?" I asked.

"The less he knows the better. I know a place in Vancouver."

"Canada again?" I asked.

"No, the other one. In Washington State, where the academy was," David said.

Callan called the ribbon. I gave him the laptop. "This might be trackable. I can't bring it back to the other side. Can you take it back to my dad with these papers? We'll try to get the password."

Callan took the bag and nodded.

Connor faded the doctor, and we headed to Vancouver. We crossed over into a wooded area which David explained was North of Vancouver.

We waited for the doctor to regain consciousness, then followed David through the woods. He seemed to know his way about here although it all looked the same to me.

After a mile or so, we came out into a clearing near a large farmhouse.

"You'd better be friends, coz I ain't asking twice," said a woman.

I turned to find a middle-aged lady in jeans and a plaid shirt aiming a shotgun at us. I froze.

"Hello, Cindy," David said.

"David? It *is* you. Well, shit! Long time no see, boyfriend."

Vince glanced at David but said nothing.

She leaned her gun against the porch and walked forward to embrace David. She pulled back and stared intently at him. "You look tired."

"I always look tired. This is how I look now," he said.

They hugged again.

"Who are your friends?" she asked.

"This is Vince, Jenna, Connor, and this is Dr. Narayan. He's from England. He's with the agency."

"Well, you're almost all welcome," said Cindy. "I got your message." She tapped her head. "Ed thought I was going crazy. I sent him up to the cabin for a few days fishing."

"I'm sorry about your mom. She was good to me," David said.

"Oh, how did...? Hey, stay out of there," said Cindy, tapping her head again. "Let's put him in the barn and we can get some food. You can tell me what's going on."

Connor and Vince chained the doctor to a post in the barn, then for good measure I pressed the nanite pen against his neck. When he was unconscious, we locked the barn door and entered the house. The kitchen was warm, and a thick stew bubbled on the range cooker. We sat at the table. Cindy had filled bowls for all of us and put one aside, I assumed for the doctor. It was more than he deserved.

"Cindy, you remember the man who was killed protecting Kim? This is his granddaughter."

"Well, it's a small world. Your grandfather was a brave man," said Cindy.

"We're just going to keep the doctor here for a few days and ask him some questions."

"Do you want my daddy's old skinning knife?" Cindy asked.

My mouth hung open.

"For effect," she added, seeing my face.

"We won't need that. Connor's got everything we need."

"Really? Well, he's a pretty Southern boy. What's he gonna do, screw the answers out of him?"

I choked on my food and Cindy laughed and thumped me on the back.

Over the next three days, Connor went into the barn many times to talk to Dr. Narayan, repeatedly fading him and asking questions, but he refused to talk. He attempted to escape several times, but to no avail. Even when he was loose from the chains, he was old and slow.

"Why do you keep doing this to me? I'm never going to

tell you anything. You can kill me if you like. I don't need to see how you fade. You tease me by letting me out of my chains, but I can't get anywhere. What's the point?"

"The point is, that eventually, you'll tell us what we need to know. Where is the cube?"

"Where did it come from? Where did we go to from my office? I've long believed there are other earths. Are we on another earth?" the doctor asked.

"You aren't expecting me to answer your questions when you won't answer mine, are you?" Connor said. "Let's have some fun fading again." He reached out and faded the doctor for the fiftieth time.

I stayed outside during these sessions, listening. It was counterproductive having me in the room. He kept trying to speak to me, as though we had some kind of connection. It was getting on my nerves.

Connor closed the door and locked it. "I'm worried this isn't going to work. Your dad might have been a fluke. I've faded this guy about thirty more times than I did your dad."

"If it doesn't work, we'll think of something else," I said.

That evening, I sat on the porch trying to make a ball of energy appear in my hand. At this point, I didn't care whether it was red or white. I just needed something.

"Your staring at that hand like it ain't yours," said Cindy, taking the seat next to me.

We talked for a while, and Cindy told me how she'd met David.

"He lived with us a while after the massacre at the academy. He was in a bad way," said Cindy

"And he was your boyfriend?"

"It never came to nothing. We had a mutual crush on each other at the start, but I realized pretty soon, long before he did, I think, that he didn't like girls. He tried to, for me, because we were so close, but in the end our love became something more like brother and sister. I was surprised to find him with Vince."

"You knew about Vince?" I asked.

"David has kept in touch regularly over the years, so I knew they'd split up. David was heartbroken. I hope Vince treats him more kindly this time."

"I think he will. Even in the short time I've known him, Vince has changed," I said.

I blinked in and glanced about, as was habit now. I looked towards the barn. A soft yellow haze escaped from under the door.

"Is someone in there with him?" I asked.

"No, he's alone," said Cindy, sitting forward, having blinked in herself.

"Where's David?" I asked.

"*What's up?*" David sent. He'd been listening, of course.

"*We're up,*" I said to him.

Cindy and I stood and made our way to the barn.

The doctor was lying asleep in the straw.

David, Connor, and Vince arrived behind me.

David chuckled softly and turned to Cindy. "Well, he really likes your cooking. He's dreaming about it."

The whispers woke up the doctor. He looked at us with a nervous expression.

"Where's the cube?" Connor asked.

"You might as well kill me, I'm not going to tell you that," he said.

"*He doesn't know,*" David sent.

"You know what? I don't think he knows," David said.

"Where would you guess it is? If you had to guess," Connor asked.

"*In the mountain with that prick Tomowski. The language*

he's using in his head! He really doesn't like Craig," came David's voice, translating Dr. Narayan's thoughts.

"It couldn't be in the mountain, could it. We've already breached it. They can't guarantee its safety," I said, conversationally.

"He's just going to tell us it's there and assume that the new security features will take care of us.

"Okay, I'll tell you. I think it's probably in the mountain," said the doctor.

"What's security like these days. Any changes?"

"He's seeing lots of those anti-fading posts. The ones they set up when we crossed over the first time. He's grateful for the work Dr. Philipson did with you. That gave them the idea to modulate the frequencies which stopped Vince from getting past them."

"When's the best time to go? When are we most likely to catch him in? Or out?" I asked

"Craig told him he's got a visit to Washington DC planned in a few days."

"What's the password to your computer?" Vince asked.

"I'm not going to tell you that," the doctor said.

"It's Tokyo2020."

"What happens to the faders who are captured in the U.K?" I asked.

"Killed, mostly. Some are sent to Colorado, but I'm seeing flashes of comatose girls at Hilltop and Colorado. Oh God, they're all pregnant."

I took a few breaths.

"Tell us about Project Dreamcatcher," David said.

The doctor stared up at David. He looked truly alarmed.

"There are two bases working on the project to make new faders. They have been successful so far, so they're going to roll it out to other bases soon," David sent.

"We understand it's not just Colorado and Hilltop taking part in the project. They're going to do it elsewhere." I said.

"He's thinking of other bases. They've got a research facility inside CERN in Switzerland which is currently being fitted out to house more girls."

You look surprised. You think we don't have people on the inside? We have people on almost every site. If not inside, then nearby," I said

"He's just thinking of people's faces now. I think I've got all the bases,"

"What happened to Jason Watts's father?" David asked.

"He doesn't know who that is."

"Who killed my mother?"

He said nothing and stared at his feet.

I knew, just from his demeanor, but I looked at David for confirmation. He wasn't meeting my eyes either.

"Well?" I asked David.

"It was him. He told your dad he had inserted a new inhibitor but he injected her with a slow acting poison and sent her home to him," David said aloud.

I spun back to meet Dr. Narayan's eyes. In that instant, I could see him putting it all together. He knew David had been picking the answers out of his head.

"You're turning me into one of you, that's what all the fading was for. I didn't imagine that was possible. Not after the tests," he said.

"Oh my God!" David covered his eyes and reached out to the wall to support himself, clearly having read something awful in the doctor's mind.

Sitting back on the ground, Dr. Narayan stared into the middle distance and refused to engage with us.

"He's singing *Crocodile Rock* in his head, trying to block me out. Good choice; I hate that song."

We locked up and walked back to the house and sat around the kitchen table.

"What are we going to do with him? It's too dangerous to keep him around," Connor said.

"He could fade at any time," Vince said.

"I'm not so sure. I think Dad was able to fade so fast because of the nanites," I said.

"I have no idea what you're saying right now," said Cindy. "But, please, for the love of God, don't try to explain it."

"So, we might have up to a year before he can fade," Connor said.

"He's probably going to have to come back to Broken-Earth with me," Vince said.

"Oh. You're going back there?" David asked.

"For now. They need me," Vince said.

"Ed and the boys will be back tomorrow night. This needs to be resolved before they get back. Did you get everything you needed out of him?" Cindy asked.

"I think we got more than we wanted," David said with a sigh.

"I'm going to bed before you say any more stuff that's gonna break my brain." She stood.

David reached out his hand without looking at her. She took it, and he pressed the back of her hand briefly to his cheek. The bond between the two was clear.

After a plan had been made to portal the doctor to Broken-Earth in the morning, I went to bed.

As I lay in the dark, it occurred to me that Connor was down the hall and my dad was in another universe. It seemed like a terrible waste of an opportunity. I pulled on the gown that Cindy had loaned me and opened my door as quietly as the old house allowed, which wasn't the least bit quiet. Halfway down the hallway, a door to my right opened. I was busted. I turned to find myself face-to-face with Vince. We looked at each other awkwardly for a moment. Vince shrugged, closed his door, then crept over to David's, tapped, and entered.

Good plan, I thought. Knock but don't allow time to be rejected. A thought which terrified me.

I tapped on Connor's door and entered, closing it behind me.

"Is everything okay?" Connor asked, sitting up.

I almost couldn't hear him over the sound of my pulse hammering in my ears.

"Just a second," I whispered.

"*David?*"

"*Erm... Yes?*"

"*I'm hanging a sock on the door knob of my mind.*"

"*Understood.*"

"Everything's perfect." I walked to his bed, removed the gown, and slid under the covers.

"Oh right. Everything *is* perfect," he said, taking me in his arms as we kissed.

He kissed my neck and stroked his hand down the full length of my back. "You're covered in goosebumps," he muttered into my ear.

"We must be near ley lines," I said.

Early the next morning, I woke to the sound of Cindy's shotgun. One blast. An upstairs door flew open and footsteps ran heavily down the stairs and out towards the barn.

I surmised that Cindy had shot Dr. Narayan. Nothing could be done about that now. Connor and I stayed upstairs for another hour. He traced the red and gold hexagon shapes around my arm.

"I don't know what this means, but it looks like a bad-ass tattoo," he said.

THE DISCUSSION at the kitchen table that morning became what to do with the body. I wondered if I might be able to send him into the in-between, but the thought made me sick. Even if I could do it, I didn't want to.

Connor and Vince wrapped the Doctor up in a blanket, and while Cindy and David cleaned up the mess in the barn, Connor and Vince took the doctor and stuffed him into the trunk of a huge sequoia deep in the surrounding forest.

Cindy's parting shot to Vince was "Treat him right this time, or you'll be next to see the business end of my daddy's shotgun,"

We said goodbye to her and stood apart while she and David stood with their foreheads touching, muttering words I couldn't hear.

"Jealous?" I asked Vince.

"Not even a little bit. She's his family."

We headed back into the woods to cross back over.

I WALKED with Dad through the garden.

"So, it *was* him. I wondered," Dad said.

"I'm sorry," I said.

"I would have liked the chance to grab him by the throat and—," he sighed. "Maybe not." Dad wiped tears from his face.

"It's done now," I said.

We sat on the bench by the pond.

"I miss the rose bush," he said.

"The what?" I didn't know what he was talking about.

"I planted a rose bush for her in the garden of remembrance," he said.

"The one with the red and white roses?" I remembered it because it was so striking.

"That's the one. That was where we scattered her ashes," he said, tears falling again. "Do you remember her at all? It's okay if you don't. You were only three when she died."

I thought of the memories which had been dredged up by the other. They were perfectly clear.

"I remember her face precisely. She sat me in a ball pit in the garden. All the balls were purple. She was wearing shorts and a beaded sun top. You both kept saying 'purple balls' in funny voices, and I squealed every time you said it."

"How can you remember that? You must have been about one-and-a-half years-old." He smiled, shaking his head.

"I know, weird, huh?" I said. "Anyway, you have the future to look forward to now."

He hugged me and stood. "Yes, which reminds me. I'm going on a day trip with a few of the chaps. I'm just going to keep them out of trouble."

"Ahh! Sean's Famous Secret Boys' Day Out," I said.

"You know what it is?" Dad asked.

"No, just that he's arranged something. It looks like things are going to get intense for us all soon. It's a good idea to blow off some steam. Maybe we girls should do something, too."

10

"How is a country so cold and rainy and windy in May?" Callan asked as he stamped his feet and clapped his gloved hands together, staring at the landscape of Half-Earth Staffordshire, England, from the cover of a Perspex bus stop.

"How would you know how cold countries get with your big fancy domes and perfect temperatures?" Sean asked.

"I like the big domes. It's nice to go out and not have to worry about the weather," Aiden said.

"The domes aren't everywhere, just over some of the major cities. There are new cities without domes appearing all the time, now that the danger from the storms is so far in the past," said Callan.

Callan gazed around at the landscape. "I can't believe your earth remained untouched by the storms." He shook his head and returned to stamping his feet.

"It looks like that might be about to change. It's blowing a gale out there," Jason said.

"This is nothing. The storms were unrelenting with

lightning that split the earth. This is just horrible, cold, wet weather," said Callan.

"I'm sorry, Callan, but you're representing L.A.'s finest here. You're going to have to man up," Connor said.

They laughed.

"Don't worry, the pride of Ireland is safe with us in this endeavor," Aiden said, patting Sean on the back.

"What are you representing, Leroy?" Sean asked.

"I'm here to defend the reputation of the Chicago Bears," said Leroy.

"Dude, that ship sailed," said Chester, leaping out of the huge man's reach.

"Neil?" Connor asked.

"Her Majesty the Queen, of course," he said.

"And I'm representing the north," Jason Added.

"What about you, Chester?" Leroy asked.

"I'm representing poor people who want to get rich,"

"That works for me," Connor said.

"How about you, David?" Callan asked.

"I'm representing common sense, which is why I want to get out of here as soon as possible," David said. He closed his eyes and sighed. "I don't want to give up searching for people who need us but I see the value in Sean's idea."

"Can we get out of this rain?" Callan asked.

"Let's head to the store and get what we need," Connor said.

The group of men walked into the bookshop and found maps, and books on the Staffordshire Horde. After paying, Jason ripped something off the front of a magazine called *Pets.*

"What's that?" Callan asked.

"A rubber chicken," Jason said, squeezing it to make it squeak.

They all stared at him.

"It's for my dog." He dropped the magazine into a trash can.

Outside, they stood in a huddle, leafing through the books as passersby stepped around them, tutting.

"Guys, we're getting soaked. Let's find a café to sit down and go through all this," David said.

"What time is it?" Aiden asked.

"Two in the afternoon," Connor said.

"A café!" Sean said, sounding offended. "Come on, let's find a pub."

"Oh dear!" Neil said.

They piled in through the doors of the first pub they found.

"I think the ladies planned it right, staying in," Jason said, squeezing rain out of his hair.

"Did you want your nails painted, Jason? You should have said," Sean laughed.

"David, did you get your message to Jenna before we crossed?" Neil asked.

"Yes." David smiled, wishing he could be a fly-on-the-wall when she opened that cupboard door.

"They do food. Let's get food," Leroy said.

"Dude, are you ever not eating?" Chester asked.

"You can starve if you like, little man, but I'm hungry," Leroy said.

"I didn't say I didn't want to eat," Chester said.

"I can't figure out where it goes on you. Maybe you got a portal in your throat," Leroy said, looking at his wiry friend.

"These beers have the weirdest names," said Callan as he gawked at the bottles and taps.

"Just don't try the Guinness. You don't try Guinness for the first time anywhere but Ireland," Sean said.

"I'll order for us, to save time. You lot sit down. Fish, chips, and beers all round?" Aiden asked.

"I'll have a Sprite. I don't drink," David said.

They sat at the longest table and moved another onto the end to accommodate all of them. They spread out the maps and books and started reading.

"I've seen you drink," Connor said.

"I want to stay in control," David said.

"Come on man, just one," said Chester.

"You know that place Jenna sent the two agents to?" David asked with an eyebrow raised.

"Point taken. No drinking for Dave, he's driving," said Leroy.

No one wanted to end up in the in-between.

Aiden brought over eight pints and a Sprite.

"What's this one called?" Chester asked, holding up the dark beer and eyeing it suspiciously.

"Hairy– something," Aiden said.

Chester sipped his beer and coughed. "Jeez, they don't have Bud Light?"

"No, they only serve beer," Sean said.

"What is the in-between?" Leroy asked, as he sniffed at his beer.

"I had never even conceived of the in-between before Jenna opened a portal to it. She was terrified and not even intending to open a portal. I think perhaps the lack of focus and blind panic resulted in a portal to nowhere. I don't know if it's truly in-between the worlds, but the name fits for what she saw," David said.

"How long have you known about the other worlds?" Chester asked.

"The first time I faded, I didn't know it at the time, but it was to Broken-Earth. I came back within minutes, unaware that we'd even gone somewhere else. All I knew was that I'd lost Kim. After that, whenever I emitted, it was red. I knew something different was going on and I became terrified of fading. I just didn't do it. Over the years, I began to suspect that fading might take me somewhere else but I couldn't bring myself to try. It wasn't until the day we went to Full-Earth that I truly knew." David looked at Connor. "I believed we'd end up somewhere. I suppose, when I pulled that stunt, as terrified and clueless as Jenna, we could all have fallen into the in-between."

Connor shuddered, and so did everyone else.

"So, you weren't thinking of somewhere when you did that?" Neil asked.

"I felt that another place existed, that I could make you all safe after all you'd risked to save me. Ultimately, what did we have to lose?" David said.

They read through the maps and books until the waitresses arrived with trays of food, handing out cutlery, and condiments.

"Ahh! A bunch of treasure hunters. Every time I think I've seen the end of you lot, another group arrives," said the waitress. "Right! That's fish, chips, and mushy peas for nine. Enjoy your meals."

The boys piled the books and maps into the center of the table as the waitress placed the plates. They ate quickly and, one by one, as they finished their food, they picked up a book or map and continued to read.

The waitress came back for the plates. "You know the whole area's been gone over like, a million times, don't you?" she said.

"Sure, of course," Sean said. "We've got a group project for university. We need to take soil samples of the actual location where the horde was found. We know what farm it's on but not the precise spot and we haven't found anything in these books."

"I'm sorry, I'm not allowed to talk about that. It's on private land," she said, and left.

"Are you sure the Staffordshire Horde hasn't been found on Full-Earth?" Chester asked Sean.

"I've been through all the treasure finds in England on that side. I can't see any mention of it,"

"What if the land belongs to someone," Leroy asked.

"We'll split it with them," Sean said.

"It depends where on the farmer's land it is. Some of that land is owned our side," Callan said.

"Let's just go to the farm and see how it goes," Leroy said.

They headed out of the pub and made their way to the farm to find a man working in the yard. He glanced up to see them watching him and made his way, slowly, across to the gate.

"Excuse me, are you the owner?" Sean asked.

"He's not around," said the man.

"When will he be back?" Chester asked.

"Don't know," said the man. He wasn't giving much away.

"Would it be possible to see the excavation site?" Sean asked.

"Nope," said the man.

"I'm sorry, we've not much time. It's rag week at the university. One of the trials is to half-bury a rubber chicken at the excavation site and take a picture. We get extra points if we're first," Sean said.

Jason held up the rubber chicken, making it squeak.

"We're students," Aiden said.

The man looked at David and Neil. "Even you two?"

"I'm a tutor. Just here to make sure they behave themselves," Neil said.

"I'm a mature student," David said.

"I doubt that," said the man. "Look, you might as well clear off. You're not getting on this land." He turned to walk back.

"That's okay," said Neil. "Another group are saying they've already been onto the land and done it, so it's not worth so many points. Come on, lads."

The man spun back with his eyes narrowed on the group. "What?"

"Nothing. Have a great day," Neil said.

"Just clear off," the man said before marching towards a Land Rover.

"He's probably going to check. Go with him," David said. "Get the precise coordinates."

Sean, Aiden, and Chester faded and jumped into the Land Rover as it pulled away, heading for the fields. The others waited. Half an hour later, they had all the information they needed.

"It's a bit late to start digging now. Are we all okay to come back tomorrow?" Sean asked.

"I've got work tomorrow, you carry on without me," Callan said.

David prepared to portal them back to the Full-Earth. He stood still, turning his head this way and that.

"What's the holdup?" Chester asked.

"Dude, we're getting soaked here," Leroy said.

"Shh!" Connor stared intently at David, knowing he was listening to something important.

"Matthew? My name is David. Are you Jason's friend?"

Jason turned and was at David's elbow in a second.

"Is it him?" Jason asked.

David held up his hand to silence Jason.

"I see. We will be with you in a minute." David turned to Jason. "We must be near a ley line or I wouldn't have picked that up. He needs help. His friend is injured. We need to go back to Full-Earth. I can portal us from there," David said.

They stepped over to Full-Earth.

The moment they appeared, Callan's communicator beeped, and he stepped away to speak.

"Can we do this now or do you need to rest?" Jason asked, fidgeting.

"We can go now," David said.

"Wait, we need to get back. Jenna and Orla are missing," Callan said.

"What?" said Neil.

"Jenna? Jenna!" David tried to reach out to Jenna with his mind, but it was like her mind wasn't there anymore. He tried Orla with the same result. He didn't want to think about what that might mean.

"I can't find her. She might be travelling again," he said.

They all knew he meant that she might be in the in-between.

"Jason, it's your op. Do you want to delay it?" David asked.

"I don't think we should. Let's get this done. Quickly. Are you okay with that, Connor?" Jason asked.

Connor paused but said, "Okay."

"Callan, take everyone back to the residence. Jason, Connor, and I will deal with this," David said.

"I'm not letting my only sister's boyfriend get himself killed without me, she'll murder me. Besides, they're probably shopping," Sean said.

David emitted and tried to home in on exactly where

Matthew was. A minute went by. Sweat poured from him as he concentrated.

"Apparently, we're not *that* close to a ley line. This is a real struggle," David said.

Suddenly, it was there, in the mist, shapes shifting in what looked like an alley. David turned to find Callan had set up a ribbon gate right behind him. The men nodded at each other.

"Let us know when you're back and where you are. We'll come get you."

Callan passed David a communicator.

Jason leaped through, followed by Connor, Sean, and David.

"Okay, everyone, through the gate," said Callan, flashing his tag and stating the destination. As one, they faded and stepped through.

11

———

"Good morning, ladies," Heidi said, coming in from the garden with a bagful of supplies.

"What have you got there?" Orla asked, suddenly alert.

"Face creams, hair curlers, and nail paint," Heidi said.

"Great! Movie morning can commence," said Jodi.

"Right. We've got *Eat, Pray, Love, Dirty Dancing*, and *P.S. I Love You*," Orla said, flicking through the DVDs.

"Ahh, the old ones are the best," Sofia said.

"How is the DVD player working?" Jodi asked.

"David jury-rigged an adaptor. It's hooked up to a little cube, running on Jenna Power," Orla said.

"I'm a freelance energy provider now," I said, placing a box of Dooley Cola and eight cups down.

"We should have popcorn," Jodi said.

"I should have thought of that," I said.

"I love *P.S. I Love You*," Orla said.

"I haven't seen it," Jodi said.

"I haven't seen any of them," Heidi said.

"Oh good, you haven't started your movie yet," David sent.

"*Hey, this is girls only,*" I sent back.

"*We're heading off for our adventure. I left a couple of gifts for you in your bedroom closet, for your girls' day in,*" he sent.

"You did?" I squealed, jumping to my feet.

"*Thank you.*"

The girls looked at me.

"I forgot to use my inside voice. David left something for us in my cupboard." I ran out of the room and nearly knocked Brother Damon off his feet. They had just arrived through the gate down in Zoe's room.

"Oh! Sorry, Damon. Hi, girls. Hey, Justin. David left a surprise for us. I'm going to see what it is." I glanced briefly at Zoe and the anger inside me flared. I looked away.

The others rounded the corner into the living room, and I headed to my room.

I opened the closet door and jumped back as its contents, packed in from bottom to top, spilled out across the floor.

"No way!" I squealed.

Hannah and Zoe peeked in to find me surrounded by bags of Cheetos, Doritos, strawberry laces, and other treats.

"Can you help me take these through?" I asked, still trying not to look directly at Zoe for more than a fraction of a second.

They each picked up armfuls of treats and staggered out of the room.

Heidi walked in. "You're doing it again," she said. "I felt the flare of anger from the living room."

I dropped onto the bed. "I know. I can feel it. I don't understand why this is happening."

"Look, the Brothers are here, just talk to them," she said.

I dug the heels of my palms into my eyes. "I just want to stop seeing it. If I could just stop seeing it."

"*Yes,*" came a chorus of voices at once in my head. I jumped.

"Need more hands?" Zoe asked from the door.

I glanced up and away, but then looked back to her. It was just Zoe. Nothing weird, no freaky ribbon going into her head. Just Zoe.

"Oh! Yes, please. There's a couple of packs of Parma Violets here. They must be for Orla," I said, my face screwed up in disgust.

She took them. "I don't know how she eats these things. It's like chewing perfume, they're foul." She turned and left.

Heidi was staring at me with a puzzled expression.

"I can't see it anymore. It's gone," I said, shrugging.

"So has your anger," she said.

"Well. That's good then. Let's watch the movies." I shrugged and smiled.

Heidi patted my shoulder. "Let's get the rest of this pile of tooth decay to the others."

We headed into the living room where the screen was paused to start *P.S. I Love You.*

"Oh God. Heidi, you're going to be a wreck," I said.

"Are you saying I'm hashtag lame?" Heidi asked, settling onto the sofa next to Orla.

"That one still needs a little work, sweetie," Orla said, patting her knee.

I took Doritos and cola out to the Brothers in the garden.

"You can watch the movie with us if you like," I said.

"I understand it will be emotional," Justin said.

"Oh yes. There will be laughter, there will be tears," I confirmed.

"We'll just watch the fish if you don't mind," Damon said.

"As you wish," I said.

I walked back into the house and sat with my friends, feeling lighter than I had for days. I didn't know what this thing inside me was, but it had listened, and I was relieved.

Two hours and six minutes later, Heidi's eyes were swollen from crying.

"But it had a happy ending," Orla said.

"I know," Heidi howled.

"I'm not sure Heidi can take another one like that," I said.

"I don't think anyone dies in *Dirty Dancing*," Zoe said.

"Okay. That's next then," I said.

"But next time, we'll get *Ghost* or *The Fault in My Stars*," Orla said with a malicious grin at Heidi.

"No!" said everyone.

After three movies and a lot of snacks and pizza, we put some music on, made coffee, and talked about everything and anything.

"Do you have any ideas for names, Sofia?" Jodi asked.

"If it's a boy, Carlos after my father. If it's a girl, we think Vanessa."

"That's lovely," I said, my voice wobbling. It was unexpected.

"Aww, Jenna, don't cry," Hannah said, hugging me.

"Please don't. I've only just managed to control myself," Heidi said.

I reached up to my cheek, wiped a tear, and examined it, feeling momentarily as though I'd never experienced crying before. My mind flipped through instances of when I had cried in the past. I fell over as a toddler, I couldn't sleep, and my mum wasn't there anymore, thinking I'd lost my dad, finding Dad again, discovering what Marcus was.

"Jenna?" Heidi said.

I looked up at her.

"That's a lot of emotions at once," she said.

I smiled at her, and whatever was inside me felt so much love for her, it took my breath away. Facing each of my friends, I had a similar feeling. In that moment, I lost any fear of what was inside me. I still didn't know what it was, but I was no longer afraid that it would hurt me, or the people I loved.

We all hugged Hannah and Zoe before they and the Brothers faded to step into the ribbon in their room.

I walked Jodi and Heidi to the ribbon in the garden, and they left.

"I'm going for a lie down," Sofia said.

Orla and I cleaned up.

"You're quiet," Orla said. She put down the tea towel and turned to me. "Can I just say, you've been a bit weird, for–well, as long as I've known you, I suppose." She smiled. "But more so over the last few weeks."

"I've been scared. Too scared to talk to anyone." I sighed. "Sit down with me."

Orla poured two coffees and brought them over to the table.

"After I did the stupid thing with the nanite pen and the red mist," I began.

"You mean the stupid thing that saved my parents and boyfriend?"

"Yes, that's the one." I readied myself for being called crazy.

"When I portalled back, I think I picked up some hitch-hikers." My heart was racing.

"You mean like fleas?" Orla grinned, but seeing my serious face she said, "Sorry, go on," She put down her mug and leaned in.

"There's an awareness, an 'other' I suppose, or 'others'. They've spoken to me a couple of times."

"At the ceremony?"

"Yes." I was surprised. I wondered for a moment if she'd heard it, too.

"You looked like someone had sneaked up and shouted 'boo' in your ear. You were half out of your seat; I remember wondering what it was." Orla gazed into her coffee. "So, what did they say then?"

"They said 'abomination' and they didn't say it; they screamed the word."

"You heard them the night we went out. You thought I'd said something, but it was these voices, wasn't it?"

I nodded.

"Does Heidi know? I know she's concerned about you but never said why, and I've noticed the two of you are always off in a corner, talking."

"She doesn't know about the voices. There's something else," I said.

"Oh great, let's be having it then," Orla said.

"You remember in the ceremony, when the fader mist left Zoe and the walls glowed? I could still see the ribbon, coming down from above, and through Zoe."

"Until when?"

"About four hours ago. I just begged to be no longer able to see it, I heard the voices say 'yes', and it stopped."

"Are you sure the voices aren't someone communicating with you the same way David does?"

"I feel strongly that it's something inside me. It's been pouring through my memories. It's very distracting. But I think it's something to do with this." I pulled up my sleeve to reveal the red and gold hexagons.

"Do you think it might be the little nanite things? I hate

thinking about them, they give me the heebie-jeebies." Orla shuddered.

"I don't think so. I hadn't considered it."

"Right. These voices. Have they ever asked you to do anything? To hurt anyone or yourself?"

"No. Never. In fact, I can sense that whatever this is, loves us."

"So, is it an 'it' or a 'they'?"

"I'm not sure. It speaks like a lot of voices all at once, but all at the same time and all saying the same thing."

"And I'm the only one you've told?"

I nodded.

"Have you asked them what they want?"

"Yes. They won't talk to me when I ask."

"Right. Whatever this is, they are clearly capable of communicating. You need to make them answer you."

"You believe me?" I was stunned.

"You believe you, and that's good enough for me right now. Have a think. See if there's any way you can force an answer out of them. Honestly, Jenna, I don't know if it's just you or something else in there, but I think the response is the same. Face it down, find out what's going on."

"I'm going to lie down for an hour or so," I said and headed to my room.

I propped up my pillow and lay on the bed.

"Well?" I asked out loud.

Nothing.

"Why won't you speak to me?"

Nothing.

"What's the point of being in here if you're not going to communicate with me?"

Nothing.

"*So that's it? I'm just going crazy, and they're going to put me away forever?*"

"*Jenna,*" said the voices.

Goosebumps rose along my arms.

"*What are you?*" I asked

"*We are what we are,*" said the voices.

"*You are not blowing me off with that half-arsed answer. Why are you here?*"

"*We felt you cross between the worlds. We sensed the abundance of energy. The white and the red intermingled. But when we joined with you, we saw there was no blue. You are not the One.*"

"*So, you hopped on the wrong bus? Can't you just hop on to a different one?*"

"*There is a disturbance in the balance of what you call the ribbon. We need you to redress the balance.*"

"*How am I supposed to do that? What is this imbalance? What's causing it?*"

"*We can show you how to become whole, and you will be our instrument.*"

"*Become whole? What does that even mean? Why can't you do it?*"

"*We cannot act within the mortal worlds, but the One has not yet arrived.*"

"*What are you? Who are you?*"

"*You may call us Hive.*"

"*Hive. Well, that's not creepy, is it!*" All I could think of were bees and ants. I shuddered.

"*Our children are dying; you must help us. You must learn to use your power. Learn to step between the worlds.*"

"*But that's not my ability, that's David's. Are you sure it's not him you want?*"

"*It is yours now.*"

"Our children are dying."

I got up from the bed.

"How can I help? Where are your children?"

"They are screaming!"

"I don't know what to do," I shouted, thinking even if I could create a portal again, I'd go straight to Major Tomowski and deal with him.

Feet came running and the door flew open. Orla came towards me. I wobbled. I tried to step back. I was no longer in my bedroom, and neither was Orla. We were back at the Colorado academy.

We were standing in Major Tomowski's office.

"Well, that was a hell of a ride. I hope you can get us out of here," Orla said.

There were papers scattered across the desk in front of us. We began to gather them together. A box lay on the table and I flipped up the lid. It was the cube. I couldn't believe my luck. As I reached out to grab it, the voice of Hive shook me to the core.

"Danger," it screamed in many voices, simultaneously.

There was no mistaking its intent. I spun around to find the major standing in the doorway, facing us with his gun drawn. Before I could think to get us out of there, he fired.

Orla dropped to the floor.

"Orla. No." I kneeled down next to my friend.

Her white t-shirt was turning red. She howled with pain. I didn't know how to save her. I didn't have a nanite pen. I applied pressure to the wound, and blood just pooled up through my fingers. I heard the compression of a dart gun and the world began to drift away. My vision reduced to a pinhole. The major took out his cell phone. He stared at us briefly, then turned and spoke.

"The Banks girl is here. I tranq'd her and shot the Irish one. Send my transport round."

I woke on a gurney in a brightly lit room with glass walls on three sides. Darkness lay beyond the glass walls. The anti-fading posts gave off a high-pitched whine of around me. I guessed I was inside the mountain base but I hadn't seen this level before. I jumped to the floor. Orla lay on the gurney next to mine. She looked unconscious and deathly white. Blood pooled along the side of her body. They hadn't done anything to help her.

"What's wrong with you? She needs help," I called.

"Shh! Can't a girl get some sleep around here?" Orla said weakly, her eyes still closed.

"Orla," I tried, but I broke down into sobs. "I'm so sorry."

"I'll be fine after a nap," she muttered.

"You have to help her," I shouted. I knew they were watching and listening.

"You can help her," came a woman's voice.

"I don't know how." I lifted Orla's t-shirt to see how much damage there was. It was a small hole. I couldn't believe it was responsible for so much blood.

"Press the button in on each of the cubes, please," the woman's voice replied.

"What?" I looked up to a speaker in the ceiling. I took in my surroundings. There was a small, wheeled, stainless-steel trolley against one wall. It held four cube-like devices and something in a small metal cage.

Some of the cubes were dark and some contained light. I blinked in to see they were yellow. He'd done it. He'd succeeded in creating energy cubes. The little cage contained another cube. It was possible to push the button, but not to remove it from the cage. It was the original. Once I touched those things, it was game over. I knew that.

"If you press the buttons, your friend will receive medical assistance," said the voice.

I stared at the cubes.

"Are these your children?" I asked silently, still unsure what this entity was.

There was no answer.

"If you let her die, you'll have no hold over me. Then what will be the point?" I asked.

As I looked out into the darkness, the area outside got lighter.

Across from me was a glass room like the one we were in. A man lay on a gurney, hooked up to cables and tubes like David and Jodi had been when we found them. To the left and right of him were similar glass cells. I guessed they were all waiting for their turn at the cubes. I looked to my sides to find one empty cell and one occupied. A boy was staring straight at me. He jerked, blood ran from his eyes and nose, and he dropped to the floor.

"You didn't need to do that," I shouted. "Just to make a point? What's wrong with you?"

I turned back to Orla.

I wanted to try and create a portal but I knew the anti-fading posts would stop me.

"Can you help her?" I asked silently into my mind.

"Why do you seek from the outside, that which is already within you? You are the portal, the gateway. The power you seek is already yours."

"But I don't know what to do," I cried.

"Press the buttons..." said the agent.

"Give yourself to us. You shall be our instrument."

I didn't give it a second thought. If saving my friend meant giving up my life, I'd do it.

"Yes," I shouted to Hive.

"*Yes,*" Hive responded in every corner of my mind.

Power coursed through me. Showing me what to do. I turned to Orla and placed my hands on her.

"*Remain still. We are healing her,*" said Hive.

Orla's eyes flew open. "I heard that," she said before sliding away again.

I stood there. I didn't know how long for. I drifted as the energy surged through me.

A metallic tinkle sounded as something fell on to the gurney. I looked to find a mashed-up piece of metal. The bullet. Next, I watched as another object rolled along the surface. An inhibitor. They'd injected them into us again. I didn't know why they'd even bothered with Orla if they were just planning for her to die. My neck hurt as an inhibitor was also pushed from me.

"Awake," came the voices.

I realized that sound of many voices came from my mouth.

Orla woke and sat up. "Are you okay?"

I tried my voice. "You're asking me? I'm fine. How are you?" I relaxed with relief. It was just my voice.

"Your eyes are looking a bit weird," Orla said.

Feet came running, and several figures arrived at the door.

"What did you...?" came Major Tomowski's voice.

I turned. He stared at my face, his eyes wide. I was a little worried about what he might be seeing.

"*You could call upon your power and use it with abandon.*" Hive said.

I could feel it then. My ability was back and so much stronger than it had been.

"*Calm down. Let's not get ahead of ourselves,*" I sent back to them.

The major and his goons were frozen to the spot. I stared him in the eyes while I disabled every anti-fading device and every machine delivering sedatives to people in these glass cubicles.

"Grab those cubes," I said to Orla as I created a portal.

I turned, breaking my control over them.

"No!" came the major's panicked voice behind me. His running steps turned to silence as I took one step of my own towards Orla, and we were back at the residence.

We left my room and made our way to the living room to find Zoe, Hannah, Sofia, Heidi, Justin, and Damon there.

Hannah screamed at the sight of the blood over Orla's clothes which brought David in from the garden.

"I'm okay," Orla said, still a little dazed. "I mean, I've been shot, and unshot, or something. Don't ask. What are you doing here?

Orla pushed the trolley holding the cubes to Heidi.

"We're keeping Sofia company. Almost everyone's out looking for you, or in jail," Zoe said.

"In *what*?" Orla asked.

"Some of the boys got into a scrap. Callan's gone to bail them out," Hannah said.

"Would the ones in jail include my brother and boyfriend by any chance?" Orla asked.

"I, erm, can't remember," Hannah said, still staring at Orla's blood-soaked t-shirt.

"Where were you?" Zoe asked.

"It's my fault. I accidentally portalled into Tomowski's office," I said.

Zoe's jaw dropped. "You should probably fix that."

"You are not wrong," I said with a sigh, "but I think it's fixed for now."

Justin sniffed at me, and Damon looked closely at my face. They glanced at each other with raised eyebrows.

"I think we need to get you two home," Damon said to Zoe.

"Jenna's my friend. We're fine," Zoe said.

"It's okay. I need to rest," I said, turning to leave the room.

Hannah screamed again, then fainted back into her chair.

"What?" I said, spinning back

"Erm...you've got something in your hair," Damon said, reaching into it.

I turned to find him holding the major's right hand between his finger and thumb.

"I'm going to throw up now," I said, walking away.

"I need to speak to you," Heidi said, following me.

"I don't think I'm up to a conversation. I need to lie down."

"Look at me," she said.

"What?" I faced her.

"Who are you? What are you?" she asked.

"*She needs to rest,*" said Hive through my mouth.

Heidi's eyebrows shot up, and she took a step back.

"I don't know what's happening but I do need to rest," I said in my own voice.

I went into the bathroom, stepped into the shower, and washed my hair five times to ensure the blood was out of it. Then I went to the mirror to see what had happened to my face that was so shocking to everyone. My pupils were hexagonal with a line of red around them. Of course they are, I thought. I wanted to cry but I'd accepted this, whatever this was. I headed for my bed, laid down, and slept.

12

"Matthew, wake up." The woman shook Matthew from unconsciousness as he lay on the gurney next to the one she was sitting on.

Matthew blinked groggily at the woman. He took in his surroundings and faded immediately.

"Please don't leave me," the woman sobbed. "I can't fade. They did something to me,"

Matthew moved to the other side of the room and reappeared. He crouched, naked and shivering in the cold room.

"How do you know my name?" he asked.

"It's written on the band around your wrist," she said, holding up her own with a white plastic band.

"I'm Kate," she said.

"Where are we?" he asked.

"I don't know. The last thing I remember is walking out of my hotel room and feeling a sting in my leg and neck. I looked down to see a dart sticking out of me, agents surrounding me as I lost consciousness. Then waking up here," she said.

"You're American," he observed.

"From Iowa. I came here, if we're still in England, to find my family."

She pulled the sheet from his gurney and threw it over to him. He caught it and pulled it around his shoulders.

"Have you got any idea of the date? How long we've been here?" he asked as he wrapped the sheet around his waist.

"Not a clue. When I woke up, I felt like I hadn't moved for a year. Everything hurts."

"Did you hear the voice?" he asked.

"I don't know what you mean. What voice?"

"As far as I know, all faders everywhere heard it."

"Well, not the comatose ones. What did it say?"

"It said, 'Trackers are faders.' After that, everything went crazy."

"Trackers are faders? That's ridiculous."

"It's true. I've known for years. I knew a tracker once. He saved my life."

"I'll be honest, I'm struggling with this. If you don't mind, I'll reserve judgement," she said. "So, what do you think's going on?"

"You've been awake longer than I have. What do *you* think's going on?" he said.

"Only about ten minutes longer," she said. "But this seems to be some kind of waiting room. Why would they just leave us here?"

Matthew shrugged.

Kate scrutinized the room, and her voice dropped. "What if they're listening. Maybe they think we know something."

"We're not going to find out anything sitting here. I'm going to take a look around."

"You're not going to leave me here, are you?" Her voice squeaked.

"I'll come back," he said, removing the sheet and dropping it to the floor before fading.

He stood there for a few moments, watching her while he was faded.

She stood and paced the room looking like a trapped animal.

He moved into the hallway to find two bodies in agents' uniforms. He materialized and pulled an electronic pass from one of the bodies. He looked into the room across the hall but it was just a storage room. There seemed to be several doors on one side of the hallway but only two doors other doors across the hall, indicating much larger rooms. He decided to get back to Kate.

When he opened the door, with the pass, she was crouched behind the gurneys. Matthew picked up the sheet and threw it around himself again.

Kate crept to the door and poked her head into the hallway, seeing the two bodies, on the floor.

"Did you...?"

"No, I just found them. Let's get moving."

They walked past the bodies.

"How long do you think they've been there?"

"It can't have been long. No more than an hour or so," Matthew said.

"How can you know that? What are you, about twelve?"

"I was twelve when I went to sleep. I can't tell you how old I am now. Being hunted makes you age faster."

"I've spent my life in the country. I'd heard about agents and trackers, of course, but I'd never seen one before the day they got me," Kate said.

"Lucky you,"

"What happened to them? There's a lot of blood."

"They've been shot," he said.

Matthew peeked through the glass panel in a side door. It was an office which seemed empty so they entered. Another body lay on the floor, that of a woman. Matthew was ready to move on, but Kate touched his arm. "Wait, let me get something."

Kate made to step over the body. She drew back her foot and walked around it instead.

Grabbing a lab coat from the hanger, she dropped the sheet and put it on. Matthew looked at her.

"What?" she asked. "I can't fade. There's no point in me walking around naked."

"No. I was thinking that might not be a bad idea. We might be able to just walk out of here." He stepped back into the hallway and relieved one of the agents of his trousers and jacket. He sat on the floor lining his foot up with the dead man's.

When he returned to the office wearing the trousers and carrying the jacket and boots, Kate had scattered the contents of a gym bag across the desk and changed from the lab coat to a pair of yoga pants and a cropped top. She had her foot on the desk, lacing up a pair of low-top sneakers, and a protein bar was sticking out of her mouth. She gripped onto the bar with her teeth and waved her foot at him.

"Hey, they fit," she said through her full mouth.

She put her foot back on the floor and threw a protein bar over to him from a pile on the desk.

His stomach gurgled the second he caught it. He ripped through the packaging and devoured it. His stomach just gurgled all the more.

Kate inspected the desktop. Her gaze fell on a photo. Kate smashed it down, her face contorted in disgust.

"They call us the monsters," she said.

Matthew was about to ask what the picture was, when Kate turned around a desk calendar so he could see it.

"I've been here for months," Matthew said.

"I'm pretty sure I've been here for a year and a half," replied Kate.

Kate pulled a bottle of water from the bag and drank. She passed the bottle to Matthew who did the same.

"You should probably put the lab coat back on, and her ID. We might pass at a distance," Matthew said.

Kate nodded and gingerly pulled at the lanyard around the woman's neck. She shivered and instead unclipped it from the lanyard and attached it onto the top pocket of the lab coat.

"Apparently, I'm Vera Richards now," she said, reading it upside-down.

She put the remaining protein bars into the bag and searched the remaining drawers, pulling out a letter. "This is addressed to Hilltop Military Academy. Do you think it's where we are?"

"Probably. This is where my friend was stationed, and I was near here when they caught me," Matthew said.

"What was his name?" she asked.

"Jason. I hope he's okay."

"I hope so, too. I think we need all the help we can get," Kate said.

They made their way along the deserted hallways using their stolen IDs to get through doors. As Matthew opened the door to the stairwell, the sound of a storm increased his level of anxiousness.

"God, it's blowing a gale out there," Kate said.

They passed several offices where windows had been left on the latch. Wind whistled eerily through and blew the vertical blinds about.

"This is so creepy. Where is everyone?" Matthew said.

"You took the words right out of my mouth," Kate replied.

Almost at the front entrance, there was a slight drop in the wind and they looked in horror at each other as a voice shouted, "get inside, we'll talk in there."

Matthew dived down behind the curved reception desk, and Kate followed.

The front doors opened and closed, and leaves blew under the desk to where they crouched hidden from view.

"There's a few more down on basement level. They're ours, so don't throw them on the truck with the others. Put them in body bags. They'll be sent to a war zone to be found, identified, and returned as the heroes they are. You, come with me for the paperwork, then take the truck to the incinerator at the back of the property."

They squeezed together under the desk until several pairs of boots had moved past them, down the hall, and some started up the stairs. Matthew cast a brief look out to see no remaining feet. They crept out from beneath the desk and headed to the glass doors. A truck was parked outside. A pile of bodies lay on the back of it, at least twenty.

"We're going to have to get onto that to get out of this compound," whispered Matthew.

"To be incinerated? Why don't we just look for a side entrance? That way, we haven't been that way yet," Kate was looking at him, horrified.

"We'll jump out as soon as there's cover," Matthew said. He didn't wait for an answer. He opened the door, and the strength of the wind knocked him back a step. He leaned into it through the doors, down the steps, and Kate followed, repeatedly glancing behind all the way down.

They climbed on to the truck to wait for the driver to

come back as rain and wind lashed at them and onto the pile of corpses. After a few seconds, Matthew studied the naked and half-naked bodies more closely.

"Take your lab coat off, we're too covered up, we look different," Matthew said quickly. He unzipped the agent's jacket and stuffed it beneath him.

Kate made to do the same, but the rain and blood had made the bodies slippery. She fell forward and hit her head on the side of the truck, cutting it. She wiped at the cut, then seemed to freeze, staring at the blood.

"Quickly," Matthew said, worried she might be about to lose it.

"Well, I can't really complain about it here in front of these souls who have lost their lives," she said.

Kate positioned the lab coat so that the edge of it would lie between her face and the body beneath and laid back down.

"I feel sick," whispered Kate.

"It'll be okay, Kate. Just try not to think about it," Matthew said, squeezing her hand.

The door to the building banged open, and they lay still. Footsteps stopped at the back of the truck. A heavy tarp was pulled over them but left unsecured on one side. The tailgate was slammed up. Kate's hand twitched in Matthew's and he squeezed back. The driver secured the tailgate, but it was difficult to tell what direction he had walked in from the noise of the storm. The weight of the truck shifted as the driver climbed into the front and started the engine.

The moment they pulled away, Matthew made his way towards the tailgate. He lifted the corner of the tarp to watch as they drove out of the main compound, away from the Academy buildings and onto a tarmac road.

"This place looks pretty out in the open," Matthew said.

Hearing no response from Kate, he turned to find her peeking out directly behind the driver's head. He felt his eyes bulge as he stared.

Kate dropped the tarp and surfed over the bodies, trying to keep the lab coat between them.

"I can see a large chimney ahead and to the left. If that's it, he's got to turn any second. We should get ready."

Staying as low as possible, they each took a side and quietly dropped the tailgate. The truck slowed to turn, and the two of them rolled off the back and dived into the shrubs at the edge of the road.

"Damn! I left the bag," Kate said, putting the lab coat back on.

"Don't worry. We'll get to better cover, then get out when it goes dark," Matthew said, pulling on the agent's jacket.

"You speak like you're ten years older. This life really does make you grow up fast, doesn't it," Kate said.

"I grew up the day they took my big sister," Matthew said.

"Well, now we've got the set," said someone from the other side of the shrubbery.

Matthew felt trapped. He wanted to fade but he didn't want to leave Kate alone. He looked at her. She nodded her head as if to say *just go*. He shrugged and didn't fade. He stood and faced the man with the gun.

"You should have secured the tailgate. It was swinging and hitting the back of the truck," said the man.

Matthew closed his eyes, and a shot rang out. The thud of the man's body hitting the ground ahead of him, made him open his eyes. He turned to find Kate standing there in her bloody lab coat, with the wind whipping wet hair across her face, shaking. A handgun still pointing where the man had stood.

"Where did you get that?" he asked.

"It...it was in the gym bag. I took it out in the truck and stuffed into the pocket here." She indicated the lab coat.

"Why didn't you tell me you'd found a gun?" he asked.

"You're a kid. I'm not giving you access to a firearm," she said.

Matthew guffawed. "Well, you saved our lives. We're lucky you knew how to use that thing," Matthew said.

"I'm American, Matthew. We all know how to use these things." She dropped it back into her pocket.

"You can call me Matt," he said.

They dragged the agent into the shrubbery, took his wallet, phone, and jacket, then ran for the fence.

"We can't wait for dark now. Someone's going to find that truck, it's not exactly hidden," said Matt.

The cover of the trees at the perimeter gave them some relief from the deluge.

"It's got spikes all over the top," Kate said, looking at the fence.

"That's what the agent's jacket is for," Matt said.

"Stay back. The fence might be electrified." He tapped the fence to ensure it wasn't electrified. It wasn't.

"You tell me to stand back and then you poke it?" Kate was incredulous.

Matt shrugged.

"And you wonder why I didn't mention the gun," she said.

Kate took off her shoes and threw them over the fence. Matt did the same.

While Kate put the agent's jacket on top of the spikes, Matt sent a text from the agent's phone. *Meet in place 11. Burn your phone, M.* It had been months. He didn't even know if his uncle Adam was still alive. He pulled the SIM out and smashed the phone. Then they climbed over the fence and ran.

It was nearly dark by the time they reached the closest town. The shops had closed except for the chip shop. They were soaked and shivering with the cold. Kate's lab coat had blood all over it from the bodies in the truck. The cut on her forehead had swollen up. She looked like something from a horror movie. Matt, wearing black, was better able to be seen in public. He bought two bags of chips and two Cokes with the agent's money.

"You're brave coming out in this. I was just about to shut up. I haven't had a customer all day," said the man behind the counter.

"I get double pocket money for going," said Matt with a smile.

"Ah, you'll have some game you want to buy, I expect. I can't get my lad away from the X-Box." The man smiled as he passed the chips over.

Matt went back to the end of the shopping precinct where Kate was hiding in the shadows.

"Come on, we can get some cover in the alley while we wait," he said, handing her a bag of chips.

They entered the alley and headed towards the sheltered loading dock at the end.

As they walked past, a shadow separated from the darkness, and Kate was hit from behind and dropped to the ground. Matt spun around to find his uncle Adam with a baseball bat.

"Matthew? It's really you? I thought it was a trap," Adam said. He took the boy in a fierce embrace.

Matt kneeled down to check Kate was alive.

He looked up at his uncle. "But you came anyway?"

"Of course I did. I couldn't not come. I'm sorry about your friend. Who is she?"

"Her name's Kate. She helped me get out. We need to get her somewhere safe, somewhere out of this storm."

"*Matthew? My name is David. Are you Jason's friend?*" Matt launched himself backwards across the ground, looking around himself for the speaker.

"What's wrong?" Adam asked.

"Didn't you hear that?"

"Hear what?"

"It's the same voice. The *trackers are faders* voice," he said.

"I can't hear a thing," Adam was looking at him strangely.

"Yes. It's me. I just escaped from Hilltop but my friend's injured," he said.

"*I see. We will be with you in a minute,*" came David's voice.

Matt held up his hand, listening to the voice. "Help's coming, they're close."

"They are?" Adam asked.

They moved Kate out of the rain.

"How hard did you hit her?"

"How hard should you hit an agent? You're lucky, you were going to be next, dressed like that,"

They sat sharing Matt's chips.

Are you still in the flat over the shops?" Matt crouched to check on Kate.

"Yes, but I'm on my own now. The others went back to Manchester. They took the car, so I haven't even got wheels right now. I've just been sitting in that flat hoping to hear from you. I didn't know what else to do," Adam said, his voice wobbling.

"I think we can help give you a ride to somewhere safe," Connor said, appearing with Jason, David, and Sean.

Matt blinked in. A red mist surrounded the newcomers.

"Connor. It's been a while. What's with the red mist?" Adam asked.

"Jason," Matt said. It had been a long time since they had met at the Manchester shopping center when his sister had been taken by the agents.

"Matthew? Well, you've grown. Let's get you out of here," Jason said.

"If you don't mind me saying, you picked a shitty day to need rescuing," Sean said.

"We don't need rescuing. We already escaped," said Matt, a little offended.

"Sorry. Transporting then," Sean said.

"She can't fade," Matt said. "They did something to her. Then uncle Adam brained her."

"That's okay. I might be able to fix that." Connor crouched, pulling a nanite pen from his pocket and tapped it on her neck and held her as she came around.

"What happened?" she asked groggily.

"I happened. Sorry," Adam said, waving his bat.

She looked over at him and squinted but wasn't focusing.

"Can you stand?" Matt asked.

They got her to her feet. She stood with her eyes closed, wavering like she was about to faint.

"We're not near a ley line. We're just going to have to land directly on the other side," David said.

"What?" Adam asked.

"Just fade, we'll take care of everything else," Sean said.

"You're okay. Just one little step," Connor said, standing behind and fading her.

The others faded and David portalled them across. When Connor let go of her on the other side, she reappeared, dropped to her knees, vomited over a woman's purse, and collapsed.

"Oops!" Sean said, looking around.

The diners in the restaurant they had just appeared in stared at them in horror. They looked back.

"I am so sorry," David said to the woman.

"She's injured," Matt said.

"I'm not feeling too good myself," Adam said, gripping his stomach.

"They're Broken," someone said.

13

"And it just went from bad to worse," Sean said in the kitchen of the residence as Orla tapped the nanite pen, not quite as softly as she could have, next to her brother's cut eyebrow.

"Who threw the first punch?" Orla asked.

"Ah, that would be me. The guy was building up to it, but we hadn't the time to wait," Sean said.

"So, you started a fight you weren't capable of winning," Orla said.

"We would have been more than capable of winning, but we had a sick woman, which didn't help. I think that's why they thought we were from Broken-Earth. Young Matthew was crouched over the sick lady, and Adam here was dizzy from his first crossing."

"Of universes," Adam said. Clarifying that he had a good reason for his temporary lightheadedness.

"Anyway, it turns out the rescue...," Sean began.

"Transport," Adam corrected him.

"The transport was the only useful thing to come out of the whole day. There's been a big announcement on the news today that a horde of Saxon gold has been discovered in Full-Earth, Staffordshire by a farmer. What are the chances!" Sean said.

"So that was your great plan? Treasure hunting? You're a bunch of eejits," Orla said.

I stood in the doorway of the living room and listened to the conversation, building my nerve to enter. I was tempted to just go straight back to bed; I was still exhausted.

Heading straight for the coffee machine, I marched in.

"It's my life-saving superhero. How are you this morning, sweetie?" Orla asked.

"I'm okay," I said.

It was unusual to wake up without the smell of breakfast wafting through the house.

"Where's Sofia?" I asked.

"She's in her room with your dad," Orla said. She was looking everywhere but at me.

I looked over at the unfamiliar face who I assumed was Adam. "So, you're Adam. Is Matthew okay? Jason's been worried about you both."

"Matt's great. We picked up a new friend, Kate. She erm, bumped her head. Jason's with them at the hospital. We hadn't heard from Jason for months. That's why we were in the vicinity of the base when Matt got caught; we were trying to find him. I wondered where he'd gone. I've got to say that living in an alternate earth was pretty far down my list of guesses. I suspected he was dead with so many of the others."

"Are you staying here? I'm sure there's room. We could get Matt into a school with a class full of other faders," I said.

"We're still hoping to find Matt's sister," Adam said.

"I hope you do," I said. I was doubtful, knowing what I knew from Dr. Narayan's mind.

"So, are we going to talk about the hexagon-shaped elephant in the room?" I asked Orla.

"Do you know what it means, the voices and the groovy eyes?" Orla asked.

"Not a clue," I said.

"I guess we're not going to talk about it then," Orla said. "Do you want some toast?"

"Well, I know one thing. I don't imagine they'll be letting Zoe anywhere near me for the foreseeable future."

"It's not that. It was just chaotic with all the new people," Orla said.

"What new people?" I glanced at Adam, but there was only one of him.

"The ones you brought last night. Sofia had a hell of a shock with twenty people banging the doors to get in when the sprinklers went off."

"I don't know what you're talking about." As I said it, I was getting an idea of what I might have done.

I walked around from the kitchen and sat on a stool at the breakfast bar. Orla was staring at my feet.

I looked down. They were filthy. "How did I not notice that?"

"They all told pretty much the same story. They'd escaped from the Cheyenne base when the anti-fade devices failed. I guess these are the ones who found the stairs or lifts. They were running around on the mountain, lost and confused. Next thing they know, they found themselves stepping into the garden here. A woman with funny eyes"— Orla did air quotes—"gave them blankets and food. Actually, you gave them the latest consignment of goods for Broken earth; we'll have to replace it. David's been dropping them at various safe houses since five a.m. this morning. They don't seem to know they've been on a different earth."

"Jenna agreed to be my instrument," said Hive in her many-voices from my mouth.

Adam dropped his coffee mug. It smashed on the floor, and black coffee splashed everywhere. I looked at him.

"Sorry," he said. He looked frightened and picked up the pieces of the mug. I threw over a tea towel before taking a mug out and pouring him another coffee. I put it on the dining table, and Orla passed it over.

"Erm...thanks," Adam said.

"Well, maybe next time, wake her up. It's not right to use her body without her being aware of it," Orla said, looking at me, but it wasn't me she was talking to. I looked back at Orla and smiled. She was fearless.

"Also, we need some rules about who gets to use my mouth, and when. Here comes my dad. Please don't freak him out any more than necessary."

"Hi, Dad, sorry about the strangers," I said quickly, to get control of my own tongue first. I smiled at Sofia standing behind him, she was carrying a suitcase.

"Dad?" I asked.

"Who am I speaking to?" he asked, his voice raised.

I jumped.

"Me," I said.

It was like he was staring at a stranger. It frightened me.

He looked at me with an eyebrow raised as though that hadn't answered his question.

"It's Jenna. Believe me, you'll know the difference," Orla said.

"Why are you still here?" he asked Orla.

"She won't go," Sean said, flapping his arms dramatically, indicating that he had done his best with her.

"I'm going nowhere. Jenna's my friend, and whatever that is in there, saved my life last night," Orla said.

"Whatever that is, put your life in danger in the first place," Dad said.

"It was an accident. She was mid-portal. I just walked in," Orla said.

"Mid–?" Dad sighed and pinched the bridge of his nose. "What is it? Is this those bloody nanites?"

"*I wish to speak,*" said Hive within my mind.

Oh great, I thought.

"You wish to converse?" said Hive's many-voices.

Dad stepped back. He looked brokenhearted.

"What are you?" Dad asked, still too loud.

"You are frightening Jenna," said Hive.

"I'm frightening *her*?" Dad took some deep breaths. "We need to do this later." He shuddered.

"Where are you going?" I asked.

"Sofia's visiting with Anna for a few days. I'm just getting her settled and I'll be right back." He put his arm around Sofia, steering her away from me, keeping himself between us.

They disappeared into the garden, and Dad didn't even look back. Everyone stared at me. I burst into tears and ran back to my room.

I had been crying for about twenty minutes when I lifted my head to the raised voices outside the door.

"You're not going in there." Sean said.

"And you're going to stop me, are you, big man?" shouted Orla.

Seconds later, Orla appeared in my room.

"The dope seems to have forgotten I could fade and just walk straight through him."

"He chose his new family over me. He looked at me like he didn't know me." I burst into tears again.

"He's scared. No one knows who your new friends are. Give your dad time. Will this cheer you up?" Orla reached back and pulled a packet of strawberry laces from her pocket.

I laughed through my tears. We sat on the bed and opened the packet and worked together to knot them all end to end.

"Don't tie them into one long string, or we'll have to snog like *Lady and The Tramp* when we get to the middle, and I love you, Jenna. Just not that much."

I laughed. I felt like I hadn't laughed so much in years, even though we'd only been watching movies the day before.

"I heard them, you know. When they spoke to you in your head as they were healing me. To be honest, up to that point, I'd thought you might be going a bit crackers," Orla said.

"Aren't you scared of it? Like everyone else?" I asked.

"Don't be daft. Whatever it is, I don't think you'd let it hurt the people you love and I don't think it wants to hurt us anyway."

"I hope everyone else comes around to that way of thinking."

"Hmm," Orla said after a few moments, as though she were considering something vexing.

"What?" I asked.

"I wonder how Major Tom's doing without his hand," giggled Orla.

"Don't remind me. I can't believe that thing was hanging in my hair. I wonder what Damon did with it?" I said with a shudder.

"Why? Did you want it back?"

"Not really, I just don't want to find it around the house. Like, in a drawer or something."

"But if it is still around, maybe we could paint the fingernails with glitter and send it back to him. Just open a little portal above his desk and drop it down in front of him."

We squealed at the disgusting and hilarious thought.

There was a knock at the door, and it opened immediately afterwards. It was Sean.

"Manners," Orla said.

"Sorry. I just wondered if you wanted a cup of tea," he said.

"Thank you, Sean. That would be lovely. Jenna prefers coffee."

The door closed, and we laughed.

The spell, however, was broken. I sighed.

"I don't know what this all means, but whatever it is, I promised I would help and I'm going to do that. This thing saved your life, and I owe it a debt."

"Just don't let it get you killed. I couldn't forgive myself," Orla said.

A few minutes later, the door knocked again, and in walked my dad with my coffee.

"I need to chat with Jenna." He passed the mug to me.

"Well, I need to nip to the shops. I'll be back soon. Don't be mean to her, or I'll be throwing you out," Orla said. To me she said, "Maybe I'll pick up a glittery nail polish."

I laughed.

"What's that about?" Dad asked, taking a seat next to me on the bed.

"Orla wants to paint Tomowski's fingernails and send his hand back to him," I said with a smile.

He sighed. "You're you, but you're not you. I don't know what to make of it. What is it?"

"It's described itself to me as the life force of the ribbon," I said.

"Do you know that to be true? Could it be lying to you?"

"I don't think it is. So far it has saved Orla's life and a bunch of faders from the mountain. Honestly, Dad, I think this could change our luck for the better. Tomowski and his whole army might not stand a chance against me now."

"I think I've heard enough," Dad said.

The pressure of a nanite pen at the back of my neck surprised me. Dad took the mug out of my hand as I passed out.

I opened my eyes. I lay there, trying to process what Dad had done to me. He hadn't liked what I was saying and he'd just switched me off, like I was nothing.

I jumped up and stood there, seething. My jaw hurt from being clenched so hard. I took several breaths. I checked the time, not even ten minutes had passed. I wondered if it had been less effective because of Hive or had I been tranquilized so many times over the last few years, I was growing resistant.

I turned to the closet and took a bag from the bottom of it. I lay out clothes from my drawers and stuffed them into the bag. Within a few minutes, I was ready to leave. I decided to take one last look around the residence before leaving. I didn't bother to open the door, I just created a portal and looked through it. Most of the house was empty. My dad was sitting with Sean in the dining room.

He lifted his head. His face was pale and his eyes red.

"I've lost her. I've lost my little girl. I don't know what to do." Dad's voice disappeared and the end of the sentence came as a whisper.

His head dropped down and his shoulders shook with tears.

I closed the portal.

"*He is frightened,*" came Hive's voices inside me.

"*He taught me to face my fears. He's a coward.*" I was furious.

"*He loves you,*" said Hive, plucking memories of Dad carrying me on his shoulders at a theme park.

"*That's no excuse, and stop that!*" I didn't want to be reminded of the day I thought he was dead. I wanted to be angry with him.

"*Hello, little duck,*" came his voice from the memory of seeing him in Colorado.

I sighed.

"*Rest. We still have much work to do.*"

"*Why? What's going to be hexagon-shaped when I wake up next time, my ears?*"

"*You do not need to sleep.*"

I took the clothes out of the bag and put them away again. Looking over to the dresser, I saw that my coffee was still there. I picked it up and picked up a copy of Rene Descartes Meditations on First Philosophy. I wondered what Hive would make of Cogito Ergo Sum, I think therefore I am.

I returned to the bed, got comfortable, and started reading.

"You did what?" came Orla's outraged voice from the kitchen.

"Just leave her to rest, she'll be out for hours," Dad said.

The voices were coming closer.

"I'm going to check on her, and if you try to stop me, you'll be getting a black eye."

I chuckled softly.

My bedroom door opened. I kept my attention on my book and turned a page. In my peripheral vision, the two of them stared at me. Dad marched off, and I looked up and winked at Orla.

"Sweetie. Don't disappear without me, okay? If you need to go somewhere, take me with you. But give me a second to put some shoes on and maybe a Kevlar vest,"

"Understood."

"Even if it's not me. Take someone. Whatever you're going through, you just don't have to be alone with this."

"I'm never alone," I said with an eyebrow raised.

Orla smiled.

"You know he loves you, don't you?"

"That's what Hive keeps saying. I was ready to set his hair alight."

"The creepy space fleas are starting to make more sense than you right now," Orla said.

"Space fleas?" Hive asked.

"Just a joke. I'll be off." Orla closed the door quickly.

I sensed amusement in Hive. *"There's hope for you yet,"* I sent.

I continued to read, but after a few minutes found myself bothered by the itching in my arm. It seemed to be spreading.

I raised my sleeve to find the hexagons continued up to the top of my arm.

14

———

Adam and Jason entered the hospital room.

"Thanks for getting me out of that house. It got a bit freaky," Adam said, shuddering at the thought of the strange young woman speaking in several voices.

"Jenna's a great person. Whatever's going on now, it's not her."

"How's she looking, Matt?" Adam asked.

"She's waking up," Matt said,

"Where am I?" Kate asked. She sat up.

"You're safe. We're all safe," Matt said. He'd been told to not drop too much detail onto Kate straight away, but it was clear that he was bursting to share the exciting news.

"What happened?" Kate touched the back of her head.

"I conked you on the head. Sorry about that. I thought you were an agent," Adam said.

"Matt, are you okay?" she asked.

"I'm great. This is my uncle, Adam."

Adam smiled, hoping to appear less threatening, and Kate shifted uncomfortably.

"And we're where?" she asked.

"We're in a hospital in Coventry," said Matt with a smile.

She studied her surroundings. It looked like a hospital room. There was a curtain to go around the bed and controls to sit her up. It sounded like a hospital. People walked busily down the hallway outside her room and appeared to be in scrubs, but Adam could see she was sensing that something was off. She would be noticing there were little things that didn't seem normal.

"Okay, what is it? Something's not right," Kate said.

"Can I tell her? She doesn't seem too freaked out," Matt said.

"That comes after you tell her," Jason said

"When I said you're safe, I meant you really are safe. The agency will never be able to get you here," he said.

"So where is here?" Kate asked.

"Okay, you know when you fade—sorry, when you used to fade—and it feels sort of like you're not fully in the place you were? Well, there's another place. Another earth. It's full of faders, and the agents can't get here."

"Have you been stealing someone's meds?" she asked.

"Take a look out of the window," Matt said.

She checked under the covers and arranged the hospital gown she was wearing. She climbed out of the bed and walked to the window.

Looking down, she said "well, the storm's passed. I see a man with a lawn mower on the grass and people walking along. Everything seems normal."

"Look up," Adam said.

She turned her gaze to the sky and stared. "What's that?"

"It's a dome. They're all over this earth," Matt said.

Adam walked over to join them at the window.

"Look more closely at those people on the street," Adam said.

She glanced back down to the street as two people hurrying towards each other, both fading and reappearing seconds later, fully clothed. Her jaw dropped.

"Did you see that?" Matt Asked.

"I don't understand." She gazed around the room.

"I know. It's a lot to take in, isn't it," Adam said.

She stumbled, and Adam caught her. He helped her back to bed. When she made to cover herself with the blanket, she stopped and gazed at the silver pattern on the back of her hand.

"What's this?" She rubbed at it, unable to remove it.

"That's your nanite tag. I'm sorry. There was nothing they could do about your fader gland. They're not certain what the monsters did to it."

"But what is it?"

"It's your ID. Yours is silver because you're what they call an inc. That means incomplete, because you can't fade. I'm sorry. Mine's gold because I'm a fader," Matt said.

"I want to go home," Kate said.

"But you're safe here." Matt said.

"What if we can't get back? I have family. I want to go home."

"Sure, Kate. You can go wherever you want to," Jason said. "We have a safe house in the Cotswolds on our earth. You can stay there until you've located your family."

"Thank you. I just... I need to put my feet on my own earth. This is terrifying," she said.

"But it's also kind of cool, though, right?" Matt said.

Kate laughed nervously. "Kind of. I promise I'll think it's cool in retrospect," she said.

Matt leaned over and hugged her. She appeared

momentarily shocked, then smiled and hugged him back.

"Thank you for saving me," he said.

"Thank you for saving me first," she said.

"The nurse was going to get you some clothes. I'll see where she is with that," said Jason. "Matt, where's the nurse's office?" Jason and Matt left the room.

"I really am sorry I conked your head," Adam said.

"There doesn't seem to be any lasting damage. I don't even feel the cut on my forehead anymore," Kate said.

"This is certainly a magical place," Adam smiled.

"I'm glad Matt found you. He's a special kid," Kate said.

"He is that. He seems a little clingy with you. I hope that doesn't bother you. I'm the only family he's got. We've lost everyone else,"

"I'm sorry. We've all lost a lot of people. Will you both be staying here now?"

"I tried to talk him into it, but he's a twelve-year-old boy who still thinks he still might find his big sister. We'll be staying at the safe house, too, running operations from there," Adam said.

"Operations?" she asked.

"There are still a lot of faders and trackers who need help,"

"Then I'm going to the right place. If I can't find my family, I will happily make the agents pay for what they've done," Kate said.

Jason held open the door, and Matt walked in with a pile of clothes in his arms.

"Here's your clothes. They're only basic but they'll do for now," Matt said.

"They're great, thank you, Matt," Kate said with a smile.

Adam pulled the curtain around the bed so Kate could get dressed.

"I'll call David at the house to get you a lift back to our earth," Jason said.

"Are you not coming back?" Kate asked.

"No, I live over here for now," Jason said, taking out a small communicator.

"Hey, Orla, it's me. Are you still at the residence? I knew Sean wouldn't be able to move you. How's Jenna? Oh, that doesn't sound good. I'll be back soon. We're just getting Kate, Adam, and Matt back to the Cotswold farm. Can Connor and David come help get them back? Great. We'll see them at Coventry Main Ribbon Station." He disconnected the call.

"Who are all these people you're mentioning? Jenna, David, Connor," Kate asked.

"Orla's my future wife, but if you meet her, don't tell her that. Jenna's a friend. She's not very well right now, and because you can't fade anymore, we need Connor to fade you so David can transport you back over to Half-Earth," Jason said.

"Half what?" Kate asked.

"That's what they call our earth here; Half-Earth. I think because it's mostly full of people who can't fade," Matt said.

"So, what do they call this? Full-Earth?" Kate laughed.

"Yes," Jason said.

Kate, now dressed, moved the curtain and stepped out.

"I think I'm a little offended by that," Kate said.

"I think we all feel the same," Adam said.

The nurse came in and took Kate's hand. She pressed the nanite pen onto it, and the little pattern disappeared. Two seconds later, a light flashed on the end of the pen.

"I've never had to remove one before," said the nurse before leaving.

"Why did she take it off?" Kate asked.

"Because you're not staying here. They know we're hunted on our Earth. They don't want to give hostile forces an opportunity to advance their technology and use it against the people here," Jason said.

"But you've still got one," she said to Adam.

"As soon as we've rescued everyone we can, we'll be coming over here" said Adam.

Kate picked up a bag from the cupboard beside the bed, containing the yoga gear and bloody lab coat.

They walked down to the hospital exit and entered what looked slightly like a bus.

"This thing has no wheels. I mean, you saw that, right?" Kate said.

"It's called a hopper. It's just a couple of stops to the main ribbon station," Jason said.

"You said that on the phone. What is that?"

"It has to be seen to be believed." Adam said.

"Like everything else. So, this residence is close then?"

"It's in Los Angeles," Jason said.

"I'm sorry?"

"They'll probably be there before us." Matt laughed.

David and Connor stood waiting at the hopper stop when they alighted the hopper.

"What a beautiful building," Kate said, looking at an old church.

"This is the Church of St. Mary. On our earth, it was restored in the nineteen-twenties but then bombed by the Germans in nineteen-forty," Adam said.

"They missed it here?" Kate asked.

"There was no World War Two here," Matt said.

"So, at some point, there were two earths where there had been one. This is fascinating," Kate said.

The hopper pulled away, and on the other side of the

street, Kate had her first glimpse of the ribbon station. They watched as people faded to step into it and appeared after stepping out of it.

"What is it?"

"It's the ribbon. It's how faders travel here. We were in L.A., less than ten minutes ago," David said.

Adam moved closer to Kate, in case she felt dizzy again.

"You're looking a lot better than when I last saw you," Connor said.

"We've met?" Kate asked.

"We brought you over to safety after you hit your head," Connor said.

"Well, someone hit my head, but it certainly wasn't me," Kate said with a wry smile at Adam.

Adam blushed.

"How have they accomplished so much?" Kate said, gazing with wonder at her surroundings.

"Perhaps faders can just do a lot of good when they're not being hunted down and killed," David said.

"I will definitely return here someday," Kate said, looking from the beautiful old church, up to the huge dome covering the city.

Jason hugged Matt.

"You look after Kate, okay?" Jason said.

"I think you'll be less dizzy if you close your eyes and just take a step when I tell you to," Connor said.

"Happy travels," Jason said after David created the red mist and located the farm.

Connor placed a hand on Kate's shoulder, faded her, and told her to take one step.

"You can open your eyes now," Connor shouted over the wind and rain.

The five of them stood in the yard of a farm, between

what sounded like a shed full of cows and a farmhouse.

"Come on into the house. We'll find you somewhere to sleep. Matt will be coming in with me and you'll be in his room," Adam said.

THEY STEPPED in through the kitchen doorway. A pot of stew was cooking on the stove, and the smell of fresh bread was in the air.

"You couldn't put us down inside the building?" Connor asked.

"Sorry, it can get complicated piling a bunch of people into a small space," David said.

"Well, trust you to turn up when the food's nearly ready," Dorothy said to Adam.

"You must be Matthew. I was so happy to hear your uncle found you."

"Hey, Dorothy, this is Kate. A new friend from your neck of the woods," Adam said.

"Hi, Kate. Would you like to rest up a little? Dinner's going to be another hour," Dorothy said.

"That would be lovely, thank you," Kate said. "So, where are you from, Dorothy?"

"I'm from Des Moines, and you sound like you might not be from too far away," Dorothy said.

"Cedar Rapids. Not far at all," Kate said.

The two women disappeared up the stairs.

"Good luck with everything. I'll be keeping an ear out if you need me," David said to Adam.

"Thanks for everything," Adam said.

"Can we do it here?" Connor asked. "I don't want to go out into that crappy weather again."

Connor and David stepped into the red mist.

15

Over the next week, Dorothy watched as Kate settled in at the farmhouse. She seemed keen to have a try at anything that was asked of her. When she wasn't being asked to help out, she would clean anyway.

"This place has never been so clean," Dorothy said. "I could bounce a quarter off those beds."

"My mother was a nurse. She wouldn't have it any other way," Kate said.

"How about your father?" Dorothy asked.

"It was just Mom, my sister and me," Kate said. Dorothy noticed a flicker of something and decided not to further pursue the subject of the father.

"How did your sister wind up in England?"

"The usual story, she met a man and the rest is history. Are you and Adam–?"

"Good heavens no. This place is a safe haven as well as a working farm. I was asked to look after things here when the owners went missing. Probably caught by the agency. It was good timing for me as we'd had to abandon the California safe-house."

"Why did you have...," Kate started.

The door flew open and Adam lurched in with Matt.

"The stable's been hit by lightning again. Ellen Degeneres is in foal but she's hysterical. We're in danger of losing both of them," said Adam.

Dorothy pulled on a coat and passed one to Kate.

"You called a horse, Ellen Degeneres?" Kate asked.

"I love Ellen,"

"Well, I love Jesus but I wouldn't name my cat after him," Kate said, laughing.

"She renamed it Ellen after she got here," Adam whispered.

"What was it called before?" Kate asked.

"Dorothy," Adam said.

"I can hear you, Adam," Dorothy said.

"I know you can, Ellen," Adam laughed.

They ventured out into the biting winds. Entering the barn, they found the mare on the floor bucking hysterically, smashing her head down repeatedly. Dorothy watched as Kate removed her coat, rolled it up and slid it under the mare's head.

"Do horses wear earplugs?" Kate asked.

"Good thinking," Adam said.

Dorothy dashed to a storage box just as the lightning flashed again, this time hitting the ground outside in the yard with a thwack. She returned with two squashy balls and an eye mask. She pushed one of the plugs into the mare's ear and after a few attempts, timed with the head thrashing, she inserted the other. Together they slipped on the eye mask and the horse became rigid, then relaxed.

Minutes later, the mare shuffled as a gush of fluid flooded the floor and the foal began to appear.

"How's it going down your end?" Dorothy shouted.

"Gross," Matt said.

The women laughed and stroked the mare's head. Ten minutes later a shivering, wet foal with long skinny legs lay sprawled on the ground.

The mare with its eyes still covered, found the foal and began to lick at it.

"I think we all deserve a hot chocolate," Dorothy said.

"I think some of us deserve something a little stronger," Kate said.

"Shouldn't we be thinking about getting out of here?" Adam asked.

"You can if you want to. I'm not leaving these animals," Dorothy said.

THE NEXT DAY, the worst of the storm had moved but the wind was unrelenting and still occasionally joined by strikes of lightning.

They all went to visit the mare and Dorothy removed the mask. Ellen Degeneres was skittish but mostly calm. They checked on the foal which seemed healthy.

"Okay then Matt, what do you think she should be called?" Dorothy asked.

"I get to name her? That's awesome. Can we call her Lightning?"

Adam groaned and Kate laughed.

Dorothy gave Matt a bag of feed. "Here, wise-ass. Feed the goats, please."

"That'll teach you," Adam said.

Dorothy stuffed a bucket into Adam's hand. "And the cows need to be milked."

"That should keep them out of trouble," Dorothy said.

Thirty minutes later, Dorothy watched as Adam leaned back while Kate tried to get closer to him with the antiseptic wash.

"Hold still," Kate said.

Adam pulled back his arm.

"I said hold still, you big baby," Kate said

"It hurts," Adam said.

"Well, if it didn't hurt, I wouldn't be trying to clean it out, would I."

"You could be gentler," Adam said.

"And you could be more careful," Kate said.

Dorothy readied to leave the room with a basket over her head.

"That's a new look." Adam said.

"My hood keeps blowing off."

"If you're going to check for eggs, I just checked, there are none," Adam said.

Dorothy pulled the basket from her head and put in on the counter.

"What happened to you this time?" Dorothy asked, wondering if their meagre medical supplies would hold out.

"I was trying to milk a cow, but it knocked me off the stool. Look at what it did," Adam said, waving his elbow around.

The sudden sting on his elbow made Adam howl.

"That's not fair, you got me while I was distracted,"

Kate and Dorothy shared a look and rolled their eyes. Kate continued to swipe the antiseptic liquid across his graze.

Kate finished up with a large plaster over the graze. "Stop picking on the cows."

She set about clearing the first-aid kit away.

"Thank you, Kate," Adam said, looking suddenly shy.

"You're welcome, Adam," Kate replied with a little smile.

"Oh well, round two, I guess. But I'm putting on a thicker coat," Adam said. He headed to the cloakroom.

"He likes you," Dorothy said.

"He's a good guy," Kate said.

"Do you think you'll stay?" Dorothy asked.

"I think if any of us stay here much longer, we're going to be hit by lightning. There's not much safe to this safehouse. But, in answer to your question, I don't think I'm going to hear anything about my family now. I haven't really got anywhere else to go," Kate said.

"There's a whole other universe out there," Dorothy said.

"Well, yes, there's that. But for now, I'd like to make myself useful in this one."

"Some of the boys are coming over to talk about an op tonight," Dorothy said.

"Can I sit in? I'd like to help," Kate said.

"I'm sure you could. From what Matt tells me, you're quite resourceful."

Adam returned to the kitchen in a heavy coat. He was leaning to open the door when it burst open.

"Son of a bitch!" said Matt, coming through the door and holding his hand up with blood running down from his fingers.

"Language!" Kate and Dorothy said together.

Kate took one look and pulled out the first-aid kit again.

"What did I tell you about feeding the goats?" Dorothy asked.

"To make sure everything I want to keep is away from their teeth," Matt said.

"Because?" Dorothy prompted.

"Because they will eat absolutely anything including me." Matt ran his hand under the tap before sitting in the chair that Kate pushed out for him.

Kate dabbed at the wounds. "They aren't deep." She set about spraying and covering the fingers with gauze and tape. "So how did it get you?"

"We both got spooked by the storm," he said.

"We're all spooked by these storms. They've been going on a while now." Adam said.

"You think that's why the chickens aren't laying?" Kate asked.

"It's possible." Said Adam.

Kate held up the first-aid kit. "Should I even bother putting this away?"

"Let's be optimistic," Dorothy said.

16

A dam sat with Dorothy, Matt, and Jason, at the kitchen table in the farmhouse waiting for the others to join them. David and Vince pushed open the door and stumbled in. Vince turned to close the door. He looked up at the sky for a moment, then closed it.

"How long has it been like this?" Vince asked.

"A few weeks. Some areas are experiencing their first floods in over a hundred years," Adam said.

"The animals are really spooked," Dorothy said.

Matt went to the bottom of the stairs. "Kate, they're here."

"Who's here?" Kate asked.

"David and Vince," called Matt, sounding puzzled.

"Oh, of course, sorry," Kate said, descending the stairs. "I'm sorry," she said, "I don't know why, but I thought you meant my sister and her family had turned up. I guess I must have been thinking about them."

"I've been listening out for the names you gave me. I'm sorry, I've heard nothing," David said.

Kate nodded. Adam felt her disappointment.

"So, what's this plan you want to talk about?" Dorothy asked.

"We've learned they're keeping pregnant girls in the sub-levels of Hilltop," David said.

"Why would they do that?" Matt asked.

"It's a tracker farm," Kate said. She looked up and seemed to notice everyone staring at her. "It's obvious, isn't it? The only thing surprising about this, is that it hasn't occurred to them before. No pesky parents to lie to. They only need to control the kids."

"Kate's correct. That's what they're doing," David said.

"How do you know about this? Have you got someone on the inside?" Kate asked.

"One of the doctors told us. Dr. Narayan. He's dead now," David said.

"Good," Adam said.

"Are you okay, Kate?" Matt was looking at Kate, who had turned white.

"I was in there for over a year. Could I have...?" She put her hand on her stomach and swallowed loudly.

"I'm sure you'd know. In yourself, you'd know," Dorothy said.

"They started the project after I sent the message about trackers being faders," David said.

"That was you?" Kate asked.

"There were consequences I didn't anticipate," David said.

"So, the operation," Jason drew everyone's attention to the papers in the middle of the table.

They rolled out the maps and drawings.

Kate shook herself and studied the map of the compound, tilting her head this way and that.

"Which building were we in?" she asked Matt.

"We were here in the basement of the agency building at the back of the med center. We jumped off the truck here," Matt said.

"So, we got over the fence here?"

"That's it." Matt nodded.

"Are you sure this building was so close to the med center?" she asked.

"Yes. That's the main office building for the Academy," Jason said.

"You're sure?" Kate looked doubtful.

"I can tell you how many steps it takes to march around the perimeter of the base."

"Oh, yes, you were a tracker. I'm sorry, I forgot. And I was in a state of pure terror when I was there. I hope I can rely on my own judgement for something." Kate smiled.

"I hope so, too. You and Matt have been in the sub-levels of the agency building. No one else has been there. What do you remember?" Jason took a large drawing pad from the table and opened it to a blank page and passed a pencil to Kate.

"I didn't see much beyond the room we started in and the reception area." She passed the pencil to Matt. "You faded out of the room we were in. What did you see?"

"Don't forget, we stopped off in that woman's office where you found the gym bag with the clothes and gun." Matt drew two parallel lines representing the hallway, and halfway up he drew two boxes representing the two rooms they'd been in.

"I don't remember how many rooms were down to the right; we turned left. I looked into the room directly opposite ours; it was a storage room. There were more doors on our side of the hallway than the opposite side. I think there might only have been a couple of doors on the other side. We went past the dead people and into the stairwell."

"The staircase went down and up. I looked over the railing; it only went down one level. We went up and left, through double doors," Kate said.

"What was in the opposite direction, off to the right?"

"It looked like a couple of offices, I think," Matt said.

"We passed some labs. I could see fridges, and lab equipment on benches," Kate said.

"Then we came out into a reception area and hid behind the desk," Matt said.

"If you've already attacked the base, why didn't you find the pregnant girls then?" Kate asked.

"That wasn't us. We're not equipped to put on that kind of assault," Adam said.

"Could it be the people from the other Earth? What if they're trying to take over?" Kate said.

"We think it might have been an escape attempt by trackers," Jason said. "We've searched the area, but if that's what it was, none of them made it out."

"Did you see any posts, like this?" Vince drew a picture of what looked like a tall, thin audio speaker with metal grids every few inches and a light on top.

"They were in the room we woke up in," Matt said.

"They were anti-fade posts. I wonder why they weren't switched on," Vince said.

"Perhaps whatever happened occurred just after they put us in there," Kate said. "The men we found outside could have been the ones who put us in that room."

"Maybe. The people we found hadn't been dead long. The boots I put on were still warm," Matt said.

Kate visibly shuddered.

"Those posts weren't in the woman's office or the lab on the ground floor," Kate said.

"Or Dr. Narayan's office," David said.

"Can you lock on to any of those places?" Jason asked David.

"I can lock on to a fader or tracker or I can portal to a place I've been before. If someone's with me who's been to a place before, I can lock on to it through them."

"But can't Jenna just go anywhere now?" Adam asked.

"Jenna's not going anywhere until whatever's going on with her is resolved," David said.

"Who's going?" Kate asked.

"Me, David, Vince, Adam, Connor, and about a half dozen others from the safe house in California," Jason said.

"When should we do this, Jason?" Adam asked.

"The weekend. Nighttime. Saturday night, I guess," Jason said.

"So. A team of roughly ten portalling straight into Dr. Narayan's office. We can only hope there's no trackers in there. If they get startled by the red mist, it might give the game away," David said.

"If we're getting down to it, I'll make tea and coffee," Kate said.

She took mugs out of the cupboard. "Dorothy, is there more sugar?" she asked, peering into the sugar jar.

"It's in the store room," Dorothy said.

Kate left the kitchen and went into the store room, next door.

"I don't feel comfortable bringing Kate in on this. I think she'll want to help. She can't fade and she's an English teacher," whispered Adam.

"She can shoot," Matt said.

"She's recently had a head injury. I don't want to risk her."

"What if she wants to go?" Matt said.

"We'll figure something out," Jason said as Kate returned.

"Out of the office and lab, through to the Agency part of the building and down the stairwell," Jason said.

"Should we do sub-level one first or go down to two, or split up?" Adam asked.

"I think we should plan for different scenarios. We don't know if they'll detect us, so our best bet is to stick together with Connor and Vince," David said.

"Why?" Kate asked.

"Connor can fade others, but he can also utilize the abilities of other faders. Vince doesn't emit, so trackers can't see him when he's faded. If we're in one group, we can't be seen," Jason said.

"How do those posts work? Can they detect us and activate to trap us?" Adam asked.

"I wish," muttered Kate. She turned to hand out mugs. "I'd have a husband by now."

Dorothy took her mug and chuckled at Kate who was blushing. Kate glanced at Adam, and he winked at her.

"Where will I be?" Matt asked.

"If this goes wrong, you and Kate will be the only people here who've been inside that place. We need to protect that information. It might be needed to get us out," Jason said.

"But I could help." Matt was unhappy and looked like he was going to kick off.

"This is primarily going to be a recce. If we can do anything, we will, otherwise we'll just be gathering information," Jason said.

"I see. I'd have liked to be on the team. But your logic is

sound. Matt and I will head up the backup team. We'll need to come up with a plan for that," Kate said, looking gravely at Matt and nodding as though they had their orders.

He straightened his back and returned the nod. She flicked a glance at Adam who gave her the briefest of smiles. Jason had played it perfectly. Kate appeared to be keeping Matt out of harm's way, but they were also keeping her safe, and she didn't realize it.

"So, back to the spouse catchers or anti-fader posts," Adam said.

"The one Craig trapped us with must have been manually operated because I heard the thoughts of the tracker. He was thinking, 'that's all of them, switch it on, switch it on'. That's when I realized something was wrong." David patted Vince on the hand.

"Who's Craig?" Kate asked.

"Craig Tomowski, the major at the Colorado base," David said.

"You're on first-name terms with him?" Kate looked bemused.

"I was a student at Washington State academy when Craig was a young agent. He and his friends killed all the kids. Only two of us escaped."

"You were there? I've heard about that. I thought no one escaped," Kate said. She looked visibly shaken.

"What's wrong?" Dorothy asked.

"All those kids. And now knowing they were faders." Kate shook her head sadly.

"Just the fact that they were kids," Dorothy said.

"You're right, it's awful," Kate said.

"Okay. Let's break out the cookies and take ten minutes," David said.

"Aren't you going out for a smoke, Dorothy?" Adam

asked, dipping his head in the direction of the door which was being rattled off its hinges by the wind.

"In that? Hell no. I'm giving up, today," Dorothy said, stepping on the peddle bin and dropping her cigarettes and lighter into it.

David made his way around the table to Kate. "Something about the academy shocked you. Do you want to talk about it?"

"I've never heard that the agency did it. I heard it was a group of faders. Are you sure?"

"I watched from the tree line as Craig Tomowski shot my friend and classmate, Chris, in the face. He walked around the building and fired into the room where there the rest of my friends were."

"I'm so sorry. I feel bad that I just believed those stories. You get to the point where you see so much bad stuff, it's easy to just believe what you're told."

"The only faders there were the children they murdered."

"But I heard that agents were killed, too. Surely someone was fighting back."

"I learned, recently, from Dr. Narayan, they had considered a certain number of deaths on their side was an expected loss in an attack. They just shot a few of their own."

"He was talkative?"

"I picked it out of his head."

"I thought you couldn't read people who aren't faders."

"We turned him into a fader."

"You–? I must be incredibly far out of the loop," Kate said. She dropped into a chair. "I think I need to sit down."

"You are sitting down," David said, smiling.

"If you don't mind, I think I'm going to lie down," she said before standing back up and heading up the stairs.

"Are you all right, Kate?" Adam asked, he had been listening to the exchange.

"I'm okay. I'm just going upstairs to rest."

"I'll give you a call when dinner's ready." He said.

"Thank you, Adam."

He hoped she might have started thinking of him kindly and stopped seeing him as the thug who had knocked her senseless in an alley.

17

———

I was bored. I'd been sitting in the house for a week. The hexagons were all over my body now. I was just relieved they weren't on my face. I'd taken to wearing a polo neck sweater. Orla had stayed with me, but I could tell she was going stir-crazy, too.

"Your dad's invited Brother Justin over again," Orla said.

I sighed and rolled my eyes.

"I'm sorry sweetie. I'm getting out of it. I've arranged to go horse riding,"

"I could have come with you," I said.

"You don't like horses. They frighten you, you daisy."

"But I've got Hive now. If they frighten me, I can blast them to bits," I grinned.

"And that's precisely why you won't be coming to visit the horses."

"Well, I'm not hanging round to have Justin sniffing at me again. They'll have to wait. I'm going to work." I started pulling my hair into a ponytail.

"It's Saturday."

"I'm going to do some overtime. Do you want to come?"

"Hell no! You've not been there all week. I don't think they'll be paying you time and a half for going in on a Saturday."

"I'll see you later then." I stood and pushed my feet into my shoes.

"I'm going to get into trouble for letting you go."

"Tell them you tried to stop me."

"I'll do that. Oh! I think they've removed your ribbon access."

"I am the ribbon," said Hive.

"I couldn't have said it better myself," I added.

"You look after her," Orla said, obviously to Hive. "I'll be letting Heidi know where you are. I don't want you being anywhere alone."

I opened my mouth to speak.

"Yes, I know, you're never alone," Orla said.

I stepped back away from Orla and portalled.

I arrived in the middle of our little office and walked to the hallway. James was in his office. I quietly closed the door. I didn't put the light on but sat at Orla's desk by the window and immediately began to stuff envelopes.

Five minutes later, I looked up at the sound of the door opening. Heidi was standing in the doorway.

"Have you come to stuff envelopes with me?" I asked.

"I can if you like," she said, smiling hesitantly.

"You don't need to be so careful around me."

"Well, you feel quite disquieted." Heidi sat opposite me at my desk. "So, is there a manner in which this should be properly achieved?"

"No, you just ram them in, seal them up, and throw them on the pile."

We sat in companionable silence for ten minutes. Heidi glanced up at me a few times.

"What do you wish to know?" Hive asked.

"Hey, my mouth, remember," I said.

Heidi giggled, more from nerves, I suspected.

"Why are you here?" Heidi asked.

"We are here to restore balance."

"What if Jenna asked you to leave. Would you?"

That's a good question, I thought.

"When the balance is restored. We will leave."

"But you wouldn't leave now."

"Jenna has agreed to be our instrument. We must restore the balance."

"What if I offered to be your instrument instead?"

I stared at Heidi. My eyes felt like they were on stalks.

"Your brightness is beautiful, but we could not exist within you."

"Is there any way I can help?"

"All are called when they are called."

"I'm not sure what that means," Heidi said, returning her gaze to her work.

I picked up a pile of envelopes and walked across the office, to place them in the box for the mailroom. I turned back to discover there were no more to do, and on the way back to Orla's desk, noticed for the first time there was mail in my in-tray. I picked up the envelope. It said 'Jenna' on the front. I hadn't received a letter addressed to me at work before, I was quite excited. I turned it over and opened it. Pulling out the paper, I unfolded it and read. I narrowed my eyes before darting them to the calendar, then to the clock. Heidi sensed my mood and looked up. Immediately, I blasted her with an energy ball.

18

A dam stood with the others assembled in the kitchen of the farmhouse, and David created a portal.

"The rest of the team is waiting on Full-Earth side, and we'll go to Hilltop from there."

"Wait," Kate said, rushing into the room.

"We're kind of on the clock here, Kate," David said.

"My name's not Kate."

David closed the portal.

"What?" Adam asked. A sinking feeling settling in his stomach.

"I'm not a fader. I work for the agency." She avoided Adam's eyes.

No one moved. No one spoke.

"They're waiting for you in Dr. Narayan's office. There will be anti-fade posts set up."

Finally, she looked at Adam and Matt. "I'm sorry."

"Why are you telling us this?" Vince asked.

"I've been struggling since this mission started, but just trying to get on and do my duty. I had already decided on leaving the agency after this mission. Then something else happened and I just couldn't do it any longer."

"Go on," said Vince.

"I was invited to join the agency after my father, an agent, died in a terrorist attack, murdered by faders." She looked at David.

"Washington State," he said.

She nodded.

"My whole working life, I've been manipulated into believing that faders are monsters who killed my father and all the kids at the tracker school, because they didn't realize they were faders, like themselves."

"What was your mission?" Adam asked, feeling sick.

"To find out what you had planned and make sure they were there to stop it."

"You told them about the other Earths," Vince said.

"Actually, no."

"No?" Adam asked. He was incredulous.

"I wasn't going back to the agency with something like that without proof. They'd lock me up."

"That's not the real reason, is it," Vince said.

"I got confused." She was blushing now. "Look, just don't go. It doesn't matter what you do with me now."

"What do they know?"

"They know around ten faders are coming, where and when. That's everything." Kate took a small mobile phone from her pocket and put it on the table.

"But you shot that man," said Matt.

"The whole thing was staged. I shot him with a blank."

"But all the bodies,"

"They were real. They were trackers. I'm sorry. I thought you were the bad guys. I thought that my whole life."

She turned and headed back up the stairs.

"I think it's safe to say the op's aborted," David said.

"What are we going to do about her?" Dorothy said.

"Shoot her, I guess," Adam said.

Adam jerked his head up and bolted upstairs. He burst into Kate's room to find her with a handgun under her chin.

"No."

"You can't see this, get out."

"You're not doing it. Give it to me." He dived for the gun, prepared to wrestle it from her hands, but she let go immediately.

"I'm not going to fight you with a loaded gun in my hand," Kate said.

"What are you doing?" Matt asked from the doorway.

Adam considered the scene as Matt was seeing it; Adam standing over Kate with the gun in her hand. "She was going to kill herself."

"It would have been for the best," Kate said.

Come on, Matt. Let's go down," Adam said.

Matt walked out ahead of Adam and stamped down the stairs.

Adam looked at the gun in his hand and then at the shelf by the door. It would be so easy to leave the gun and just let her get on with it. He kept it, and left the room, closing the door behind him.

They sat around the table. David stood at the end with his hands on the back of his chair and began to speak.

"Okay, we need to work out—"

A portal appeared behind him. Jenna stepped out of it. The red hexagons around her pupils glowed. Seeing everyone's shocked faces, David began to turn but got no farther. Jenna grabbed him by the back of his collar and yanked him backwards into the portal. It closed, and they were gone.

Everyone was on their feet. Adam realized there was

nowhere to go and nothing to do. David was gone, the portal was gone. There was no way to get to or even contact the people on Full-Earth.

"What the hell is going on over there?" Adam asked.

"Did you see her eyes? What is she?" Matt asked.

Vince reached out and held on to the back of David's empty chair. "So now we're stuck here and won't be able to find out what's going on until David gets back."

Adam glanced up to Vince as an arm appeared from nowhere and pulled Vince into a portal.

19

———

"What the hell?" David turned. "Jen... Hive?"

"It's me," I said. "How many people are in this building?"

David looked for a moment as though he were going to argue. He must have seen the desperate expression on my face and closed his eyes to concentrate.

"Sixteen."

"There's a bomb. I need you to tell me where they are, and I'll get them out. We have thirteen minutes."

"James is in there," David said.

"Then let's start with him, and we'll work our way down," I said.

"Orla told me Heidi was going to drop by."

"She did. She's at the residence now, sleeping."

"Sleeping?" He stared at me with a raised eyebrow.

"She would have risked her life trying to help."

We entered James's office. He looked up. "Jenna, you're supposed to be—."

"Read this." I pushed the letter into his hands and

shoved his chair through a portal into the garden at the residence.

"Where next?" I asked.

"Sixteenth floor. In the men's bathroom, sorry."

"Of course." I portalled into the gents' toilet.

"Zip up, mister, there's a lady present."

His zipper went up as I pushed him through.

"Next?"

"Fourteenth floor break room."

We swept the building quickly.

"Seven minutes left. There's one more, in the basement, I think. It must be an inc; I can't get a reading," David sent.

I appeared behind David and portalled him to the garden. A second later I was in the basement.

I found Maggie gagged and tied up. She looked up, relieved at first, then as she took in my eyes, she shuffled away from me.

"Typical. I should have worked bottom to top."

I pulled the gag from her tear-streamed face.

"I'm sorry. Please—" Maggie said.

"Where is it?" I asked.

"It's down here somewhere. I don't know where they put it. There was something over my head. What's happened to your eyes?"

"I'm trying a new look," I swept her through to the residence.

I rushed through the basement looking under benches, in cupboards and lockers. I peered behind pipes. I couldn't see where it might be. I blinked in, thinking that if the device used energy cubes, I might see the yellow glow, but there was nothing.

I didn't know how long I'd been there. My heart was hammering. I decided it was time to get out of there.

"The blue mist. He is here," Hive sang in my mind.

I spun around.

"What? I just looked," I said out loud, blinking in and looking around me again.

Sure enough, a blue mist had settled next to a wall. I didn't see the fader, they must have gone but I couldn't see any indication that they had been anywhere else. Had a fader placed the bomb? It didn't make sense, and why were they emitting a blue mist? Whatever was going on, someone had been there in the two seconds since I had previously blinked in. I faded and went straight to the area. I walked through the wall to find the device, hidden in a wall panel. I stepped towards it, and it exploded.

"What the hell was that?" Dad asked as the ground rocked.

The people in the garden looked up at the cloud of smoke and flames leaping so high into the air several miles away it could be seen above the wall around the residence.

"It's the bomb," I said. "I needed somewhere unpopulated and couldn't think where else to take it."

My dad turned to me, grabbed me, and pulled me into his arms. He froze slightly. I knew he could feel the hexagons were now across my back. He let go, then hugged me harder.

"I thought I'd lost you," he said thickly through tears.

Orla was sitting with her arms around a weeping, shaking Maggie. She looked up at me. "Can I not leave you alone for a minute? Heidi's going to kill you. She's furious."

"Jenna!" I turned as Heidi ran to me from the house. She hugged me so fiercely I thought she was trying to break my ribs.

"Well, she *was* furious," Orla said.

The ribbon burst into life, and David came through with Callan, Connor, and Jason.

Connor came to stand by me. "Thank God you're okay,"

"Where's Vince?" David asked.

"I thought he was with you in the Cotswolds?" Orla said.

"He disappeared through another portal straight after Jenna took David," Jason said.

"It wasn't me," I said.

"It wasn't us, was it?" I asked Hive.

"It was not. He is coming."

"Apparently, he's on his way," I told David, tapping my head to indicate where the information had come from.

The gate flickered into life for another incoming visitor, and Vince appeared.

"Don't read me," he warned David.

David's jaw dropped. He looked at me. Clearly, the warning had come too late for David, but whatever he had read seemed to involve me, and I was curious.

"Let's talk," Vince said. A private conversation seemed to be taking place between David and Vince.

"I don't know how to thank you," James said.

"If I hadn't got that warning from Maggie, we'd all be dead," I said. "Although you could have just called me," I added to Maggie.

"They were watching me. I couldn't make a call from home and one of my colleagues was a part of it. The only thing I could think was scribbling that note in the bathroom and adding it to the mail for your floor. I thought the message would get to you in plenty of time. I didn't know you hadn't been in the office because we hadn't spoken in a while." Maggie blushed.

"You know you're going to have to come with us," said Callan to Maggie.

"What? She's a victim. She was tied up down there and left to die along with us," I said.

"It's okay. I need to talk to them. I have things to tell them," Maggie said.

"Make sure she gets good representation," James said to Callan, who was walking Maggie through the front door to the hopper.

"I'm going to change. I'm feeling a little warm," I said.

I headed to my room to change into a sleeveless top. It was about time I stopped hiding the progression of the patterns across my body.

I removed the sweater and looked at the patterns. They were subtly glowing. This was new. I pulled on the top and gazed at the shifting pattern on my arms. The red was being replaced by white and then yellow. The colors swirled inside the golden hexagons, and I was mesmerized, chasing the patterns with my gaze. I realized this was going on across my midriff, too.

"Are you okay in there?" Heidi knocked and opened the door. "What in the Divine Light!" Her hand covered her mouth.

Feet came running.

"What is this? Jenna, can you hear me?" Dad asked. "Someone call Dr. Hade."

"Like she can help," Orla said. "I'm calling Brother Damon."

I could hear them. I was paralyzed. I couldn't respond. All I could think was that Dad was right. I shouldn't have done this. Was it killing me? Was it taking over? Pushing me out of my own body? What is a hive? It was where insects were born. Was that what the hexagons were? Cocoons for creatures?

"What the hell is going on?" Dad was beside himself.

David was there.

"I'm not telling your dad the weird stuff that's going on in your head. I'm looking at you. There are no alien insects."

He shared what he could see. I was lying on the bed. The hexagons were glowing and rippling in red, yellow, and white all over my body.

"I thought I was standing," I sent.

"That was hours ago. You've been there for most of the day."

I had been completely unaware of the passage of time.

"I've got her. She's in there," David told the others.

"She's scared," came Heidi's voice.

"I'm here, little duck."

Through David's eyes, I saw everyone around me. Dad, Orla, Heidi, Damon, Justin, and Connor by my side with red-rimmed eyes.

Something was coming.

At the same time, Heidi and David said, "I think we should—"

The power of the energy moved through me. Connor and Dad were pushed from my sides as a nimbus glow pulsed from me.

"Hive, what are you doing to her. For the love of God, please don't hurt her," Orla cried.

My mind filled with images of fire pouring from my fingertips, raining down on Major Tomowski and the skin peeling from his bones.

"Why are you doing this?" I asked.

Agents falling beneath my feet.

"This is the power," said Hive.

Explosions deep within the Cheyenne base and the mountain collapsing in on itself, all caused by me.

"What about the captured faders and all that wildlife on the mountain?" I thought to Hive.

I watched as the Citadel tore apart and the rocks rained down on what was left of it.

"*What about all those people, the Brothers, Zoe and Hannah? This cannot happen,*" I cried out into myself.

David's voice came to me from a memory. "Just because you can do something, doesn't mean you should."

"*We chose well,*" said Hive.

Then it began.

My mind opened to the memories of Hive and the reality of what it actually was. Eons passed by in the blink of an eye. I watched as civilizations grew and died. I could never have been prepared for the loss of so many, to mourn billions. My heart broke a billion times but grew a billion times larger.

"*Grief is the price of love,*" said Hive.

And there *was* love. I was expanded and filled with it. I felt pride in every good thing and sorrow in every sadness.

I opened my eyes. Everything looked sharper and brighter than it had before.

"She's awake," Connor said. He was holding my hand again.

I lay there, trying to take stock. Wondering what I was now.

"Are they everywhere now?" I asked.

"I don't understand," he said.

"The shapes," I said.

"The hexagons have gone. Except the ones in your eyes, but they're gold now. It's kinda pretty," he smiled at me.

I lifted my arm. Sure enough, they'd gone, but my skin was a strange, shifting, metallic, glowing pink. The colors had merged.

"You're rose gold now, like an Apple accessory," Orla said from the door.

I smiled.

Brothers Justin and Damon were in the room.

Justin looked at Connor. "I've never sensed anything like this."

"Have you ever heard of faders who emit a blue mist?" I asked.

"Blue? No, never. Why?" Damon asked.

"I saw it in the building just before I found the bomb."

I didn't catch his response. I closed my eyes and went back to sleep.

We woke and sat up. The room was empty except for Connor, asleep in the chair next to the bed. We moved to the edge of the bed and stood. We felt different.

"Is this what we are now?" we asked

"For now," we replied

We were truly one.

We left the room, Connor woke behind us. "Jenna?"

We walked through the house. Orla, Heidi, and Jason were in conversation in the living room, Neil, David, James, and Callan in the dining area. Conversations ceased as we passed. We approached Damon and Justin in the garden. The others followed from the house.

"Jenna trusts you. She believes you will help us," we said.

"We may be able to help if what you need is not at odds with the people of my world or the Divine Light," Damon said.

"What are you?" asked Justin.

"We are the Light," we said.

"Are you saying—?" he said.

"We are the balance and the scales." Our voices rose and filled the air.

We stood upon the grass in the center of the garden. We

held out our arms and we shone. As we spoke, we became louder, and our brightness filled the space and lit up the faces of those around us.

"With this vessel we will right this injustice and end this abomination. Our children are dying, our need is at odds with this world, but you are tied to our cause by virtue of promise. By blood and sacrifice shall you make amends for the horrors that you have wrought, for we are the Divine Light, and we demand it of you."

Damon and Justin dropped to their knees. We turned and spoke directly to them.

"Stand, Justin and Damon, sons of Divine Light. And know the truth."

Justin and Damon stumbled to their feet and walked towards us. We reached out and touched their heads. They fell back to their knees and sobbed.

We walked to the doorway and faced David. "*That which Vince has been unable to keep from you shall never be shared.*"

"*As you wish,*" David sent with a slight bow of his head.

We turned to face those who were gathered.

"This vessel requires rest." We walked through the house and laid down.

I woke up. We were separate again, although they were still inside me.

I looked around the room to find Dad in the chair, looking at me.

"I'm starving," I said, happy to hear my own voice.

He smiled, sighing. His body sagged a little. "It's good to have you back."

"Oh, the gang's all still here, but I feel like me again," I said.

"I'll get Sofia to make something for you."

"She's back?"

"She refused to stay away any longer. She's right, I never should have done that. I'm sorry." He left the room.

I walked to the closet and opened the doors.

"Yes!" I pulled out a large bag of Cheetos, went back to the bed, and started munching.

There was a knock at the door, and Connor put his head around. "Can I come—?" He stared at me as my cheeks bulged with Cheetos.

"This vessel requires Cheetos," I attempted through a mouthful of snacks.

"I see your body's still a temple," he said, taking a few out of the offered bag and sitting next to me.

"Sofia's making you cheese on toast," he said.

I swallowed. "Great."

"So, you're the Divine Light now. Although, I always thought you were divine."

"Cute," I said as I licked orange flavoring off my fingers.

"Damon and Justin are in the garden. They haven't stopped praying since you came in here about four hours ago. They look devastated."

"We showed them something awful." I put the bag down. It all came back to me. "Did they tell you?"

"No. They didn't know if they should, because your friends in there didn't tell us."

I leaned into him, and he held me.

"We have to get Zoe, Hannah, and her parents out of the Citadel."

"The Citadel? I thought this was about Cheyenne mountain."

"I knew something about Zoe upset them but I didn't understand why."

I headed out to find everyone waiting. Heidi lurched to

her feet. I thought for one awful moment that she was going to drop to her knees.

I sat at the breakfast bar, and Sofia placed a plate of cheese on toast in front of me. I stared at the food. I was hungry, but everyone was gawking at me, and I felt horribly uncomfortable.

"That'll be the holy toast," Orla said.

Vince roared with laughter, followed by the rest of us.

People started talking amongst themselves and Heidi opened a tin of cookies.

"Thank you," I mouthed across to Orla.

She smiled. I looked around at everyone, realizing these people were my anchor. I ate my food.

"How are the wedding plans going?" I asked Sofia.

"They're on the back burner for now," she said.

I was disappointed.

I finished my food. Refilled my coffee and turned back to the room.

"David, can we get Kim and her friends from Broken-Earth and the team from our Earth? This involves them; they need to hear it."

David headed out to the garden. Five minutes later, we were assembled.

"No Adam?" I asked.

"We have an agency infiltrator. It turns out Kate wasn't Kate," David said.

"How did you discover that?"

"She just admitted it. We were about to head out on a mission and she told us they were waiting for us,"

"Why would she do that?" I asked.

"It could be some plan I don't know. I think she's grown quite close to Adam and Matt. Maybe she had a change of heart," David shrugged.

"I didn't know agency operatives had hearts," Orla said.

"Adam stayed to watch her, and Matt stayed to make sure Adam doesn't put a bullet in her. She does seem to have changed her allegiance, but who can tell," Jason said.

"Heidi can tell," I said.

I portalled to our earth to find Adam sitting in the kitchen of the farmhouse. At the end of the table sat Matt, and on the opposite side of the table sat his prisoner.

"Vera?" I was shocked. I hadn't seen Vera a.k.a Nerd Two since she was sticking electrodes to my head at the Colorado base.

"Jenna. You've changed," said Vera carefully.

"I hear I'm not the only one," I said.

"You know her?" Adam asked.

"Sure. Vera and I go way back. We're having a family meeting. You're late."

"I'd prefer to die on this earth if you don't mind," said Vera.

"Jeez, Vera, not everything's about you."

We portalled back to the residence. Heidi was on it immediately and I stayed in the kitchen to listen in.

"Have you been to Full-Earth before?" Heidi asked Vera.

"Yes, once. It's very nice here." Vera glanced up seeming to notice that Adam and Matt were standing nearby.

"You look uncomfortable," Heidi said.

"Quite frankly, I'm not sure if I'm here to be killed,"

"Well, my cookies aren't great but I think you can risk it. Excuse me I have to speak to Jenna,"

Heidi came over to me and we walked through to the hallway.

"Well?" I asked.

"Similar to Vince when I first sensed him. Self-loathing, shame and love."

"Love?"

"When she glanced towards Adam and Matt."

"That's interesting. Thank you." I made to turn away but stopped. "Heidi?"

"Yes?"

"Make sure you and James get a seat for what I'm about to say. I'm sorry but you're going to need it."

We'd moved out into the garden. There wasn't enough space in the house for the number of people gathered. Sean's tracker friends and his girlfriend Sam had also arrived along with Jodi and the girls. The moment I walked out, Milly launched herself into my arms and patted my cheeks.

"I love you," she said. I knew this time that she wasn't speaking to me.

"We love you, too, little one," said Hive.

"I knew you were there," Milly whispered.

"We know. You sniffed us out," said Hive.

I smiled and put Milly back down.

"*Since you're here, maybe you could tell them.*" I didn't want to have to be the one to do this. There was no answer. It was up to me. There would be no getting out of this. I spoke.

"Many years ago, a storm began on this Earth. It was the beginning of the end for this world, its energy was depleting, the ribbon fading. For years, the storms got worse. In some areas, crops failed, whole communities died of disease. In other areas, they built the domes to protect themselves. Then a group of Benedictine monks discovered a way to stop the storms. They had a Brightling, probably originally from another Earth. They used a red-mister and somehow connected the Brightling to the energy ribbon of that earth. Over the years, through the Brightling, they siphoned the energy from that earth to this one. They are still doing it now, although that Brightling must be very old now and the energy coming through is much diminished. Of course, after the storms on the other Earth started, the sun sickness came, or radiation poisoning as we call it. Then most of the inhabitants of that earth died as a result of what the Brothers did."

Quiet sobs came from Justin, seated at the back of the group. Kyle and Eric stared in horror at him.

"No one here today knew of this. Don't misplace your anger," I said.

"The storms on our Earth. That's what it is, isn't it? It's Zoe," Jason said.

"Yes."

"And what happened to Broken-Earth will happen there?" Orla asked.

I nodded.

"How can we stop it?" Sofia asked.

I looked at James and Heidi. Heidi sighed. She knew.

"This all began with our Earth dying. If we stop it, our Earth will continue to die," Heidi said.

Vera opened her mouth, then closed it again and looked down.

"Did you have a question, Vera?"

"Vera! The nerd from Stalag 19. I knew I recognized you," Orla said. She shook her head, looking perplexed.

"Can it be stopped?" Vera asked.

"The Five must be stopped. The Divine Light wills it," Justin said.

"The Divine Light?" Vera asked.

"Jenna's divine now, Vera. You have to keep up," Orla said.

"Justin's right. We're not here to discuss if we do it. We need to work out how," James said.

"You're some kind of God now? Can't you stop these storms from destroying any Earth? Vera said.

I instantly regretted bringing Vera over. That was a good question and everyone was waiting for an answer.

"Firstly, I'm not the Divine Light, I'm their instrument. It's a fairly recent situation and I'm not sure what I'm capable of. I think I could destroy a planet but I honestly don't know if I could save this one."

20

Later, I sat with Justin and James in the garden.

"Where's Damon?" I asked.

"He's back at the Citadel. We're supposed to be watching the Brightling. We've both spent too long here."

"I understand," I turned to James. "This must be difficult for you."

"Difficult. You have no idea. That bomb should have taken me. I'd have preferred that," James said.

"Then why are you helping us?" I asked.

"Because it's the right thing to do. A whole world of people has been murdered by the Brotherhood, and now they're starting on another world. I love this Earth, but what they're doing is wrong. It can't continue. It's taken what, seventy years to destroy a planet. It will take that short time again to destroy yours. There are no more Earths. We're not buying ourselves much time, and the price is too high. More than anything, I wish I didn't know. I wish that you had just gotten on and done whatever you need to do, because the weight of this is too much to bear."

"Will you tell anyone else?" I asked.

"No. We can't expect help with this. If anyone else found out about this, we'd probably be killed. You'd better hope that no other mind reader like David stumbles across us before we carry out the plan." James said.

"If we ever agree on a plan," I said. "Justin, tell me about the Five."

"I've heard they are untouchable," he said. "They are rarely all seen together. There's usually always one or two missing. That might be for security, I don't know. It's either Peter or Rachel who are missing when they congregate."

"There were three men and a woman at the ceremony so I guess that was Peter missing. Who are the others?"

"Benedict is the oldest. He's the blind one you thought was looking at you," Justin said.

"Are you sure he's blind?" I remembered him. I'd been convinced he was looking at me from across the room.

"He has no eyes. He was captured and tortured by Brokens when he was young. His eyes were burned out."

"Good grief, that's horrific." I shook my head.

"Gabriel and Noah are the remaining two."

"Do they have abilities?"

"I don't know. I've never seen any of them fade."

"The binding ceremony. What did it do to Zoe? Is she physically bound to this Earth?"

"I always thought it was ceremonial. Like, a marriage, she's making a commitment."

"Did the previous Brightling ever leave?"

"We didn't work with her. I don't know."

"I think the first thing we need to do is get Zoe off this Earth."

I left the garden and headed into the house. I found Orla and Jason in their room throwing shoes into a box.

"What are you doing?"

"We'll have to leave here, won't we? I'm not leaving my shoes," she said.

"I'm pleased to see you've got your priorities straight." I smiled. "To be honest, I thought you had more."

"David took the first three boxes over to the vineyard already," Jason said.

I shook my head.

"Can you call Zoe to see if they can come over for a movie day?" I asked.

"I'll get on it." Orla took out her communicator.

I found Dad and Connor sitting together, looking unhappy.

"I know," I said.

"What do you know?" Connor asked.

"There's no way either of you can keep me out of this. You can't distract me or send me to my room. I know you both want to protect me, but it's not going to happen that way this time. Hive will do their best to keep me safe. This isn't only their fight. Zoe's in the middle of it, and that makes it our fight, too."

"Don't forget, Jenna will be unmatched in this. She's the Divine Light. They won't know what hit them," Orla said from the doorway with her box of shoes.

"How did it go?" I asked.

"They're just getting ready. They'll be along in a few minutes."

"I suppose I should pack my stuff up, too," I said.

I went to my room and threw clothes into a bag. Sounds around the house indicated that the others were doing the same.

"Hello," called Zoe from the room downstairs.

I stayed out of sight as Orla walked into the living room with them.

"What's with all the bags?" Hannah asked.

"We've got something to tell you, sweetie. You might need to sit down." I closed my door and let them get on with it.

A few minutes later, there was a knock at my door. I had changed into a vest top. I thought it best that they see the full effect.

"Come in." I didn't look as they assessed me from the doorway. I stood folding my clothes and laying them in piles on the bed. I wanted to give them time to take in my strange iridescent skin with its shifting patterns.

"Well, it's nicer than the hexagons," Zoe said.

They came in and hugged me.

"Oh, are we allowed to hug you, being divine and everything?" Zoe asked

"I'm not divine. I'm the Divine Light's Uber. I'm how they get around."

"I knew this was all too good to be true," Hannah said.

"I'm going to miss our little house," Zoe said.

"We need to get your parents out of there," I said to Hannah.

"It's going to look suspicious, all this ribbon activity," Zoe said

"Then sooner rather than later, please," Hannah said.

"Let's do that now. We don't need to bother with the ribbon." I pulled on a sweater and took Hannah's hand. "Think about where they live."

The portal showed their house. They were doing the dishes.

We walked into the kitchen.

"Hi, Mom," Hannah said.

Her mom saw me and shrieked.

We gave them ten minutes to pack up and brought them back to the residence.

The garden was filling up with our Half-Earth friends getting ready for David to take them to safe houses. I planned to get Zoe and Hannah out first.

"Is everyone ready?" I asked the few assembled in the living room.

They nodded, so I created the portal. Orla went through, helping Hannah's parents with their bags, then Damon went ahead of Zoe, and Justin stood behind her. Zoe began to walk in to the portal, then stopped. It was like an invisible barrier was barring her way. Zoe couldn't get through. She was being pulled and stretched in two directions and screamed, and I closed the portal.

David came running into the room. Zoe was sitting on the floor with her head in her hands.

"It was like I was being ripped apart," Zoe said, shaking and sobbing.

"David. Can you go to the vineyard and let them know Zoe's okay, but we can't get her off this Earth?"

He nodded and turned to go to the garden.

"Just take mine," I said. I opened a portal, and he ran straight through.

"Stay with her," I said to Justin. I went to pour a glass of water for Zoe who was still sobbing. The crying suddenly stopped. I looked up. There was no sign of Justin.

A woman in a robe stood next to a shocked-looking Zoe. I recognized her from the ceremony. It was Rachel, one of the Five. She looked at me, produced a red mist, grabbed Zoe and stepped into it. They were gone.

I ran into the living room to find Justin on the floor, bleeding from a wide gash across his throat. His arms were flailing about. I crouched beside him and tried to cover the wound, knowing I would be ineffective. He pulled my hands away from his neck and took hold of them in his own hands.

"*Do something,*" my mind screamed.

Beyond that, I was without words, but Hive came forward and calmed my racing heart and mind. I watched as our hands in his grew brighter, our skin became a living ribbon of light. Our mouth opened, words of comfort and promises of a glorious afterlife that I alone could not have had the capacity for, flowed from our lips. Justin's face became enraptured and joyous. The life left his eyes, but a haze of light moved from his hands into mine, and Hive retreated. I staggered to my feet and noticed for the first time that Damon and David had returned.

Damon dropped to his knees and held the lifeless body of his friend. He looked up at me. "What you gave him at the end is more than anyone could hope for. Thank you."

I didn't feel I deserved that. I'd let him die. If I'd stayed with Zoe, that wouldn't have happened. I felt wretched.

"What happened?" David asked.

"Rachel was here; she took Zoe. It happened so fast. I didn't know what to do, but Hive came forward."

A loud piercing scream came from behind me. I turned to find Milly staring at Justin on the floor. I lifted her into my arms and ran out into the garden and passed the hysterical girl to her mother.

"The rest of you have to leave now. They could return any second."

I watched as Jodi and the girls walked through the portal to the vineyard followed by Anna, Sam, Chester, Leroy, Aiden, Sean, and his parents. Sofia hugged and kissed my dad, then went through.

I sat at the dining table with Connor, Damon, Dad, and James.

"Dad, you can't stay here. You need to go back. You can't leave that child fatherless before it's born."

"I know. I've gone through this argument in my head already. It just ends with you pushing me through a portal."

'Sounds accurate." I smiled. "Tell the others, if they want to help, they shouldn't go too far. If I do need them, I don't want to get there and find no one in."

"I'll lock them all in and guard them with a rifle," Dad said.

"It's extreme, but I like it."

"Take care of yourself, little duck." He hugged me then pulled away and looked sternly into my eyes. "Take care of her," he told Hive.

We hugged again, and he went through the portal.

"I thought that would be more difficult," I mused.

I looked at Connor.

"Don't even think about it. I'm going nowhere," he said.

"Was it wise to send them all away?" Damon asked.

"I won't have anyone else dying needlessly. The first thing we need to do is get Zoe back."

"How are you going to find her?"

"I can always see her."

"Hive, turn it back on, please."

"It is done."

"I need to go to the Citadel. David, we need Vince."

David walked into the garden and returned minutes later with Vince.

We portalled to the Citadel and arrived in the square, in front of the sealed ribbon gate. Guards stood at the gate, but they were unable to see us. Standing holding hands, Connor, David, Vince, and I were invisible. I looked up at the subtle rippling of what I now knew to be the fading ribbon of energy coming from Broken-Earth into the top of the tower.

"Is she there?" Connor asked.

"No, but someone is," I said.

We portalled to the top of the tower. A man sat in front of a red mist portal reading a book. A very old woman lay surrounded by machines which seemed to be keeping her heart pumping and lungs breathing.

"*Are you there?*" David asked the prone figure. Being connected with him in this way, I could hear them.

"*I am here. I am so tired,*" the sleeping woman responded.

"*You are the Brightling?*"

"*I was, but I am dead, or as good as.*"

"*We're going to try to free you,*" David sent.

"*There is only one freedom I desire. I am so tired.*"

"*You will rest with us, child. Your work is done,*" added Hive.

"*Thank you.*"

I materialized and stepped towards the man. He looked up in shock and dropped his book as he tried to fade and escape through his portal. He wore the mantel of the Five but I didn't recognize him. I deduced this was Peter.

I faded and grabbed his arm, pulling him back to solidity.

"You can't do that," he said, trying to fight me off.

I looked at him with Hive's bright, glowing eyes, and he stopped struggling.

"Give her the peace she prays for," Hive said to the others.

Peter continued to stare into my eyes, mesmerized while Connor and David turned off the machines.

"Where is Zoe?" I asked.

"I don't know. She's Rachel's charge," he said.

"*He's telling the truth. He doesn't know.*" David sent.

"And where's Rachel?"

"She asked me to take her shift. She was supposed to take over here an hour ago. She said she felt Zoe trying to leave. They're connected, like I am to her," he said.

"Close the portal," I said.

"I can't. She's connected to it," he said.

"She's dying," David said.

"What? Do you know what you've done? This world will end. Everything we've built will be destroyed."

"I've been to Broken-Earth. I know what that looks like," Vince said through gritted teeth.

"But we also know that's not what you think is going to happen here. David said.

"She's gone," Connor said, closing the Brightling's eyes.

"You like portals, don't you," I said.

As he watched me, his eyes flickered to the sides, indicating that he was becoming aware of something creeping around the edges of his vision. He looked around himself and struggled again when he realized the blackness slipping up and around him was an endless void. He was mostly no longer in the room. The void was closing in. His feet on the floor became unstable, and suddenly, he was balancing on his tiptoes and cartwheeling his arm. I let go. He drifted away, screaming. I closed the portal.

"Won't he just be able to red-mist his way out of it?" Connor asked.

"There is no return for mortals from what you call the in-between," said Hive.

"What now?" Vince asked.

"I don't understand why I can't see the ribbon," I said.

"Maybe they're not on this earth anymore," suggested Vince.

I created a portal to the residence, but looking through, I

could see it was being searched by Brothers and officers. I moved around to get a better view and found James and Heidi being guarded by Callan.

"Where are they?" Callan asked.

"They didn't say where they were going," James said.

"We're getting a thought reader, so you might as well tell us."

"Do you know what the Brothers are doing?" Heidi asked. "Have they told you about the worlds they're destroying?"

"Don't even talk to me. I can't believe you've fallen for this nonsense. You're implicated in a murder, Heidi," said Callan.

"It was Rachel who murdered Justin," Heidi said.

"Really? Then where is she? Did she turn into the cat?" Callan shouted.

"She's a red-mister," James said.

"I can't believe you're such a dumbass moron-head," Heidi said.

"Get these two out of here," said Callan.

"You can consider yourself single," Heidi said.

"Let's move," I said. "No, wait."

I watched as Felix dropped down from a chair and walked as though he hadn't a care in the world, towards the portal. Only Heidi seemed to notice as he stepped through it. He sat at my feet and licked his paws.

"Surely that's just showing off," Vince said.

David indicated to Vince to pick up the cat.

Vince took a step back. "Don't look at me. You know those things hate me."

David chuckled, picked up Felix, and we portalled to the vineyard's winery. I opened another portal and connected it to the residence ribbon gate on Full-Earth. James, Heidi, and an officer stepped out. The officer reached for a weapon, but by the time he drew it, he was standing back in the garden of the residence alone.

Heidi hugged me. "Callan is an asshat."

"Thank you. Things had taken an awkward turn," James said, and then to Heidi, "And you're too good for him anyway."

"Where's Damon?" David asked.

"They accused him of killing Justin and took him away immediately."

"I thought they were blaming me," I said.

"They're blaming everyone," James said.

"The next time I go to the Citadel, I am not going to be nearly so quiet." I was aware that my eyes were glowing.

I created another portal, and we walked straight through into Vanessa's study at the house. I looked around the room. I could see Connor was feeling it, too.

"She was alive when we last saw this room," I said.

"I remember, taking the maps off the walls," Connor said.

"Who?" James asked.

"Vanessa, my grandmother," I said.

"She was very brave," Heidi said.

"It must run in the family," James said.

We headed out of the office and found the others moping around. At the sight of me, Orla jumped up. "They're here."

Dad and Sofia came running out of the kitchen.

"No Zoe?" Hannah said.

"Not yet," I said.

"The storms in England make sense now. It didn't take long for them to build up," David said.

"They've been going nonstop and getting worse from the

very day you said that ceremony took place. Almost to the minute, in Glastonbury." Adam said.

"Did it start immediately?" I asked.

"Not everywhere. It's been working its way outwards from that point," Adam said.

"I think we need to speak to Kim."

I opened a portal, and Vince went through. A moment later, he was back with Kim, Kyle, and Eric.

"How's the weather at your end?" I asked.

Kim came straight to me and enveloped me in a hug. "Thank you,"

"How did you stop it?" Kyle asked.

"We found the guy doing it and, well, I'm not sure what we did to him, but it didn't look good from where I was standing," Vince said.

"Was that the Brightling?" Kim asked.

"The Brightling was about a hundred years old on life support with no idea what was going on. She died peacefully," David said.

"When did it stop?" I asked.

"About an hour ago. The wind died down like it just lost momentum," said Kyle.

"But it didn't stop here at all? What about in the last hour? For a few minutes maybe?" I asked Adam.

"Not at all. We could ask Dorothy, she's back at the farm. I couldn't convince her to get out of there."

I made a portal.

"Erm...she's not fond of those things. We'll need to go over there," Adam said.

I let him go ahead first to speak to her.

I watched Felix as he looked around the room and spied Scruffy asleep next to Jason's chair. He walked over, stretched, and then curled up to sleep between Scruffy's front and back legs. Scruffy lifted his head, licked Felix's ear, batted his tail on the floor a couple of times, then went back to sleep.

Looking back at the portal, Adam and Dorothy were jumping up and down waving into the corner of their kitchen where the portal was.

"Oops," I said, stepping through.

I was almost knocked over by the two of them running through the portal as it became visible on their side. An incredibly loud crash of thunder had me following them.

"Couldn't you hear us?" Adam asked.

"Sorry, I had you on mute," I said. Adam just stared at me.

I opened my mouth to ask my question "We were wond–."

"How big can you make these things, these portals?" Dorothy asked.

"I'm not sure. What were you thinking?"

"As big as a barn door? I need to get the animals out of there. The barn and stables have been hit by lightning three times, we've had fires and the barn's falling apart," Dorothy said.

"What's the best place?" I asked, throwing the question to the room.

"Over here would be okay but for the long term, closer to the equator. The storms took a long time to get there," said Kim.

"We part own a farm in Chile," Connor said.

"You do?" I asked.

"*We* do," he corrected me. "You do understand that you're Vanessa's only living heir?"

"Is any of what she owned or part owned in her name?"

"Well, no but–,"

"Then it's not mine." I said.

"At the moment, I'm responsible for everything. It's a bit much. I was hoping you'd help,"

"Dad, can you help us run a company slash guerilla movement?" I asked.

"Sure, sweetheart."

"See? You're a natural," Connor said.

We wrote down the numbers of livestock.

"Take me to Chile," I said.

"Can I come?" Dorothy asked.

I took Connor's hand and opened a portal.

21

We stepped through and were surrounded by farm buildings.

"It's perfect," Dorothy said.

"Señor Connor?" came a voice from inside the barn.

I pulled up my hood, took the sunglasses from my pocket, and rammed them onto my face.

"Mateo, how are you?" Connor turned to shake the man's hand.

I shoved mine into my pockets and looked around the place showing an inappropriate amount of interest in buckets and shovels.

"This is Jenna and Dorothy."

"Hi." I half turned and gave a quick wave.

"I'm pleased to see you well, Connor."

"Have you got space for a few sheep, cows, pigs, goats, horses, ducks, and chickens?"

"You're asking if I have space for another farm inside my farm?"

"These are the numbers." Dorothy handed him the sheet.

"Oh, very small numbers. We can take them. They can go in with our own, once I know they're healthy."

"They're healthy. I have all the documentation." Dorothy said.

"May I ask why they need to be transferred?" Mateo asked.

"Have you seen the weather reports coming out of the UK?" Dorothy asked.

"Yes. It looks very bad. When can you get them to us?" Mateo asked Dorothy.

"In about an hour or so." Connor said.

"An hour?" Mateo's eyebrows shot up.

"Do you also have space for some friends to stay?"

"Your friends are like us?"

"Three are, one isn't." I was pleased Connor didn't try to start explaining Vera.

"How are the additions coming along?" Connor asked.

"They are finished, you want to see?" Mateo led us to a patch of ground out back of the farmhouse with a walled well and a bucket attached to it.

"The steps are here. If you fade and just start walking, you'll go down."

We faded and went through what was apparently, not the ground, and down a set of steps. Mateo switched on a light and a huge room was revealed ahead of us.

"We could house about fifty faders down here comfortably. There's no physical access, you have to fade in. The air comes from ducts about half way down the well. It's possible to fade in through the basement in the house too. We have kitchen and bathroom facilities as you'll know from the plans."

"This is incredible," I said.

Mateo tried to subtly glance at me for about the tenth time in a few seconds.

"I have a skin condition," I said.

"Apologies." He said, looking awkward.

Turning back to Connor, he continued. "So, as you can see, I always have the space for your friends. This is the nature of our deal, my friend. Your other friend can stay up in the house."

"I had no idea you'd completed it already," Connor gazed around. "The timing could be quite fortuitous."

"Are you staying for dinner?" Mateo asked.

"I'm sorry, we need to get this organized." Connor said. He turned to head back up the steps but Mateo touched his shoulder and he turned back.

"Connor, I heard that Vanessa passed. I'm sorry. She was a wonderful woman"

"Thank you. We need to head off."

Back outside, as we walked around to the front of the house, Mateo looked around confused. "Where's your wheels, man?"

"My friend here has an interesting talent."

Connor and Dorothy stood by me, and we portalled back to the vineyard.

"Okay, it's sorted. We need a team," Connor said.

I portalled the men over to the farmhouse.

"Dorothy, can you start packing up whatever you need for now?"

The animals were going crazy. We ran the short distance to the barns. I made a portal across the doorway. I expected this to be difficult, but the animals could see the warm dry day through the door and just headed towards it. When all the animals were across, Dorothy came over with folders full of paperwork confirming their health. They wanted to bring over feed and hay, but Mateo insisted he had enough and could order more. Finally, Adam, Vera, and Matt were there, and Connor and I were just about to leave.

"Jenna?" Dorothy called. "Were you going to ask me something?"

"Oh right. Yes. Did the storm let up at any time today? Even for a minute?"

"It never let up, not once," Dorothy said.

I glanced over to Mateo he was looking at me and crossing himself. I sighed, and we went back to the vineyard.

"I think we've been conned," I said to Connor as we entered the living room.

"Conned how?" he asked.

"I think you're right," David said, sitting up, having already gleaned it from my head.

"I should have been able to see Zoe and the ribbon leading from the portal directly to her, and I think Hive should have been able to sense it. I need to think about this."

I noticed two strangers in the room. They were drinking from mugs and had blankets wrapped around them. They were staring at me, of course.

"This is Mohammed and Meena. I just picked them up from Karachi," David said.

"Hi," I said.

"They don't speak English," David shrugged.

"So, get on your fader loud speaker and find an interpreter," I said.

"I was just waiting for you to open a portal to a ley line and get me a better signal,"

"Oh, righto. On it. What language do they speak?" I asked.

"I've ascertained that it's Urdu."

"Okay, you're good to go,"

"I'm looking for a fader who can translate between English and Urdu for me," David sent. I heard it in my mind, as did everyone else.

"I stood there for a couple of minutes with the portal open and tried to ignore the scrutiny of the couple,"

"Okay, I'm done. I've found Safira, a nursing assistant in Chicago willing to help,"

We went to Safira who was in a medical supplies room inside a hospital.

"How did you?" she broke off staring at me.

"I know, I look weird. Sorry."

"I thought you'd need time to get here. I don't get off work for another four hours,"

Connor was poking his nose into boxes on the shelves.

"Can you give us ten minutes now?" David asked.

"I guess–."

David took her hand and walked through the portal.

"It's really useful knowing where all this medical equipment is," Connor said.

"I know, that's what I was thinking,"

We stepped across to the living room.

"Hey, Beautiful. Do you want a coffee and bagel?" Connor asked.

"Yes please," I smiled. Connor kissed me and headed for the kitchen.

"I'm going to the office" I said to David. "Let me know if you need help getting her back to work. Make sure she knows the danger she's in, working in a public place like that," I said as I opened the office door.

Dad looked up from behind a mountain of paperwork. "Can I change my mind?" he asked.

"What is all this?" I asked.

"Well it's not everything," said Sofia working on another pile at the table in the corner. "David was transporting the files to us when he got called away onto another job."

"Yes, I just met them," I said.

"Did he get his translator?" Dad asked.

"She's in there with them now,"

"Your father nearly jumped out of his skin when he heard David speak in his head. It was funny," said Sofia.

"You won't believe the properties Vanessa bought. All over the world, it's incredible," Dad said.

"Are they all farms?"

"There are apartments too, here and there. But mostly, it's farms, small airstrips, anything with a good reason to be out of the way. A few ships too."

"That's fantastic. Is there any way to find out where the ships are?" I asked.

"I'll let you know," he said.

"*Portal please. You can do it from there,*" came David's voice.

I created a portal while I spoke to Dad.

"Going somewhere?" Dad asked.

"No. Jenna-power for David."

"*Thank you. Safira's back in the hospital and the siblings have gone to their aunt's in Lahore,*" David sent.

I closed the portal

DAVID CAME into Vanessa's office as I sat there staring at the wall, thinking.

"Sorry, did you want the office?" I asked.

"I'm worried about Damon. Can you make a connection to the ribbon? I want to look for him," David said.

"Where?" I asked.

"Anywhere. I just want to look."

I made a portal, and David emitted his red mist and listened through it. I stared at the Citadel, seeking the Five. There was nothing.

"I've got him," David said.

"Where?" I asked, looking into the portal as though I might see him through a window in the Citadel.

"Los Angeles Police Department Headquarters." David had been listening much farther than I had realized.

David took my hand, and as he listened in, he guided me to where they were. I centered the portal, and we watched as Damon was being interviewed by Callan.

"You've been a fool, Damon, you know that, don't you," said Callan. "I'm not judging you. We were all taken in by them. We were fooled into helping them fight their war which was none of our business. We were fooled into helping the Brokens."

"Divine Light, take me unto thy place of heavenly light as thou took my brother after he was cruelly struck down by Rachel—" Damon started.

"He wasn't struck down by Rachel, one of the Divine Five. His throat was cut by Jenna the off-world freak. She's probably killed Heidi by now. They took her earlier today, and James." Callan was red-faced now, shouting in Damon's face.

Damon turned away from the spittle flying from Callan's mouth. Callan was swinging an electro-baton around menacingly.

"I heard his voice," Heidi said from the doorway. "That's not him. There's something wrong." She had tears in her eyes.

"Let's ask him," I said, preparing to portal across into the room.

"Wait. You don't understand. I'm not saying that's not

like him. I'm saying that's not him. That's someone else." She was shaking. "I can feel it from here."

"Are you sure?" I asked.

Heidi marched into the room and touched the portal. Callan looked immediately up, straight into the portal, as though he could see right through to us which he shouldn't have been able to do.

Heidi lurched back in shock.

Callan smiled an ugly smile, which seemed out of character with his face. He swung the metal baton, and smashed it into the side of Damon's head. Damon flew out of the chair he was chained to and fell to the floor, bringing the chair down with him.

Callan, or whatever looked like Callan, twisted the end of the electro-baton so that it hummed loudly, and plunged it down. I disabled it before it was able to electrocute Damon.

Hive blew out of every pore in my body and we flew through the portal, blasting Callan with energy balls which, somehow, he deflected with a flick of his wrist.

We grabbed Callan around the throat and screamed in our voices, "Reveal yourself."

Callan's face cracked and pieces of it fell away as though from a plaster mask. When the semblance of Callan had fallen away, it revealed burned-out eyes staring back. He faded away, and our arm was left holding nothing. David and Heidi were there. Heidi picked up some items from the floor and pocketed them. I stroked my finger through the chain holding Damon to the chair, portalling a section of it to somewhere. We lifted the unconscious Damon back through the portal and lay him down on the couch at the house. Hive healed him as the others looked on silently.

"Will he be all right now?" Hannah asked.

"We have healed what we can. Time must heal the rest," we said.

We sat beside him all night. In the morning, Orla came into the room. She could tell who was behind my eyes.

"Jenna's exhausted. You need to let her rest."

We nodded and stood to leave the room but turned at the door and said, "He should not have been able to fade away from us like that."

We went to our room, but there was one more thing we needed to do before we could sleep.

We portalled into the hallway outside the labs at Hilltop. There were anti-fading posts every few feet along the hallway. As we walked, unseen, through the building, we melted their circuits. The little blue lights remained on, but they would never trap a fader.

We walked down to the next levels, happily frying circuits as we went. Stopping at the beds of the unconscious, pregnant girls, our anger flared but settled. They would soon be free.

We opened the portal and stepped through to the mountain. This took longer. We found the pregnant ones on the deepest level, several levels down from where we had been with Orla. We returned to the house and slept.

I woke the next day to find Damon sitting by my bed.

His head looked okay, but there was blood on his robe and in his hair.

"How are you?" I asked.

"Physically well," he said.

"You know that Callan wouldn't have done that, don't you," I said.

"I know. David said it was a man with no eyes. Was it Benedict?"

"Yes, but I don't think that's all he was. I don't believe he was fully revealed to us. There was something else, behind that face."

"He faded from my grasp. He should not have been able to do that," said Hive.

"What would have been able to fade like that?" I asked.

"One like us," said Hive.

That didn't feel like good news at all.

"I think you need to clean up," I said to Damon.

"I'm going to do that now," he said, indicating a pile of clothes at his feet.

"I'll see you back downstairs," I said.

As I descended the stairs, the familiar smell of a Sofia-made breakfast almost brought tears to my eyes.

Connor came to me and put his arms around me. He kissed my temple. I leaned into him and inhaled.

"You smell lovely," I said.

"I found a girl's shower gel in the bathroom. I'm thinking of swapping brand."

"You found my shower gel, you cheeky bugger. You're as bad as Zozo," Orla said, brandishing an almost empty bottle. "Look, it's nearly gone."

"I'll buy you another one, sweetheart," Jason said.

"But it's not from this Earth." Orla marched into the kitchen and dropped onto a stool at the breakfast bar.

I walked into the kitchen. It had been a lifetime since I had been in this room. I went to the storeroom cupboard and put my hand on it.

"That's where you first faded. Anna told me," Heidi said. "You were chastising bullies even then."

"That wasn't long before I met you," I said.

I looked at her red-rimmed eyes. She sat at the dining table with some objects on it in front of her.

"I said it wasn't him. I was wrong," she said. "Everything here was his. This is what he took out of his pockets every night before bed. His communicator, his security bracelet controller, and this. A little thing from your world. The only artefact he ever owned. I bought it for him."

I picked it up. It was a guitar pick with Led Zeppelin printed on it.

"I'm sorry, Heidi." I wept at the loss of Callan. I'd convinced myself that Callan might still be alive somewhere.

"At least I know he never became horrible at the end. It's what that monster did to him," she said.

"Benedict did it thinking we would believe it was Callan. But he didn't realize that you would see right through it," I said.

"He used Callan to make us weak. But instead, he'll make us stronger." Heidi put the pick into her pocket.

"May I join you?" Damon asked, in ripped jeans and a Jack Daniels t-shirt, and smelling suspiciously of Orla's shower gel.

"Of course. You look different," I said.

He did. He was actually pretty fit. I glanced at Orla with a speculative expression.

"You'll be going to hell for having those thoughts about a man of the cloth, Mrs.," said Orla.

Dad put breakfast plates down onto the table and across the breakfast bar. He walked to the door and shouted, "Come and get it."

The thunder of feet turned out to be Ava and Milly. When Milly saw Damon, she dived onto his lap and hugged him. She missed Justin, and so did he. No one told her to leave him alone.

"So, what's the plan?" Sofia asked.

"Food. Then let's all head into the family room for a meeting. I'd like everyone there," I said.

After breakfast, we headed into the large room and were joined by the Broken-Earthers and the team from Chile. I winked at Milly, and she wandered through the room, sniffing at people. She even got down onto her knees and sniffed at Felix. Then sneezed. Damon's gaze followed her. He smiled, then his lip trembled before he gripped his jaws together and looked away. David sat quietly in the corner, and Heidi engaged everyone present in conversation.

"Firstly, Milly, Heidi, David. Is there anyone here who doesn't seem to be who they are supposed to be? Anyone hiding abilities or secrets we need to know? Anyone hiding malicious intent?"

The three of them confirmed that everyone present was who they were supposed to be.

"Everyone?" Adam asked, glancing at Vera. "Does she have any secrets? I mean, more secrets?"

"None that you need to know about," Heidi said.

"Then let's get started. Last night I portalled into Hilltop and the mountain. I deactivated all their anti-fading posts so we can go and get those pregnant girls out."

"Alone?" Dad and Connor said together.

"No," said Hive.

"I have a suggestion about the pregnant ladies," James said. "If the mothers don't wake up, the babies should be brought up on Broken-Earth."

"We're calling it Stolen Earth now," said Eric. "Our world has been all but stolen from us."

"Does anyone know how long it will take to be safe again?" Hannah asked.

"If we can regain Zoe, the process will be much faster," said Hive.

"So. Our to-do list is, get Zozo back, close the portal, rescue the mothers, kick Benedict's ass, kick Tomowski's ass." Orla counted the list off on her fingers.

"About Benedict. We might have a problem," I said.

Everyone looked at me.

"We believe he is of the Divine Light," said Hive.

"And that means what?" Dad asked.

"In the days before, different factions fought over the lands of the Earth. It was decreed that never again shall the Divine fight in this realm. He cannot harm me, and I cannot harm him."

"What does that mean?" Sean asked.

"We just lost the ace up our sleeve." Dad said.

"What can kill him?" Vera asked.

"The Divine Light cannot be killed. It can be forced out," Hive said.

"Can we take a bagful of those cubes, ram them down his gullet and get Jenna to blow them up?" Orla asked.

"He will be keeping Zoe and other humans quite close to ensure his safety. If he senses a threat he will leave and take Zoe with him. We are of the Divine Light. We sense it near to us. This is why he appeared to be looking towards Jenna during the ceremony," Hive said.

"So, if he senses that we're a big enough threat, he'll take her and run. We have to find a way to attack him that he won't see coming," I said.

"We're royally screwed," Heidi said.

"Not necessarily," Vera mused.

We all looked at her.

"We have access to the biggest supply of fire power on this Earth."

"Perhaps you haven't been paying attention. But we're not exactly besties with your pals in the agency," Adam said.

"True. But I think we can use the agency's hatred of faders against them. You've seen what they do to a few faders. How would Major Tomowski react if he believed a whole planet *full* of faders were about to invade? The fact that the weather here has suddenly and without apparent cause, become apocalyptic, might help to convince him we're under attack from another Earth. Which we are." Vera sat still. She'd said her piece. She stared at me.

I looked at Vera. I tilted my head the way Hive did. It was becoming a habit.

"I like you a lot more now," I said.

Turning to the others, I said. Zoe's safe, we know that, but those girls in the base aren't. First thing's first. We need to get those pregnant women out of the agency bases."

22

We sat around the old wooden dining table. I looked at everyone surrounding me, afraid to think I was about to put them in danger. The board, once again held maps of ley lines.

"Why are the maps out again? We don't need direct access to the ley lines, we've got Jenna and Hive," Hannah said.

"Not if I die," I explained.

"You can't do that, Jenna. Zoe's depending on you," Hannah said.

"It's necessary Contingency planning," I said.

I pointed to little flags in the map. "These are the two bases where the girls are being held, they are familiar to most of us but not all. The closest ley lines are highlighted on these maps, I want you to become familiar with them. From what I saw on my walk around the mountain, it looks like we have a lot of girls to rescue and not much time to do it. We only have one Vince so we can't do both together if we want to avoid being visible to trackers. Remember, the trackers are under threat of death, they won't all stay quiet if they see us," I said.

"Hi everyone, this is Safira, I thought it might be wise to get some medical advice," David said, entering the room.

"Thanks for helping out with Mohammed and Meena," I said. "Has David explained the situation?"

"I can hardly believe it," Safira said.

Dad looked at the numbers listed. "Are these numbers of women?"

"Yes," I said. "We have two hundred and thirty-eight girls over two bases. Two hundred and twenty-four in Colorado, and fourteen in Oxfordshire."

"Do we hit the biggest one first to maximize the number of rescues?" Hannah asked.

"I think we should do the smaller site first. In and out fast so we have more people freed up to work together on the larger numbers in Colorado," Jason said.

"I think you're right, Jason. We'll do Colorado last," I said.

"Where are we going to put them all?" Sofia asked.

"We're gonna need a bigger boat," Orla quoted.

"Funny you should say that," I said. "We're trying to locate a ship Vanessa owned which should be off the coast of Greece, somewhere. Otherwise we might be able to get up to one hundred at Chile and the rest in the wine warehouse and around the house."

"Mateo said he had enough space for fifty," said Connor.

"He said fifty comfortably. They don't need to be comfortable, they just need to be safe," I said. He nodded.

"Excuse me," Safira said.

"Yes, Safira?" I asked.

"I'm sorry to interrupt, but where possible, could you

please get any paperwork, laptops, charts. Everything you can find?" Safira asked.

"What specifically should we be looking for?" Orla asked.

"Firstly, we need to be aware of any medical requirements, gestational diabetes, complications like that. Then going forward, you should know who the fathers are. Do some babies have the same father? If so, they should be kept in a family unit or separated completely, to avoid future inbreeding."

I stared at her. We all stared at her.

"I would never have thought of such a thing," Orla said.

"Okay, teams. Each team needs someone who can make portals, and someone who's been to the site," I said.

"We'll start with Hilltop but they might be expecting us, so I'd like to use Matt to get us to that storage room. He won't have to cross over," I said to Adam.

"That's fine. He'd like to help," Adam said.

"Sarah can you stay on Broken-Earth and David here, in case something happens to me, you two can connect with Vince.

"Operation One. Hilltop. Matt on this side, making the connection for me. Adam and Jason. Sofia, we'll need someone at the house to coordinate the incoming patients," I said.

"What about me? I'm familiar with Hilltop too," Orla said.

"You're also familiar with Colorado. If we have a problem at Hilltop, we can't have all our best people in one place," I said.

Orla nodded.

"Then, assuming we all make it back okay, the same team plus a whole bunch more. There are a lot of sleeping ladies who don't even know they're relying on us. Jodi, can you wait down at the wine warehouse with a couple of helpers to coordinate incoming down there. Dorothy, the same at the bunker in Chile?" I asked.

The ladies nodded.

"Connor, you're going to be busy. Assume they've all got poisoned or explosive inhibitors. You'll have a few minutes to get around the twelve from Hilltop before we start on the mountain,"

"Okay," said Connor.

"Vince. You know your role. Just keep us hidden for as long as you can."

"I'd like to help. I can't just sit around crying. My own emotions are getting on my nerves," said Heidi.

"As would I. I guess I need to earn my keep while I'm here," James said.

"We need portable gates, nanite pens and cubes,"

"The gates might not work if your tags have been barred on the system. If you swiped your tag on Full-Earth, you'd probably get a dozen officers around you." James said.

"You won't have to swipe or travel through it. Just use it so David can make contact and bring you back if there's a problem," I said.

"I'll contact Yolanda, she can help with that. David can you help me make contact?" James said.

"Sure, we can do that now," David said.

David and James left the room.

"What can I do?" Damon asked.

"You'll have your work cut out for you, praying your butt off that we all make it home," Orla said.

"I could do that. But I'm ex-marine corps. I'm sure there are other ways I could help," Damon said.

'Then hop onboard, my friend," I said.

"You kept that quiet," Dad said to Damon.

"Why do you think we were Zoe's security detail?"

"I'll admit I never thought about it," Dad said.

I FOUND James on the balcony looking out at the lush vines.

"One of the workers is emitting," he said.

I walked to a button on the wall and pressed it three times. The loud hoots went off. The workers in my eyeline, stopped work and looked at themselves and each other. The emitting man picked up his tools and ran towards the winery.

"I can't believe you have to live like this," James said.

"We're the lucky ones," I answered. "What are you going to do? You know you're welcome to stay here, don't you?"

"I'll have to face the music. Is that correct? Heidi's been teaching me the Half-Earth language."

"I recommend not paying too much attention to that. She's getting it from Orla, and well, you know Orla."

"I fecking do," James said with a smile.

"How did it go with Yolanda?"

"I was just coming to tell you. I've spoken with her. She's managed to get hold of four portable gates and would have taken them with the latest delivery of pens and cubes over to Heidi's apartment but she hasn't heard anything more about the investigation. It just seems to have died down. She's suspicious and concerned that she might be being followed so hasn't taken them herself. She gave them to someone else. They should have dropped the equipment at Heidi's place by now,"

"If anywhere is being watched, surely Heidi's apartment...,"

"It should be alright. Someone invisible will be doing it," said James.

I assumed he knew someone with the same ability as Vince.

"Great, I'll get them. If Heidi's ready," I said.

WE PORTALLED across to the apartment. The first thing I saw was Maggie, dressed as a cleaner. I shook my head, 'someone invisible,' an inc. She was standing by the apartment door with her back to it. She looked upset.

"Maggie, are you alright?" I looked around thinking someone might be here.

"I know I was only supposed to leave them here, but I didn't know what to do,"

"You're alarmed. What's wrong?" Heidi asked.

Maggie pointed towards the bedroom. Heidi walked that way.

In that moment, Hive came forward and we were 'we' again.

"Stop," we said.

Heidi froze.

"You are not armed," we said.

We moved towards the room, passing Heidi, and entering to find Callan lying in bed. His face was grey, wrinkled and dry. It was like his life force had withered.

"Callan!" Heidi shrieked from behind me. She ran to him. "He's still alive. I feel him."

"Is it him you feel?" we asked.

She sat back, her face puzzled. "And another."

We leaned over Callan and put our hand on his head.

"Begone," we cried. A bright light shot from our hand and flooded Callan.

"Benedict will know we have done this. We must move him now," we said.

"Heidi, get what you need. If he's been relying on Callan for energy, this might have knocked him back a little. But he could still appear at any moment," I said.

"I thought he was dead," Maggie said.

I rushed to Maggie. "Sorry," I pushed her through a portal to the vineyard.

"*David, I need you and one of the guys,*" I sent.

Heidi stuffed various items of clothing into a bag.

David appeared with Jason and they got Callan through, I moved a portal over the equipment, putting it on the other side.

"What about this suitcase?" I asked, pointing at a case by the door.

Heidi looked at it. "It's not mine," she said.

We stared at each other and it. Unsure of what that meant.

"*Bring it,*" David sent.

I threw it through.

"Okay. Ready?" I asked Heidi.

"One second," Heidi said, grabbing a book from the shelf, adding it to the two photos in her hands.

I started to feel like we were being watched. Heidi froze for a half second. I could see she felt it too. We headed through the portal and I closed it behind us.

"Was that–?" Heidi started to ask.

"Yes," Hive said.

Callan was laid on the sofa. He appeared not to have moved for several days.

David and Safira appeared with saline in drip bags. Safira started sorting out the equipment.

"It's okay, we don't need that part," said Heidi indicating

the needle. She drew the solution from one of the bags, up into the pen and held it against Callan's arm.

"It's shouldn't go in too quickly," Safira said.

"It's okay. The nanites will regulate the distribution of the saline," Heidi said.

"The–?" Safira managed.

Heidi held Callan's hand. "I'm sorry. I'm so sorry I left you there. I thought you'd died. I thought it was you," Heidi was sobbing.

"Benedict must have gone to your home, made a psychic connection with Callan and left him there to die," Hive said.

"Safira, can you stay?" I asked.

"Am I needed?" Safira asked, turning the nanite pen over in her hand.

"You are most certainly needed," I said.

Safira took out her phone and made a call. "Hi. It's Saffi. I'm calling in sick. I have the flu. Yes, I was. I felt ill and just came home. Thank you."

She returned the phone to her pocket. "Okay, I'm all yours."

"Let's move him upstairs," Connor said.

"Where are you set up for the patients?" Safira asked.

"We've cleared the wine warehouse and the gym," I said.

"Is all the machinery in place and confirmed operational?"

We all looked at each other.

"Machinery?" I asked.

"You've got to be kidding me," Safira sighed. "Okay, get him upstairs. We need to talk."

The guys lifted Callan and headed upstairs with him.

I looked out in the entrance hall at the suitcase.

"So, whose is this then?" I asked.

"That's mine," Maggie said. "I was going to ask if I could

come to your world. I'll make myself useful. I can help out around the place–,"

"Well, you're already here but you're welcome as far as I'm concerned. If you change your mind, you can go home. While you're here, your help would be appreciated. You don't need to be a fader to be a valued member of this team. Don't forget, faders are hunted here. We need all the help we can get. Although if you want to be a fader, I think we can help with that too," I said.

"I can stay? That's great. I thought you'd say no," she said.

"I'm not the boss of where you live. Go and speak to Sofia. She's in the office, over there. She'll have a better idea of where we need help."

Maggie hurried off to the office.

"If these girls have been kept in a drug induced coma for long enough, they'll probably be brain-dead. Taking them off the ventilators will kill them. They can be kept off for a couple of minutes maybe, but no more. How mobile are the ones they're using, do you know?" Safira asked.

Dad came out of the office and leaned against the wall, listening to our conversation.

"I saw the ventilators at the bases, but I don't remember them so clearly. Just a second," I said, closing my eyes. "*Hive, can you help with this?*" I asked.

The memory came to me of walking, faded, through the mountain, melting the wiring on the anti-fading posts. Destroying all but the little blue indicator lights. Seeing the girls attached to machines. Flitting my gaze across the machinery. The picture froze on one of the machines.

"PX01-D. That was the model number on the machines in Colorado. I don't see a manufacturer name." I opened my eyes.

"No, that's on the side. It's just a logo of a bird on the front," Safira said.

"Yes, that's right," I said

"That's the same machine we use at the hospital. You have a remarkable memory," Safira said.

"I had help," I admitted.

"Unfortunately, those machines are too unwieldy to move in an operation requiring speed. How about the British ones?" she asked.

I closed my eyes again and read out the name of the machines at Hilltop.

"I don't recognize that one. I'll check online we need to find some manufacturer locations. You're not going to be getting those girls right now, you know that, right? You're just not ready."

"I'm getting the message. We're going to have to wait until night to get the ventilators,"

"I don't think you'll need to wait at all," said Dad.

"We won't?" I asked.

"They're probably made in China. It'll be the middle of the night over there. The best time for acts of grand larceny as I understand," he said.

Connor joined us. "He's comfortable, still out. Heidi's with him. What's happening here?"

"We're planning a heist," Dad said. He was looking more excited than I felt was appropriate for a science teacher.

We went into the office.

"Was everything okay with Maggie?" I asked Sofia.

"Yes, she's taken her case upstairs. She's taking Heidi's room. Heidi's going in with Callan," Sofia said.

"We need to find a manufacturer or supplier of portable ventilation machines. Preferably in China so we can go now," Dad said.

Sofia clicked at the keyboard. Here's one in Beijing. She pasted the address into a maps app and in moments we were looking at the factory.

"That's a big place. How will we find the right area of the factory?"

Connor looked over my shoulder. "Look at the direction the vehicles are facing. It's a one-way system around the main building and the lorries are parked over on that side. Can you go to street-view here?" He asked, pointing at the screen.

Sofia panned around to see a wire fence and a loading dock.

"Goods Outwards. Great job Connor," Dad said.

"I *am* the COT of this company," Connor said.

Dad thought for a moment. "Chief Operating Thief?"

"You got it! I'll gear up and meet you in five," Connor left the room.

Sofia printed some sheets from the website and handed them to me.

"This is the product name in English and in Mandarin and here's the product's SKU, its own code number and a bar code, I don't know what good that will do you."

"Who do you want with you?" Dad asked.

I thought about it, stood in the entrance hall and shouted "I'm going to China to steal some stuff. The first five who are front and center are in."

Feet came thundering from the kitchen and down the stairs. Sean, Aiden, Chester, Orla and Jason were in front of me in seconds. Leroy stopped three steps from the bottom looking at the others and slumped his shoulders.

"Come on big man, you're in," I said.

I opened a portal and we stepped through. Factory sounds came from the building.

"I thought they'd, you know, be in bed," Orla said.

"I'll admit I was kind of hoping for that too. Okay everyone, it sounds like this place goes throughout the night so we'll just do our best to avoid the employees if we can," I said

Faded, we entered the building through the loading dock. We found one little, elderly man with a clipboard standing next to a printer. We watched as the printer spilled out some sheets which he tore off and scanned. He clicked a couple of keys on the hand scanner, then sat down, took out a newspaper and read.

"How do you want to proceed?" Jason asked.

"I could put my hand around his heart and get him to lead us to the ventilators. "Connor said.

"Or we could just surround him and intimidate him," Chester suggested.

"Hands-up who wants to duff up the hundred-year-old man," Orla said.

"Who probably doesn't even speak English," Sean added.

As we watched, a beep sounded and the roller doors to our right began to rise.

The man winced as he rose from his chair with his hand on his hip. He walked into the center of the floor and stood as a fork lift truck brought in a pallet of boxes.

He watched calmly as the truck came towards him.

"Jeez," Aiden said.

"I can't look," Orla said.

Leroy began jogging towards the old man but stopped as the truck halted an inch from his nose. The old man chuckled.

Leroy walked around the truck. "Hey, ain't nobody driving this thing."

We walked out to watch more closely. The fork-lift truck had stopped at a line marked on the floor. The man scanned one of the boxes, taped the paperwork to them and scanned it again. The truck placed the pallet down and retreated back through the doors.

"I like Connor's suggestion, but leave his heart alone. Give his bladder a little poke," I said.

The man checked the printer, nothing else had printed out. He returned to his seat. I watched as the faded Connor crouched down beside him. A nanite pen appeared, and Connor tapped him on neck. His hand came up and he looked around but there was nothing to see. I expected him to slump down but he didn't. A moment later, he stood and headed, in an unexpectedly spritely fashion, out of the room.

We rushed across. Connor had taken out the sheets and found the one with the bar code. He picked up the scanner and waved it across the barcode. The screen was showing some Chinese symbols, a flashing cursor on the screen followed by "X fifty slash two thousand.

"What do you think?" Connor asked.

"Type five, zero," Leroy said.

"Are you sure?" Connor asked.

"It's saying there's two thousand machines in stock and they're packed in groups of fifty. We want five packs of fifty. Hey don't look at me like that, I used to work in a warehouse, okay?"

"That's more than we need though," I said.

"If we ask for a part of a pack, it's gonna need human intervention. I think we should keep humans out of this," Leroy said.

"Good call," Connor replied.

We heard a door swing.

Connor typed and pressed the green arrow key. It flashed more symbols and went blank.

"Did it work?" Chester asked.

"No idea. I guess we'll know in about five minutes or so. Let's wait on the other side of the shutters," I said.

"What did you do to him?" Jason asked.

"I gave him something for the arthritis," Connor said.

"And that's why I love you," I said.

"I'll keep an eye on the old dude," Chester said.

We faded again and the rest of us headed through the shutters as the old man walked back to his seat.

Five minutes later we watched as a fork-lift truck drove towards the shutters. A few minutes later it was parked in the wine warehouse in California. We unloaded the pallets and portalled the trucks back to the warehouse. I sent one hundred ventilators to Chile.

"What else do we need?" I asked Safira.

"Do you have generators?" she asked.

I looked at Connor. "I think so but I don't know how many. I'll asked one of the guys,"

Connor looked around. "Cheng?" he called.

A man walked over.

"Dude," Chester interrupted before Connor could speak. "Are you Chinese?"

"Yeah," said Cheng.

"And do you speak Chinese?" Chester asked.

"Mandarin, sure. My lao lao, grandma, taught me" Cheng said.

Chester stared at Connor.

"I don't know what to tell you man. I forgot," Connor shrugged.

I punched his arm.

"Do we have generators here?" Connor asked.

"Yeah. There's two in the little annex in back of this building and one in the shed in back of the house,"

"Thanks man," Connor said.

"Power strips and, wait, I'll give you a list," Safira went into the little office and started scribbling.

23

"Are you all set up?" Dad asked as we stood in the house. I nodded.

Matt held my hand and guided my portal to the right place. The small storage room at Hilltop looked like it might hold five of us, unfaded, at a squeeze. Damon, Vince, Adam and Jason came through with me. We faded through the side wall, straight into a room with sleeping, pregnant girls and an agent with a remote in one hand and an automatic weapon slung about his body.

"Would you like me to–?" Damon began.

"No. He's got a remote. He could probably kill all of them at once. I can do it from here. I just need to move the cameras," I said.

I watched the cameras on the walls move. When they were sufficiently altered, I stood behind him and materialized. I created a portal and yanked him in.

"What the–?" and he was gone.

Connor went straight to the girls and removed their inhibitors. Jason detached the breathing tubes from the machines and I severed any other wires and tubes. We freed them one at a time, passing them through to the teams waiting for them in the gym at the vineyard. Adam collected the charts for each girl and sent it through with her. We went around the room, moving the cameras as we went.

"Let's check next door," I said.

We faded through the walls to see what was on the other side of the storage room and found eight children, trackers, being kept in cages and an agent guarding them.

We moved around the room remaining in contact with Vince. We couldn't risk the kids seeing us and starting a commotion while the agent had the remote. Connor took inhibitors out of them. One by one, they winced or yelped.

"Keep it down," the agent said. Connor took the inhibitors, put his fist in the guard's stomach and let go of the little capsules. I appeared before him.

"Move an inch and I'll kill the lot of them," he said, holding up the remote.

"I don't think you will," I walked towards him and he fumbled with his rifle while pressing the remote. His eyes flew open as he gripped his stomach and dropped to the floor with blood pouring out of his mouth.

The children started to rattle the cages.

"David?" I sent.

"I'm here,"

"I'm sending eight tracker kids through to the house, can you let my dad know?"

"Will do. This seems to be taking longer than expected,"

"Just a few more minutes,"

"Silence," said Hive. The children looked at me, terrified.

"Can you help me out, it looks like they're all going to start screaming,"

I heard *"I'm David. I'm the one who told you trackers were faders. This is a break out. If you don't trust us, by all means stay.*

Please keep the noise down, my friends are trying not to get killed rescuing you."

"Did you get your translator?" A young Asian boy asked

"I did. Thank you." David sent.

I portalled the children to the house.

WE CHECKED out the other floor but there were no more faders. From what David had told me, Dr. Narayan had been thinking there were more, but it appeared that now they were gone. I didn't want to think what had happened to them, but I couldn't help remembering what happened to Dad's research mice when they thought he was dead. We portalled back.

"Where's Safira?" I asked.

"She's downstairs with the girls. They're all unconscious but alive, in the gym on yoga mats. Matt looked at them as they came through, hoping to see his sister but he doesn't recognize any of them. Your dad and Orla are with the kids in the kitchen. A couple of the older ones recognize Orla," said Hannah.

When I entered the gym, I saw the girls were all on the portable ventilators. Safira was looking at the charts. "Most of these girls are brain-dead. This is obscene. We need a doctor here,"

I could only think of one. I opened a portal to find her sitting in her office alone.

I stepped over and pushed her chair straight over. Dr. Hade stared at me in shock as her chair rolled across the wooden gym floor and bumped into a yoga mat."

"What–?" Dr. Hade started.

"Safira, update the doctor. Her technology might be able

to help them," I said on my way up the stairs. I turned to see Dr. Hade taking in the girls around her.

"Okay everyone, ten minutes and we head out," I shouted.

A large group of us met in the hallway, faded and headed out through the portal, leaving Dad, Sofia and a few of the others at the house, warehouse and at the bunker in Chile. We walked straight into the bottom level of the mountain where they were keeping the girls. This time there were half a dozen staff members with remotes hanging around their necks, and twenty anti fade posts around the room, which I knew didn't work.

"Oh Jeez. Will there be these many agents in every ward?" Connor asked.

"Maybe not. It looks like they're doing rounds," an unexpected voice said.

"Safira? What are you doing here?"

"We need those beds. Do you know how to operate them?" she asked.

"Good point. But you'll show the others how to do it and you'll be going back with the beds,"

A young woman glanced up. I noticed a metal collar on her neck and her eyes bulged. Her face went placid and she turned away.

"*Was that you?*" I asked David.

"*Yes. The man in front of her has the control for her collar. He likes to press it to see if she wets herself.*"

"*What a charmer,*" I sent.

I slowly moved all the cameras but one of the staff members saw one move and looked around the walls at the rest of them. He opened his mouth to say something. I portalled him away. No one noticed.

I reached out to the agents in the room. I felt the electrical impulses in their bodies and I paralyzed them as they stood.

"Connor, remove the inhibitors. Damon, get the remotes. Safira, show us how to make these beds roll," Connor and Damon moved, and the rest of us stood around a bed while Safira indicated the mechanism for mobilizing the beds.

Loud thuds filled the air and I looked up in time to see Damon snapping the necks of the last two agents. I'd never seen anyone move that fast.

"Damon, what are you doing?" I asked.

"I'm sorry. I don't like seeing them float off into nothing. It upsets me," Damon said.

I nodded. It upset me too.

"Some of the girls don't have inhibitors," Connor said.

"They're the brain-dead ones," the tracker said.

We moved the first bed. It glided silently and smoothly. I created a portal to the bunker in Chile and Sean pushed the first bed through. Leroy followed up and the others followed quickly. I sent the tracker through after Connor faded her to remove the metal collar.

"I told you to go," I said to Safira who was unplugging equipment,"

"These are vital signs machines. We need at least five of them," Safira said before wheeling two of the machines through the portal to Chile.

"I've got to admit. I'm getting a bit of a girl crush on her. She's the absolute business," said Orla rolling a bed past me.

The door swung open and a man came through and froze, staring at us. I flicked an energy ball at him. he flew into the wall, and slid down to the floor.

I looked at my watch as the team assembled for the next ward.

"Fifty girls in nearly half an hour. This is taking too long,"

"Move all the beds down to the other end of the bunker, we need to speed this up," I shouted through the portal.

We walked to the door. The next ward was on the other side of it. It was empty of staff. I stopped and looked down at the remote around the unconscious man's neck. I removed it and threw it into the in-between.

"Connor," I started.

"I know, inhibitors," he said.

"No. We're going to try something else. Everyone on breathing tubes, leave the tubes on the beds. Push the beds in a couple of feet away from the walls but leave the machines back by the walls. Unplug three more of those vitals machines and put them in the middle of the floor. Then get to the other end of the room.," I said

I stood at one end of the room. I created my portal and stretched it wide, like I did across the barn door. Then I stretched it further. I could see the bunker. Mateo and Dorothy were down the other end frantically attaching breathing hoses.

"Some of you go through and help them," I said.

Orla, Aiden and Damon ran through.

The portal started to wobble and wave in the air. I stopped to get my breath. I was getting a little dizzy.

"*Can you help?*" I asked Hive.

"*The power is within you to accomplish this,*" Hive said.

"*Could you possibly give me directions?*" I asked.

I closed my eyes and remembered the feeling of the power flowing through me when I first accepted it. When I healed Orla.

"Isn't it big enough now?" asked Connor.

I looked to see the portal almost touching the walls. I

pulled it in a few inches. Then I walked the length of the room and the beds just appeared in the bunker behind me as I went.

"Well, that went a lot faster," said Connor.

The door opened into a main hallway with the next ward on the other side.

We faded and moved into the hallway. The anti-fade posts flashed.

"Stop. We appear to have a new edition to the security since I was last here," I said.

"Are we trapped?" Chester asked.

"Have you met my friend Jenna and her friend Hive?"

I looked at one of the posts. I melted the wiring, then I kept melting it. Soon the smell of burning plastic reached the air.

"Hey, Beautiful. Do you have a plan for when the fire alarms go off?" Connor asked.

"Sorry. I was...," I started.

"Showing off?" Orla asked.

"Yeah maybe. Sorry."

I melted the wires on the other posts and we continued, faded, through the door into the next ward.

Three agents in lab coats and one in uniform.

I moved the cameras, froze the men, Damon went into action. The remotes were removed and necks snapped.

Tubes were disconnected from the machines, beds moved from the walls and vitals machines moved to the front of the beds. All, without me saying a word. I opened a portal in the middle of the floor beneath the dead agents, and closed it after they'd drifted off. Damon looked at me with his mouth agape.

"Did you want to keep them?" I asked. He closed his mouth.

"Next time, clean up after yourself. I don't think Sofia would be happy to see them appear on her floor."

"I never thought of that," he said, chagrinned.

I opened a portal to the wine warehouse. I could see the equipment all set up and ready. Dad was pacing and Jodi was sitting next to Dr. Hade who had a nanite pen in one hand and a couple of empty cubes in the other.

"Orla, get those cubes please," I said.

She bolted through the portal.

I need a few guys to move the beds on the other side and help with the tubes.

Damon and Leroy jogged through.

Orla came back with the cubes and I clicked them. Instantly they were dazzling and she returned them to the doctor.

"Oops," I said as the portal wobbled.

I stretched the portal and started to walk.

The last two wards were completed in no time.

When we returned, Connor removed the inhibitors from all of the girls who had them fitted, at both locations.

I sat in Vanessa's study with Vera and Heidi.

"Are you sure you want to do this, Vera? You know how risky this is." I said.

"Absolutely, it's the least I can do,"

"If we could pull this off..." I said.

"I know these people. I know how they think," she said.

"Heidi?" I looked over to her. She nodded once.

"I think I need David, Vince, and Connor. And I think it might be time for a vacation."

.   .   .

"Tomowski," said the voice on the other end of the line.

"Major, you're back at work after your unfortunate accident. Good for you. Sorry for your loss, by the way." I said.

"Would this be Jenna?"

"It might very well be. How are you? Hello? Have I lost you?"

"I'm here."

"Was that you giving the order to have the call traced? If not, I can wait because I'd like your full attention. Tell you what, I'll save you the time. We're in Brazil, visiting the statue of Christ the Redeemer. Not many people here, it's a little windy today. Not as windy as it's going to get. Hang on, wait. I'll send you a picture. Dad, come here. We're taking a picture for Major Tom. Get the postcard in."

We took the photo. Orla snatched the phone before I could send the picture and added a filter to disguise the strange color of my skin. Then we sent it to his mobile. We were all in sunglasses and flipping him the bird, with a postcard in Dad's hand which read *Glad you're not here.*

"Oh, for the love of God. Who drew a penis on the card?" Dad asked.

"Have you lost anything else lately?" I asked. "Like an awful lot of pregnant ladies?"

"I've got plenty more faders and trackers where you can't get a hold of them,"

"Oh, hang on, Major, I might lose you. I'm going through a tunnel. Sorry about that. Let's send the major another photo."

We sent him a picture of us at the Statue of Liberty, with Dad holding the *New York Times.*

"What is the point of this nonsense?" he shouted.

His assistant popped his head in. "I'm sorry, sir, I thought you were alone." And he left.

"What?" Major Tomowski turned and looked around himself. "I am alone, you idiot."

"Helloooo. One more picture, yes?" I said and sent through the picture I'd just taken showing the back of his head, with a Christ The Redeemer postcard stuck to the back of the chair.

I heard him leap up and rip the taped postcard from the back of his chair.

"What the hell is this?" he said.

"Major, I have Vera Richards on line one."

I disconnected and looked over at Vera who nodded.

"Major? Thank God. I'm sorry, sir, I've been off the grid. About as far off the grid as you can get. This is my first chance to contact you. They've gone off to meet up with Jenna Banks somewhere. Look, I'm going to do something, and it's going to freak you out. Try not to shoot me. I've got a lot to tell you."

I portalled Vince and Vera straight into the major's office. I didn't see a tracker but Vince and I remained hidden.

The major shot out of his chair and I prepared to portal Vera if he went for his gun.

"It's this," she said, holding up the nanite tag on her hand. "It's some kind of technology. Sir, I've been on another Earth."

"A what? Have you lost your goddam mind?" His hand rested on the butt of his gun and I kept my eye on it, ready to get us all out of there.

"Apparently, at some point there was some kind of split, and it caused two Earths. The other one is almost exclusively populated by faders. They're attacking our Earth, and the storms in the U.K., are just the beginning," Vera's eyes kept flicking to the bandaged stump where his right hand used to be.

"An accident," he said, glancing at it. "I thought you were dead until Cavendish told me you'd made contact. How did you get away?"

"I'm free to go where I want to over there. They mostly leave me looking after that kid we used to infiltrate them. A team came over here to participate in an operation to retrieve the subjects from project rebuild. I managed to get a single message out about that but then they took me across to this other world. I can't cross the worlds without a fader so I've just been stuck over there with no way to warn you about what's coming. They think I'm an English teacher and of no use in an operation. I asked to come over with the group today. I said I wanted to get some things from my apartment. I'm either out now, or I need to meet up with them in England to cross over to the command center. That's where they're attacking from. There's some kind of portal there, and it's sending some terrible storms."

"So, we just need to nuke England," he said. He didn't appear overly concerned at the thought of it.

"I don't think that will do it. From what I understand, a bomb that size would just collapse the portal doing no damage to the other side. They would just open another one somewhere else. I think a missile would have to be small enough to go through the portal itself. Is that enough? Am I out?"

"You've managed to avoid being seen by Jenna all this time?"

"Actually, no. She's seen me a few times but hasn't looked twice at me."

He stared at her with an eyebrow raised.

"You know how it works. My hair was scraped back, I

wore spectacles, and my head was behind a screen most of the time while we were working together. I've been wearing cosmetics and keeping my hair down since I've been with them. I avoid wearing anything that hints of a white lab coat, and I smile so much she probably thinks I'm simple."

"Let me see that thing."

Vera walked over to the major and held out her hand. It was rock steady.

Damn she's good, thought Jenna.

"I've seen this before. The Banks girl and her friend had them. I thought they were from a nightclub or something. Do you know what technology is behind this? How it operates?"

"Just that it matches my DNA so I can travel instantly."

"What if someone else tries to travel with you?" he asked.

"I haven't seen that. I don't know what happens."

I thought that was an interesting question because he already knew what getting too close to a portal did.

"Lopez, get in here," he shouted.

"Yes, sir. Oh," he said, spotting Vera.

"I need you for something. Stay there."

"How are things with the kid?" he asked Vera.

"How are things? I haven't killed it yet, if that's what you mean. It's clingy, thinks I'm its surrogate mother. It's going to be surprised when I finally shoot it in its whiny face."

"What's this other Earth like? What is their military capability?"

"They are advanced, sir. They can travel across the world in a matter of moments. There are a few humans but they're basically slaves. They have one military for the whole planet. I don't know the size."

I had to admit, the part about human slaves was a nice touch.

"You can't fade. Why aren't you a slave?" He asked.

"As far as they know, I'm a fader who was brutalized by the humans on this Earth. I'm a wounded hero," she said.

The major sat back and bit at the skin on the inside of his cheeks while he thought. "You don't know exactly where this portal is?"

"Not yet, sir."

"I'm sorry, Vera. You're gonna have to go back in."

"I thought you'd want to keep hold of this tech, sir," she said.

"It seems they've all got them. It's a risk but I'm sure we'll get hold of one again, and if I have to give one to R&D to play with, I'd rather it not be attached to one of my best agents. Unless you want to join my new club," he held up his stump.

She didn't react.

"Okay, get ready to head back in," he said.

She didn't dramatically sigh or sag her shoulders. She was an agent. She waited a beat, that was the only outward sign of her disappointment, then she nodded once.

"Where are you meeting them?"

"At a gas station outside Oxford. Sir, if I can speak freely. You don't look all that surprised."

"This happened just before you showed up," he showed her his phone, the picture of the back of his head, and something on the chair. He flipped over the postcard on his desk. She looked at him, probably about to say that she didn't understand. He took the phone, found the first photograph and turned it around so she could see it. She did a double-take. She looked up and around herself as though faders might jump out of nowhere.

"This job's gonna give me a heart attack, sir."

"There's nothing wrong with dying for your country, Richards. Are you supposed to return immediately?" He asked while shuffling around in his drawer. He came out with a cellphone.

"I NEED to pick up some stuff that looks like it came from my apartment. In fact, that's a good idea. I'll get some of my own stuff." She looked at the silver tag on her hand. "This tech is incredible, and it's tech we should have, sir."

"I'm not crazy about sending you back out into the field with it. I'm calling General Cavendish to get him ready to mobilize. The second you know the exact location, I want you to call Cavendish, but magic yourself back here."

"Yes, sir."

"How does it work?" He asked.

"I touch the tag and take a step, then I'm wherever I want to be in the space of a step," she said.

"Lopez, stand directly behind Agent Richards. Step when she steps."

"Yes, sir," said Lopez with a confused look on his face.

To Vera he said "Keep in touch," handing the cellphone to her.

Vera touched the tag and stepped. The agent was too close, and I couldn't close the portal fast enough. The front half of the agent slid onto Vera's carpet, and she jumped out of the way. The rest of us remained faded.

Vera picked up her phone and called the major.

"Tomowski."

"Sir, I have half of Lopez on my carpet, which would appear to answer that question. I assume you have the other half? The cleaners will find a spare key with my downstairs neighbor." She hung up the phone, silently threw a few things into a bag, then straightened the picture of her father on the wall. She touched the nanite tag, clearly assuming the room was under surveillance, and stepped into my portal.

24

We stepped out from the rear of the gas station and were nearly blown over. I portalled us once more, directly inside the fast food restaurant next door. We all stepped out of the portal and sat together at a table. The place was empty and it looked like the electricity was out.

Vera silently lifted the bag onto the table and placed the cellphone inside. She passed it to me, and I threw it into the void.

"You didn't actually want any of that, did you?" I asked.

"No, you did the right thing. The phone will have tracked us to here, then disappeared, which is exactly what I told him would happen," said Vera.

She dropped her head into her hands. I am never setting foot in that apartment again. They can burn everything I own, I don't care. Especially that carpet," Vera shuddered.

A haggard-looking young man came in from the back and looked surprised to find four customers.

"How did you get in?" he asked.

"Through the door," Connor.

I didn't have my sunglasses on me and I waited for him to recoil at my eyes and metallic skin.

"I thought I'd locked it," he said, walking up to us, narrowing his eyes.

"We expected it to be locked and were thankful it wasn't," said Vera.

"What are you driving, a tank?" he asked, looking at me with no reaction whatsoever. In fact, he was staring at Vince way more. I don't think he even noticed me.

"Something like that," I said. The absence of furtive glances or outright horror was confusing the hell out of me.

I examined my hands. They looked normal. I looked up to find the others staring at me with eyebrows raised.

"*Why am I looking normal?*" I asked.

"*I did not wish to disturb the man*" Hive said.

"*Wait. That's an option? You can just turn that off?* I was incredulous.

"I can do cans or bottles, the electricity's off so they'll be a bit warm, but the register is also off, so it's on the house. There's not much in the way of food, I'm afraid. I'm only still here because I got stuck here in the storm. I've been eating the profits for two days. I'll probably get the sack. I guess that doesn't matter since it's, you know, Armageddon and everything. I hope you don't want fuel. It's all switched off out there, too."

"What happened here?" Connor pointed to a poorly boarded-up window.

"A motorbike flew into it. That was when I knew I wasn't going to make it home by myself."

"I guess you didn't want to drive in that," Vince said.

"No, it was my motorbike," the waiter said. "Would you mind moving to a table further away from the window?"

"You might be right. I'm Vince," Vince said, standing and

shaking his hand.

"I'm Andy. The emergency services are supposed to be sending someone to pick me up, but I guess I'm pretty low down on their list. I'm sorry, you look really familiar," he said to Vince.

Suddenly, before our eyes, regular Vince burst into Fabulous Vince

"Tell me Andy, have you ever been to Las Vegas?"

"You're the magician. The Great Shadow," Andy looked stunned. "Let me get you some warm Irn Bru," he said, darting into the back.

"I'm putting my foot down. We're not leaving this kid to die here," Vince said.

"No one suggested...," Connor started.

Vince grabbed a serviette and clicked his fingers. "Someone, pass me a pen,"

We all stared at each other.

"There was one in my bag," Vera said.

Connor dug into his jacket pocket and passed Vince a pen.

Vince spoke as he wrote. "To my very best friend, Andy. May you weather many more storms and emerge triumphant. Your buddy Vince, The Great Shadow," he signed his name with a flourish.

"What do you think? Are kisses too much?" Vince asked.

"Yes," we all said.

Andy returned with four cans of Irn Bru and a box of Cadbury's Heroes.

"Andy that's so kind of you. Please take this as a token of my personal appreciation of your kindness,"

"Hey, thanks," They shook hands again.

"Where do you live?" I asked.

"In the town. I live with my parents."

"We might be able...," I began.

"We'll get you home safely to your family, Andy. Have no fear," Vince interrupted.

"Show me on a map?" I said.

He took out his phone. "Oh, it died yesterday."

"Let me see." I took his phone before he could decline and switched it on while simultaneously adding energy to the battery.

"It's not dead. It looks like you might have switched it off," I said, handing it back.

"What? But! Hey, look, it's at seventy percent." He shook his head and opened the maps. "That's where I live."

"Okay, get together whatever food you might need. Milk, bread, anything. You might find yourself trapped inside for a while," I said.

He disappeared around the corner again.

"Do you know your eyes–?" Connor began.

"Yes, I know. And believe me, we're discussing it right now," I said.

Andy came back out less than a minute later with two bulging bags. One with milk, bread, bacon and eggs sticking out of the top, and the other filled with bottles of water.

"I was worried you might have gone," he said, looking around.

"We wouldn't do that to you Andy, we will never abandon you," Vince said.

"Are you good to go?" I asked.

"Yes. Are you his Personal Assistant?" Andy asked.

"Gosh, I hope to be, one day," I said. "Think of us as Emergency Services for now,"

I reached out and put a hand on his arm.

"Quick question, Andy. What color are your bedroom walls?"

He stared at me.

"I know it's been a couple of days but you can't have forgotten that quickly," I said.

"Erm, blue," he said. That had him thinking about the destination. It was good enough."

"Good luck, Andy, and bear in mind if you tell people about this, they will think you're insane," I said. I created a portal.

"Hey, that's my bedroom," he said. I pushed him through.

"Let's get the hell out of here," I said.

As we stood there, I looked at Vince. "You actually look taller."

"I feel taller," he smiled. He had returned to his normal voice, the flamboyant persona gone.

I patted his arm and smiled. "If you forget those chocolates, you're walking back for them,"

Connor laughed.

I glanced at him, "And the Irn Bru."

BACK AT THE HOUSE, I wandered into the family room to find Dad sitting with Sofia.

"How are all the girls?" I asked.

"I've been having a philosophical debate with Dr. Hade about them," he said.

"It's called an argument, darling," said Sofia.

"But, we're scientists, so it's called a debate," he insisted.

"So, what was it called when she threw that cube at your head?"

"That's called a heated debate," he said.

"What's all this about?" I asked.

"Dr. Hade thinks she can wake them up using the

nanites," Sofia said.

"Even the braindead ones?" I was stunned as Sofia nodded.

"That's fantastic. What's the problem?" I asked.

"Whether it's better for them psychologically to be woken up while pregnant or after they've had the babies?" said Dad.

"Wow!" I dropped down onto the sofa. "That's big."

"Safira and Dr. Hade been through the records and charts. Each child was fathered by a different fader donor,"

"What do you think, Jenna?" Sofia asked.

"I think they should be woken up now,"

"Don't you think it's unfair on them emotionally to be woken up and put through labor with a child they didn't consent to making?" Dad asked.

"I think that's happened to them and nothing is going to unmake it. At least if they're awake they might have a chance of bonding with the baby when it's born. Surely that's best for the babies. If the mothers don't want them, that's another issue but doing it the other way is just taking another choice away from them," I said.

"That's what Dr. Hade said. Except it makes more sense when you say it," Dad smiled.

"That's because you and Dr. Hade don't like each other, darling," Sofia said.

"Do you know where Jodi is?" I asked.

"I think she was putting the girls to bed. I'll get her," Dad said before doing a double-take. "Oh! You look like you again."

"You only just noticed?" I laughed. "Hive's still with me. Apparently, the skin and eyes were optional extras," I said.

"You could call them armor. We will need them again," said Hive.

"I can go and find Jodi," I said.

"No. You sit down with Sofia. I'll get Jodi. Obviously, I've got an apology to make to Dr. Hade too," Dad began to walk away.

"Would you mind asking her if she'd bring the girls down?"

"Both of them?" Dad asked.

I smiled. "Yes, thanks." I turned to Sofia. He was keen to go, what's going on?"

"I have something I wanted to ask you. Will you would be my maid of honor and my baby's godmother."

"Both? Wow! I'd love to. I'm so honored. But seriously, if a priest takes one look at me in my battledress, he's more likely to give me an exorcism," I said.

"I think it will be okay. It's fortunate that you've called Jodi down. I want to ask the girls too," Sofia said.

"They're going to be thrilled," I said.

Jodi came down with the girls behind her. She looked relieved to see that I appeared back to normal.

Milly walked up to me and looked up. "I thought you were gone but you're still there. Are you hiding?"

"Not from you, little one," said Hive.

"If it's okay, I'd like to try something with the girls' abilities," I said.

"I don't want you putting my girls in danger. I know you're the Divine Light now, whatever that means, and I don't mean to be disrespectful, but this is up to me," said Jodi.

"I understand. But right now, we're on a planet that's doomed to destruction, so they're already in danger. We all are," I said. "Sorry to put doom and gloom onto your announcement," I added to Sofia.

"Par for the course these days, honey," Sofia said.

"Let's go into the study," I said to Jodi.

I thought, I wonder where—?

"I'm here," David said, coming down the stairs.

"Of course, you are." I smiled.

We walked in with David and closed the door.

"I'd like Milly to try to sniff a room on the other side of the portal," I said.

"She doesn't have to go through?" Jodi asked.

"No, I just want her to snoop on the room from this side," I said.

"Milly, David's going to communicate with you, so that you don't have to speak out loud, and we'll all be very quiet. Just in case they can hear us. They shouldn't be able to see us, though." I shuddered at the thought of Benedict staring straight at us through the portal.

The girls nodded.

I created a portal into the room at the top of the tower in the Citadel. The room through the portal appeared empty. The body of the Brightling had been removed. Milly stood in front of it with her mother behind, wrapping her arms tightly around her. I looked at David; he looked at Milly. I knew he would be asking her if she could smell anything unusual.

She shook her head and took a step closer. Her mother came with her, then another step. When she tried to take another step, Jodi refused to let her move. I nodded, ready to give in.

Milly ducked her head forward, and the front of her face hit the portal. She took a deep sniff and leaped back, her face wide with fear. I closed the portal instantly.

"Someone was there, hiding, like Vince does," Milly said, holding on to her mother.

"Thank you, Milly, that was really brave. Now Sofia's got

a question for you. If your mom says it's okay, you can go see what she wants." I gave Jodi a little smile so she'd know it was okay.

Jodi nodded, and Milly skipped out of the room.

"They were in that room when we were. Zoe was probably in that room." I shook my head in disgust. How had I missed that opportunity?

"They just let you drop Peter into the void? It doesn't make sense" David said, shaking his head.

"They weren't getting very much from the old Brightling. I guess they thought it was an acceptable loss," I said.

"Okay, Ava, your turn. I'm going to open a portal to what should be a safe place, in the middle of nowhere, okay?"

"Okay," said Ava. "I get the easy one."

"That remains to be seen," I said. "I want you to see if you can create wind on that side of the portal from here."

Ava's first attempt created a paper storm in the office with no effect on the other side. She stepped closer and tried again, then closer. When she put her hand against the portal, she pulled it back quickly. Her mother grabbed her, and I closed the portal.

"Sorry, that tickled," she said.

Jodi and I looked at each other and both blew out air.

"Do you think you can touch it again for a little longer?" Jodi asked.

"Yes, sorry. It surprised me."

"Well, you nearly gave me a heart attack," Jodi said.

The sound of Milly's squeals and cheers came from outside.

We tried again. Ava touched the very edges of the portal, and the wind picked up on the other side. When she moved her hand, the wind died down.

"Would you mind trying one more time to make sure?

We don't want to find out the hard way that it was a coincidence," I said.

Again, Ava made the wind blow and we saw the beginnings of a twister in the dust.

"Okay, that's good enough. I'd like you to try it with David's portal, if that's okay."

David created a portal. The destination wasn't crystal clear like mine, but we could make out that it was the same place. Ava had to fade to touch David's portal, but when she did, she was able to make the wind blow just as fiercely.

"I think we have a plan forming," David said.

"Do you want to go see Sofia, too?" I asked Ava.

"Aren't I a little old to be a bridesmaid?" Ava asked.

"No, but apparently, you're just the right age to be a smart-ass," said Jodi.

Ava ran off, and Jodi turned to me. "When do you start?"

"Vera and I have a visit to make in the morning. Then I'll be going back to the other side to bring my friend Zoe home."

We gathered in the family room. It had been decided that if a girl is panicked enough, she might run through the walls and suffocate underground.

We put signs up everywhere, a couple of us faded so she would know she was among other faders.

"Are we ready?" Dr. Hade asked.

"As ready as we'll ever be," Dad said.

The doctor used the nanite pen to tag the first girl, then to rouse her.

Jodi sat and read to Milly over on the other sofa. The environment was as non-threatening as we could possibly make it.

The nanites got to work, strengthening muscles, then making her lungs breathe for themselves, she was taken off the ventilator. Then they started to work their magic on her brain. We waited.

"Who's that sleeping lady?" asked Milly.

"That's Wendy. We don't know her yet but we hope she'll like us," Jodi said.

Her eyes fluttered open. Safira said, "Hi," and Wendy vanished.

I blinked in to see that she was standing, moving around the room.

She appeared by the front door, "What the hell is this?" she stared in horror at her distended stomach.

"You were captured, kept in a coma and artificially inseminated by an agency that hunts faders. These people rescued you. I'm a doctor, I woke you up," Dr. Hade said.

"Your bedside manner is the absolute worst," Wendy said. Before bursting into tears. Dorothy lead her into the kitchen for a chat.

"Well, there's nothing wrong with her cognition," Dad said.

Dr. Hade stuck her tongue out at him.

"We need a lot more nanite pens. I plan to wake up a whole mountain of people," I said.

IT WAS TIME. We'd done all the talking and planning. This was either going to work or it wasn't. I'd already set the wheels in motion with Vera.

"Is everyone ready," I asked.

Everyone nodded.

"I've got gates set up to help me portal faster," David said.

"I do not understand why you do that," Hive said.

"I can only portal across worlds. I can't fade like other faders or portal within the same world," David said.

"Whatever makes you believe that?" Hive laughed. It was the sound of an auditorium full of people all laughing at exactly the same time.

"That might be something to investigate in future," I said to David.

"Say what you like, that was a creepy fucking sound," Vince said.

I opened a portal to the Citadel. Connor, Vince, and I were just about to step through, when Vince stepped away and delivered a full-on steamy kiss to David.

"Don't die. You're my life." He turned and stepped through, Connor and I followed. We stepped into the room at the top of the tower.

"Are you sure this is going to work?" I asked.

"It's been designed to hunt down Zoe's nanites. We know she's been here. Once it goes off, we follow the path. It'll break her connection to the ribbon immediately." Vince held the device.

"Just do it, and let's get out of here. I don't want to be up here when the weather changes," Connor said.

Vince placed it on the floor and we stepped through a portal which actually opened to the corner of the same room. We stood, connected, not emitting, watching the room. After a few seconds, a man appeared and walked forward.

"Damon says that's Gabriel," David sent. He was watching through his own portal which was just outside the window.

I didn't know what Gabriel's ability was. If it was sniffing, we were screwed. If it was telepathy we were screwed. If it was sensing he was being played, we were equally screwed.

He was about to pick up the device. I looked away, and the others did the same. Connor pressed the button on the remote, and the flash bang went off in his face. He screamed and kept screaming.

"*David, get ready,*" I sent to David.

"*Ava's approaching the portal, she's ready.*" David sent.

Rachel appeared. "Keep her hidden. This could be a trick."

She went to Gabriel and pressed a nanite pen to his neck. He went silent.

"*Now,*" I sent.

Ava started a breeze blowing through the room, then gave it an extra little gust.

"Okay, I'm closing the portal," Rachel said. "It's closed. We need to get her connected again, then take her somewhere else. Stay close to us and don't mess up. If Benedict hears about this, we'll both be going the way of Peter. Let's just get it done."

A man appeared with Zoe, unconscious in a wheelchair.

The three of us moved quickly to the back of the room, hidden by the abilities of Connor and Vince. We made our way around to Zoe.

I grabbed Rachel by the front of her robe. She tried to portal but we pulled her back.

"Here. Use ours, we insist," I said as I pushed her into a void I'd opened behind her.

As Rachel fell into the abyss, she grabbed the back of the wheelchair and pulled Zoe in with her. The portal closed. Everything froze for a second.

"*I will not lose her,*" Hive screamed in my mind.

We entered the portal. It was vast and dark. The expanse and absence of anything to orient myself by, terrified me. I screamed.

"You must do this, Jenna. I cannot. It is not permitted. Zoe is depending on you," Hive said to me.

"But the darkness is everything. There is no universe," I said, and I knew it. This was the truth of the in-between. In as much as there were universes, this was the absence of one. A reality where a universe did not appear. There was no big bang, no divine spark. This was the opposite to existence.

"You exist. And your love is wider than this expanse. This is your Cogito," Hive said.

"Amo ergo sum," I said, I love therefore I am.

MY EYES GLOWED, the only light in all of everything. I found Zoe right next to me. Had she been right there, floating in the blackness beside me all along? Or was she there because I wanted her there. There was no sign of Rachel.

I wrapped my arms around Zoe and tried to open a portal but I couldn't.

"Remember, there is no returning for mortals. I must do this part," said Hive. She revealed a doorway of mist, through which I could see the inside of the house. We went through the mist and dropped to the floor.

Hannah came running. "Is she okay?"

"I don't know," I said. I heard my own voice, it was a little wild. I felt somehow bereft. Something was missing, what was it? I turned back to create a portal to the Citadel again.

I looked through. There was no sign of Vince and Connor. There was, however, a very angry Gabriel with balls of fire in the palm of each hand. Oh, that's his ability, I thought. I noticed then, the scorch marks all over the walls. I wondered for a moment if everything had gone wrong.

"Come out, you cowards," Gabriel shouted. His face was burned. Whatever Rachel had done with the nanite pen, she hadn't healed him. I figured she'd probably just knocked him out to shut him up.

Things needed to move along. Where was Benedict? I remembered how he had previously been able to see us through the portal and decided it was too dangerous to keep this one open. I stepped through, closing it behind me.

"You!" screamed Gabriel.

He threw his balls of fire at me. I faded out of the way.

I realized what was missing. I couldn't feel Hive.

"Erm... Hello? Jenna to Hive,"

He was getting ready to throw some more but I'd had enough. I hated doing it after what I'd just experienced, but I opened a portal under his feet. He seemed to hover over it for a second, before dropping through with a look of pure horror on his face. I looked away.

Connor and Vince appeared, walked to the portal and looked down as it closed.

"Is anyone else thinking Wyle. E. Coyote?" Vince asked. Connor and I both stared at him.

"Dude, you're dark," Connor said, shaking his head.

"He totally lost his shit. We've been dodging him for the last fifteen minutes," Vince said.

"Fifteen minutes?" I thought it had been seconds.

Connor pulled me close and hugged me. "When I saw you go in there. I thought that was it. My heart went in there with you. Did you get her back?"

"She's back home," I said. "I don't know what condition she's in."

"It doesn't matter. I'll get her back. Or another Brightling," said Benedict, appearing in the room.

"I don't think so," I said. I was beginning to be concerned about where Hive was.

"A clever little ruse," Benedict said.

"Speaking of clever, burning your eyeballs out was a good way to hide that you had been taken by Divinity, if a little extreme," I said.

"So, bring forth your divinity. Let me see who you are. I am amongst the oldest."

"Dude, this is a pissing contest you do not want to get into," Vince warned him.

"You have work to do," I said to Vince and swept the two of them back to the vineyard.

"I'll show you mine if you show me yours," I said. Where the hell was Hive?

"I have claimed this world as my own. You are going to have to find a different world."

"But you keep destroying them."

Benedict's skin glowed, and a light burned from his eye sockets. As he stood there, I saw the shadows of three figures. "I am called Dolos, Anansi, Loki, and Taliesin. These are each my name, and I claim these worlds."

This guy was an actual god, with god names. I was in trouble.

"Taliesin's not a god. That's cheating," I said. "*Come on Hive, anytime now would be good.*"

"Not a god, but a name by which I have been known."

"Then you can call me JennaBanksy. That's my name on social media."

He strode to within a few inches of me. "Name thyself," he screamed.

I panicked. I punched him in the face.

"You know the rules," he said as blood ran down his mouth from his nostrils.

"That wasn't a god. That was me," I said and squared up to punch an old, blind guy for the second time.

I froze. My hands dropped to my sides. The hexagons

began popping out all over my body. *Oh, not these again.*

My head raised up to face him and my eyes glowed brightly

"Thou hast used our brightest children to steal the divine power from other worlds to your own ends. You are being judged." Our voice was incredibly loud. It travelled from the high windows of the tower, over the monastery.

"Better late than never," I sent to Hive.

We moved to the window. Heat and brightness radiated from us and we observed members of the Brotherhood staring up. We turned to place the window at our back.

"You can judge me all you like. You still can't touch me," Benedict said.

"Thou hast named thyself Dolos, Anansi, Loki, and Taliesin," we said.

"In this place shall we also name ourselves," Hive said.

Our word was truth and all those who heard it would know that it was so. Our chorus of voices rang out over the Citadel.

"We are Diana.

We are Minerva.

We are Isis and Heptet.

We are Kali.

We are Gaia.

We are Hecate and Freya.

We are Aphrodite, Artemis, and Athena.

We are Nemesis.

We are the Maiden, the Mother and the Crone.

We are the Named and the Unnamed.

We are the Alpha and the Omega.

And we have come to take you home."

"No!" said the gods.

"Yes!" said Hive.

25

"Cavendish," came the general's tinny voice through the phone.

"Sir, this is the gate. Are you expecting US Agent Vera Richards?"

"No. Put her on."

The guard handed the phone to her.

"General, it's Agent Richards. I understand you're already waiting for my call."

"Major Tomowski's asked us to mobilize. We're just waiting to hear where to."

"Did he explain the nature of the situation, sir?"

"In his words, he's seen some wild shit I wouldn't believe, and our planet is under threat from off-world faders."

"You don't sound convinced. Allow me to help with that."

"How do you plan—"

"Does this help?" Vera said, standing directly in front of him, portalled there by Jenna.

"Hello? Hello?" came the guard's voice though the

phone.

"I'm here," Cavendish said.

"She's gone, she just...."

"Never mind," said Cavendish, hanging up.

"I don't know how much the major has explained. The shortest version I can give you is this. As you know, I infiltrated a group of faders. They went through a portal to another Earth which is almost exclusively populated by faders. I was given this." She showed him the silver tag. "It allows me to travel via a portal instantaneously anywhere I wish. Not between worlds, or I wouldn't have been stuck over there for so long. The weather we have been experiencing is the first wave of an attack. When it dies down, the second wave begins.

"I assume the major explained we were waiting to learn the size of missiles required to get through the portal. They need to be powerful but can't be too large, or the portal will just close and be opened elsewhere. I can tell you now, they can't be bigger than eighteen inches in diameter.

"I now have the location. It's Glastonbury. Their base of operations is inside the tower on top of the tor, on the other side of course, and that's where the portal is. General, it's time to mobilize," said Vera.

The general had heard and seen enough. He was on board. Vera pulled out a map.

"I'll meet you here. There's excellent line of sight to the building. You want something that can go straight through that window. If we get this right. It could cause no damage on our side at all, while devastating theirs."

"I've learned their top people are meeting to discuss the second wave of attacks, in that room at three p.m. today,"

"What form will the second wave be taking?" the general asked.

"Radioactive poisoning. Good luck, General," Vera said before vanishing.

VERA SAT NERVOUSLY TAPPING her foot in the entrance hall of the house at the Vineyard. David had brought Adam and Matt over to the vineyard at Matt's insistence.

"Good luck, Kate. You're doing really well." Matt hugged her. He had never once called her Vera, and she quite liked that.

She watched as the doctor worked on Zoe while Hannah paced, chewing her fingernails. Hannah glanced over at her and she gave what she hoped was a supportive smile.

Connor and Vince came back through the portal, and Vera shot to her feet. "We need to move. They'll be in position," she said.

David emitted the red mist and fixed the portal location to Broken-Earth.

"Wait," Adam said. He walked purposefully over to Vera, took her in his arms, and kissed her. "Good luck, Kate."

She blushed.

"Kate, we need to go," David said.

She giggled. Connor faded her, Vince hid the emission, and they went through.

WE GLANCED AT THE TIME. It was two minutes to three. We and Benedict had been arguing for the last ten minutes, but Benedict was way over at the side of the room. He needed to be more central.

"Can we make two portals back-to-back from one place directly to another that doesn't come here?" I asked.

"The portals are yours. I'm sure you could do that if you wish," said Hive.

"David?"

"Yes."

"He's not in position. We need a second missile. It looks like we'll have to send the first one somewhere else. Have you got any ideas? I don't want to send it to the in-between, it might break the universe or something."

"Have I got an idea? Oh boy, do I have an idea." David sent.

DAVID PORTALLED BACK to Broken Earth and on to the vineyard. He called Vera on her cell.

"Vera, we need a second missile." David said.

"Yes, sir," Vera said loudly. The commanding officer turned. "I've got him right... Hello? Hello," she rolled her eyes.

Vera held the phone to her chest. "I *had* Major Tomowski on. He wants you to send two missiles ninety seconds apart."

"Of course, he does. If they come out the other side, they're being detonated before they hit a village," he replied.

David ran to the store room and pulled out boxes on the bottom shelf until he found the duct tape. He portalled back to the missile launcher and sent Connor over to the first missile with instructions. It was being raised and levelled at its target.

JENNA GLANCED AT HER WATCH.

"You gods need to come to some kind of agreement or I'm getting out of here," Jenna said, opening a portal.

"Close that portal. We're staying here until this is resolved," Hive said.

Major Tomowski was getting nervous. Agent Richards should have been back in his office by now. He was starting to get a bad feeling.

He reached for the phone. He needed to know what was going on and possibly cancel the op. It rang and he picked it up.

"Tomowski," he said.

"Hello Craig, it's David. I wanted you to know I'm finished with your lucky spork, I'm sending it back."

The time hit three p.m. precisely. The first missile flew straight at the window, into a portal to Full-Earth and straight through a second portal back to Half-Earth and into Major Tomowski's office. He never saw the little metal spork taped to it, but David knew it was there, and he was grinning on the other side of the world.

Jenna left the portal open for a few more seconds then closed it.

"Why do you not simply bend the human to your will? This one was obliterated years ago," the gods said from Benedict's mouth.

"I'm getting bored with this," I said. "If you gods can't sort it out, then why don't we humans? I'll wear a blindfold to make it an even fight."

"This body is old, that's hardly fair," said Benedict, but he was clearly curious and walked into the middle of the room.

"Well, think about it. But I'm a human body and I'm going to need the bathroom soon," I said.

"David, how long did the last one take to get to the building?"

"About four seconds."

"About?"

"Counting down, three, two, one."

"DOES your major want another missile, or can we all go home?" the commanding officer asked.

He looked around. "Agent Richards? Agent?"

I COUNTED A FURTHER ONE, two three, I opened the portal and faded. The missile exploded into Benedict. I stepped back into a portal to the vineyard and watched from there. The tower was ruined.

"Open the Void," shouted Hive inside my mind.

The gods had launched themselves out of the mush that had been Benedict. Hive shot out of me. I saw them truly for the first time. Ethereal goddesses which surrounded the few gods and carried them off into the portal I had created. The last to come out was a tiny, bright speck of light. It hovered around my face and touched my forehead, then followed the rest of the gods.

"Go," came the voice of Hive, singing outside my head.

I stepped back fully into the vineyard, and closed the portal.

General Cavendish took a last walk around the grounds. His entire life's work had come to nothing. The captured faders and trackers were all gone. Hundreds of faders in the mountain had just woken up and faded away. Even the ones they thought were braindead.

Everything was being packed away, hard drives magnetized, files burned and he was retiring, which for anyone else meant golf. For him it meant he was probably going to have an 'accident.' The possibility of a dementia-ridden agency employee was a loose-end management wouldn't accept.

He rounded the corner to see one of the gardeners at work.

"You can clear off. There's no one left to pay you," he said.

"Yes, sir," came the young woman's voice.

He continued a few steps onward and stopped. He slowly turned around. The gardener was gone, and so was the bush with the red and white roses.

"Can anyone tell me where my shoes are?" Orla shouted down the hallway.

"Everywhere," everyone shouted.

"I need lipgloss," Orla yelled, bursting into my room.

Connor and I jumped apart.

"Oh my God! Can you two not get a room?" Orla said.

"We've got one. You're in it," I said.

"Oh, right. Sorry," She said.

"It's on the dresser," I pointed to the lip gloss.

"Thank you, sweetie. Don't mess up your dress and hair, or Sofia will kill you," she ran out of the room. "Who gave those girls chocolate?" she yelled.

"What?" came Jodi's strangled voice as she came running up the stairs.

I checked myself in the mirror, smoothing down my dress of dark blue and gold brocade. Sofia had spent the morning curling the bridesmaids' hair, even Zoe's, but not Orla's, hers was a natural explosion of red curls already.

I picked up my bouquet and headed down the hall to Sofia.

I knocked on the door and entered, Sofia's black hair curled down her back with tiny diamantes sparkling here and there in the light. Her dress was simply styled white satin with a lace up back.

"You look stunning. Dad won't know what hit him" I said.

"He will if he doesn't turn up," Sofia said. I laughed.

Damon officiated at the wedding. It was held in the garden at the vineyard, next to the little red and white rosebush. I was the maid of honor and Orla, Zoe, Hannah, Heidi and Ava were bridesmaids while Milly sprinkled petals down the aisle. Sofia's uncle gave her away and Connor was the best man.

All our friends came; Kim, Kyle, Eric, and Sarah came over from Healing-Earth, that was what they were calling it now. Zoe and Hannah were living there too. Zoe's abundance of yellow energy was helping to heal the Earth and surprisingly, the people. James, Heidi, Callan and Yolanda came over from Full-Earth.

James had returned to face the music but all he found waiting for him was a pile of paperwork. Kate, Adam and Matt came from the farm in the Cotswolds. They had returned to it after the storms ended and after repairs, I helped them transport their animals, including Ellen Degeneres and her foal Oprah Winfrey to their new stables. Matt had decided he liked the show-host theme.

DAMON WAS in demand for more such ceremonies. He had been booked by Zoe and Hannah, Orla and Jason, Heidi and Callan, David and Vince and Adam and Kate, no one called her Vera anymore.

AFTER THE CEREMONY, Connor and I took a walk through the vines.

"I miss your crazy eyes and skin," he admitted.

"How ever will you live with just normal, non-goddess me?"

"You'll always be a goddess to me," he said.

"Right answer," I said.

Connor closed his eyes and leaned forward to kiss me. I

decided it was time to share some of what I'd learned from Hive. I kissed him and portalled us. He opened his eyes, clearly surprised to find us in a beautiful landscape. The sunset played across the horizon in red, orange, and purple. We stood on a rocky hillside, and the land between us and the setting sun was lush with green grass and distant sparkles reflected from a lake.

"Well, this is nice." He smiled. "Where are we?"

"Los Angeles," I said.

"I think your portal might need calibrating. I've seen all three cities of L.A., and none of them look like this."

I grew a ball of red mist in my hand and flicked it out a few feet with my wrist. It cleared, to a city which looked very much like our Earth's L.A., but not quite.

I grew more red energy balls and pushed them into the air around us. Ten, then twenty, and each one had a different version of L.A., a different version of Earth.

"There are more than three Earths, Connor. So many more."

ORLA HADN'T BELIEVED it when I wanted to learn to ride a horse.

"But you're terrified of horses, have you forgotten?" she asked.

"I am terrified, that's correct. I want to do this for Connor. It's a surprise. He can already ride. I want to learn."

Over the next few weeks, I became passable.

"You've done really well. You could have taken this more slowly you know," she said, one evening as we brushed the horses down.

"Our lives are taking us in different directions. I might

not get the chance again," I said. I touched my belly, know that my adventures would come to an end, for a little while, anyway.

HIVE SMILED TO THEMSELVES. They had moved on from Jenna now, but not completely. She was probably their favorite human. Although, there was this new life, sleeping inside Jenna, not yet self-aware. It was surrounded and protected by the Divine Light and cocooned within a glowing, blue mist. Maybe it was okay to have more than one favorite human.

"LET'S have a trip out with the horses tomorrow," I said to Orla.

"It's a shame we can't get Zoe near a horse. She and Hannah could have come." Orla sighed.

"Yes, that's a shame," I said.

I was so excited about this surprise, I couldn't stand it.

CONNOR, Orla, Jason and I rode out down the edge of the vineyard.

"What's that? Is that a covered wagon?" Orla asked.

"Let's investigate," I said.

"But it wasn't there yesterday, and whose horses are they?" Orla was suspicious.

As we neared the wagon, familiar faces poked out from inside.

"Evenin' partners," Zoe said, and Hannah waved.

"Hannah. Are you wearing gingham? Have you lost your mind?" Orla said.

"What are you up to?" Connor asked.

I smiled.

"Okay, we're here as requested, come on then, what's the deal?" Zoe asked.

A minute later we stood together, Connor, Orla, Jason, Zoe, Hannah and I, looking through the portal.

"Cowboy-Earth," Jason and Connor said together with a sigh.

We observed the town on the other side. A saloon, horses and wagons.

"Why do you think this Earth has not progressed since the eighteen-hundreds?" Orla asked Jason.

"Cowboy-Earth," he replied. The longing in his voice was palpable.

"Why don't we find out? Saddle up, pilgrims," I said.

We rode.

"Hey, look at the sun, setting ahead of us. Is this us riding off into the sunset?" Connor asked.

I grinned. "I suppose it is."

Join my VIP list for the latest news, release updates, and notifications of promo pricing from my publisher. https://dl. bookfunnel.com/olndiiuzje

Find me on Facebook at www. facebook.com/egbatemanwrites

AUTHOR NOTES

I hope you enjoyed the final instalment of this trilogy in the Faders series. Did it take you in directions you weren't expecting? Do you see why I affectionately call it the Spork trilogy?

I would like to write more in the fader world. If it looks like people enjoy it, I certainly will. Let me know what you think.

What did you think of the ending? While I don't generally ask for feedback while writing, I did have to get advice from other authors about the ending. I really liked the metaphor of riding off into the sunset. I was worried it might be seen as a cliché or a parody. I wanted to give you an ending you could visualize.

If you want to chat, I can be found at facebook.com/egbatemanwrites

It would mean a lot to me if you would review this book, wherever you like to review books, Amazon, Goodreads, Bookbub, wherever you prefer.

ALSO BY THE AUTHOR.

ABOUT THE AUTHOR

Elaine began writing her first book, FADE, in 2014. She put it aside several times to "get on with real life" before she realized that *writing* was the life she really wanted to get on with.

Elaine loves to communicate with readers and can be found on social media at the links below. She lives in England with her husband, son and three dogs (but she'd like to live somewhere warmer.)